THE BOYDS OF BLACK RIVER

New York Classics

FRANK BERGMANN, SERIES EDITOR

THE BOYDS

OF

BLACK

RIVER

Walter D. Edmonds

With a new Preface by the author

SYRACUSE UNIVERSITY PRESS

Syracuse University Press Edition 1988
97 96 95 94 93 92 91 90 89 88   6 5 4 3 2 1

This book is published with the assistance of a grant from the John Ben Snow Foundation.

The paper used in this publication meets the minimum requirements of American National Standard for Information Sciences— Permanence of Paper for Printed Library Materials, ANSI Z39.48-1984.™

Designed by Stefan Salter
Manufactured in the United States

TO KATHERINE AND CHARLIE,

TO BAYARD AND BLANCHE,

TO KATHY AND SALLY,

TO JIM AND JEANETTE,

AND TO REMEMBER K.V.V.S.

THIS IMAGINED STORY OF THE HOUSE

WHICH WAS AND IS AND STILL WILL BE THEIRS

Foreword

In the long line of distinguished New York State writers from
Washington Irving and James Fenimore Cooper to William
Kennedy, Walter Edmonds occupies a prominent place.
Born near Boonville in Oneida County on July 15, 1903, he
is particularly well remembered upstate, even though he
sold his native farm "Northlands" in 1976 and now lives year
round in Concord, Massachusetts.

Readers and television watchers know Edmonds as the
author of *Drums Along the Mohawk* (1936), one of the finest
novels about the revolutionary war ever written, but he is
equally distinguished for his Erie Canal fiction and his
award-winning books for younger readers. Almost all of his
writings are set somewhere along the Erie Canal or the Black
River. *The Boyds of Black River* (1953) is a series of closely
linked stories from the 1930s that take us back to his native
valley at a time when the automobile was a novelty.

The new preface Edmonds has written especially for this
reprint edition tells us that—contrary to the popular notion
—writers do not sit in a trance waiting for the Muse to in-
spire them, but most of all it lets us feel how deeply attached
the great writer still is to this part of his life. Those readers
who wish to learn more about Edmonds will find much de-

tail in Lionel D. Wyld's book *Walter D. Edmonds, Storyteller* (Syracuse University Press, 1982). Edmonds himself discusses his career in the essay "Writer's Way," recently published in *Something about the Author Autobiographical Series*, vol. 4 (Detroit: Gale, 1987), pp. 167–80. Kate H. Winter sheds light on Edmonds' work—including *The Boyds of Black River*—in "North Country Voices," chapter 8 in *Upstate Literature: Essays in Memory of Thomas F. O'Donnell*, edited by Frank Bergmann (Syracuse University Press, 1985).

Utica, New York
April 1988

Frank Bergmann

Preface

The Boyds of Black River was published in 1953 but the episodes that form its chapters had appeared twenty years earlier as stories in the *Saturday Evening Post*. When at the end of March in 1933 I sat down to write the first of them, which I called "The Courtship of My Cousin Doone," I had no idea that I was beginning a novel. And of course the book is not a novel, though the publishers presented it as one. It is no more a novel than, let's say, Booth Tarkington's *Penrod*. But the stories brought together do, I think, give a fair picture of a countryside and its inhabitants, animal and human, and of a way of life in upstate New York at the turn of the century. I am content with that.

What brought me to my typewriter that spring morning was money, which, whatever anyone may say, is the motivating force behind the production of literature, great, indifferent, or just plain awful. I needed money, perhaps not as desperately as I thought I did, for I owed no debts, but actuality usually has small bearing on human apprehensions. Each man must worry for himself and, as I looked ahead, the shadows of bills to come loomed large and dark.

My wife and I had just returned from a delayed honeymoon in Jamaica where Franklin Roosevelt's bank holiday had at one stroke made our U.S. money, even our express checks, valueless. All we had worth anything at all were our return steamship tickets on the SS *Sixaola*, and until the ship called in again at Kingston, we had to live on the generosity of the proprietor of the modest country hotel we had been staying at. His name was Oliphant, and he ran the hotel to help pay the bills for the horses he bred, trained, and raced. It was the simplest of establishments, but in those days my wife and I had the use of a long private beach on the north shore all to ourselves, except for a small group of Arab mares and foals who followed us with gentle curiosity; and to us it seemed close to Paradise.

When it came time to leave, Oliphant drove us down to Kingston. On the dock he presented me with my bill. "Don't feel you have to pay it," he told me, "until this crazy exchange has settled back to normal."

But of course I did. When we were back in New York my agent, Harold Ober, arranged to have the money sent to him in English currency while my wife and I went on to Cambridge to rejoin our two-year-old son whom we had left with his grandmother. It had all been made easy, but I had had a whiff of what it might be like to be destitute. Besides, my third novel, *Erie Water*, had come out in our absence and in spite of my high hopes had had disappointing sales. It was more than time to start making money. The morning following our return I went into the library of my mother-in-law's house with my portable typewriter and sat down to find out whether there was anything at all inside my head.

The library of that Cambridge house was small and rather dark, with a single diamond-paned window facing northeast. The page in my typewriter gleamed blankly white for minutes that began ominously to multiply. And then, for no discernible reason, the image of a house across the Black River and Canal from our place in upstate New York came into my mind—painted yellow, low and spreading, under tall trees that gave it its name of Elmwood. The very look of it spelled hospitality. But the people I saw in it suddenly came out of my imagination: the Boyds, Ledyard and Doone, father and son, and in the paddock outside the gray harness horse they called Blue Dandy. I did not have to think of names. They had their names already. The house was real, every detail just as I remembered it, but my imaginary characters who now belonged to it had their own reality, not only the Boyds but their retainers and neighbors, with the exception of Ledyard's best and oldest friend Admiral Porter and the white bull terrier I called Leonidas.

In real life the bull terrier's name was Florio, a splendid and dignified individual, known to a large public by photographs that illustrated the garden books written by his owner, a Mrs. Ely, who was a friend of my parents. As far as I know Florio never fought a pit fight as Leonidas does in "The Honor of the County," but in his later years he did fight off a pack of sheep killing dogs, killing three of them. I saw him the second day after his battle; he lay in a patch of sunlight on the parlor floor of the old Connecticut house that was his home, bandaged all over, barely able to move except for the gentle thumping of his tail to greet me; and later the farmer took me to the sheepfold to look at the three dogs he had killed. In those early years I longed for a white bull terrier of my own, so it was natural to have one, so long after, in my book.

The Admiral, too, was based on my recollection of another of my parents' friends, Judge Peter Barlow, who in 1907 or 1908 drove all the way from New York City to Boonville in his Packard touring car, the first ever seen around those parts, and on his second day encountered the insurmountable barrier of Meecher's farrowing sow on the Hawkinsville road. The Judge did not swear as freely as the Admiral, but he had his own variety of saltiness, for he brought my mother as a hostess present a knife with a black handle and a twelve-inch wickedly narrow blade which he assured her had been the fatal weapon in a murder but would serve her better as an asparagus knife.

I don't know why the Boyds were so instantly realized in my mind. Obviously they belonged to the countryside and the old house. But it was also true of Kathy O'Chelrie who came from the world of the New York theater. From the instant the Admiral's Packard motor car, with its brass front gleaming and the great plume of road dust behind, burst snorting from the woods, I saw Kathy whole and understood her determination to be married to Doone, which provided the motivation of the first episode and proved the anchor that held the rest of them together.

I finished "The Courtship of My Cousin Doone" in ten days, sent it off to Harold Ober, and it was accepted by the *Saturday Evening Post* in spite of its awkward length (equal to three short stories, but they brought it out in two parts). Immediately I wanted to cash in on this success and produced a real potboiler, worked up from a newspaper incident, called "Aunt Phoebe and the Big Shot." It was a spurious piece of writing. Harold backed and filled, and sent it back with suggestions. I came to my senses. The characters did not belong in our upstate neighborhood, still less to Boyd House. After that I stuck to my original people and before May was out sent off "The Honor of the County." In August of the following year the final story went down to Ober.

It did not occur to me there was a book in them until in 1952 Dodd, Mead & Company, who had been publishing my children's books, made the suggestion . However, I thought the Atlantic Monthly Press had prior claim because they had published my adult novels. I offered the stories to them. The editor turned them down, and with his cool but not unkindly note included as explanation the report of a reader (who happened to be owner of the Press) which described the stories as "the worst ham writing I have seen since I submitted a story to my sophomore English class." So the stories went to Dodd, Mead as they should have in the first place.

Sometimes a reader will ask an author which of the books he has written is his favorite. This is like asking a parent to name his favorite child. It is also embarrassing for its implication of narcissism, of a writer's going back in order to admire his own work, which is not a wholesome practice. But having said this, I must admit that writing about the Boyds gave me a great deal of pleasure, that I enjoy going back to the book now and then to refresh my recollection of certain incidents and scenes. To me they still carry a freshness and a kind of grace that seems now vanished from so much of modern life.

March 1988   W.D.E.

THE BOYDS OF BLACK RIVER

I

1

We were sitting side by side on the rails of the training track fence: John Callant with his long upper lip moving up and down over his chew of tobacco, Doone's gold watch in his fist, and his impudent blue eyes following the prances of Blue Dandy as Doone limbered him up along the backstretch; and myself, a boy of twelve, bare-legged, dividing my attention between the horse and John Callant's mouth, for he had a neat way of spitting that someday I intended to master, just as I dreamed someday of being old enough to hold the lines over the back of one of Uncle Ledyard's trotters.

It was a broiling hot, early August morning, and Doone had already had out Maidy and Arrogance and had left Blue Dandy for the last. Uncle Ledyard had watched the mares at their training and had then gone back to the house to wait for the mailman. In some way he had conceived a dislike for the grey horse, and he never had a good word to say for him, but Doone and John Callant, and therefore myself, believed in the animal's great future.

From where I sat I could see the broad low house under the elms, and Uncle Ledyard in his chair on the back verandah, tilted backward against the wall, his wide hat on the table, his beard bent against the open collar of his grey flannel shirt, and beyond him the paddock placed at the edge of the flatland over our Black River Valley, so that the colts looking over the fence seemed to be pricking their ears at the old man from the sky.

Blue Dandy came up to us on springing feet, his head up against the check, and Doone said over his shoulder, "I'm going to start him this time."

We watched him take the horse along to the gate, swing him neatly, and bring him back. Blue Dandy went up on his toe calks and tossed the bit and eyed us as he went past, knowing he was going to start. Doone was settling his feet in the racks of the sulky and drawing the loops back to his hands. And I watched him with affection, for excepting my own father, I thought Doone the finest man in the Universe.

He was past thirty then, a black Boyd like Uncle Ledyard, but taller and smooth shaven. He had a straight nose, rather long, and a thin long jaw, and a mouth that closed itself firmly when he had nothing to say. Others of us used to wonder what would become of him, living along with his father at Boyd House, training his horses, or going fishing or shooting according to the season. But I had no doubts about him, being sure that before he got through he would win all the great stakes of America with Blue Dandy.

"He's turning," said John, round his cud of tobacco, and he lifted the watch and fastened his eye on the finishing post.

Doone had wheeled the horse again, and before I knew it (for I had been watching the mailman out of the tail of my eye) they were by us and spinning out the dust for the first turn. John's lips made a note of the seconds on the watch, but he stopped chewing to follow the horse's head along the rails into the backstretch, and suddenly he began to whistle.

I could see Doone leaning back against the reins with the wind lifting his black hair and his mouth talking to the horse round the stem of his short pipe. Blue Dandy was arching his back against the rails and fighting off from them as if he was bothered by the way they slid back of him; he had always been shy of the rail; but his action was a fine and slashing thing to watch. He was a big beast, three years old, coarser than the painting of Greybriar over the mantel in the old house, but with the same searching eye, and his head put on right. He hadn't shown speed enough in his second year to be raced even at Boonville, and it was only Doone's patience and the belief he and John Callant had in the horse that kept them after him.

He came by us again with the deep even blasts of his breathing like a great bellows and he seemed that morning to cock his eye at us as much as to say, "You poor fools," and then he was making his usual wide sweep on the turn again in spite of all Doone could do with him. It was so still as they swung into the backstretch that we could hear Doone's voice cursing him gently over the roll of his hoofs against the hard dirt. And all of a sudden John's free hand lit on my knee and he stopped his whistling to say, "Oh Mary!" and I felt a shiver go through me though the sun was broiling the back of my neck; for I saw that Blue Dandy was forgetting about the rails and putting his head out against the bit and I realized that at last he had gotten the balance of the sulky under his tail. And John's whistle turned mournful on one note, as it did when he was happy.

"Watch him, Teddy," he said. "He's roused."

It looked to me as if the horse had stepped clean out of the thills and skipped three posts when he did it. Doone's face was skimming lower to the rail, his arms were flat along the topsides of the lines and his eyes half shut against the wind; and as they straightened in to the stretch I saw him leaning far inwards, the way he did when he was finishing the third heat, and the tire of the nigh wheel was carving a line in the dirt to edge the grass.

The horse's head was out in front of him; his nostrils were the color of poppies; and the thrust of his feet on the hard track came up through the rail we were sitting on like strokes of a hammer.

I heard Doone crying, "So-o-o-o, so-o-o-o," as they went past, but the horse was round the far bend and going down the backstretch before he began to get back his stature and come up on his pasterns, and he turned as if he was dancing on a spring bed, putting his head up, fluttering the dust out of his nostrils, and tossing out his mane. When he came back to us on the rail, he didn't come in for his sugar loaf, but swung away as if he scorned John Callant and me, and he had to toe around the track for a

3

lap before he stopped and put out his ears and remembered that he was a lad again.

Doone was laughing.

"What did he make, John?"

"Two seventeen," said John.

Doone whistled.

"I knew he was tearing into the last bend. And he wasn't fighting me either."

"He was running," said John. "I thought he might break, but he went off as smooth as a feather."

"He was smooth," Doone agreed, and he put his legs out of the racks and swung himself off the seat. "You'd better take him in now."

John gave him back his watch and hopped over the seat and we watched them jouncing down the track, and John's legs made me think of a frog's, the way they hung down with the toes turning out.

"Good morning, Teddy," said Doone. "Did you like him today?"

"He looks promising," said I, wishing I could spit the way John did.

Doone grinned at me, and then we heard a deep snort.

"Promise!" said my Uncle Ledyard. "Well, he may have it, but if he's got anything else you'll have to show it to me."

He had come across from the house and was leaning on the rail with his short beard broken by his forearms and the hat back on his head. His face was red with anger as Doone said, "I'll show it to you Dad," but his eyes were miserable. And it suddenly occurred to me why he didn't like the horse. He must have seen the promise in him from the beginning, and he was jealous of the memory of Greybriar. For to some men horses are very much the same as a woman, for though he may own many in his lifetime, it is rarely that he is privileged to love more than one.

Uncle Ledyard was a massive man; with hard heavy legs and broad hands and wrists powerful from training many horses. Though he was past seventy, he would still take his turn at driv-

4

ing the two mares, if Doone was away; but he had become too heavy for racing. He showed his age nowhere else unless it was in the badger hairs coming into his short beard and heavy long eyebrows. It was odd to see the resemblance between him and Doone, the eyebrows in Doone not yet so long; but the eyes and nose the same, the eyes dark brown and silent; but with a light of the devil in them when they were angry with each other. And they both smelled of horses and tobacco and clean hay.

"I'll grant you he's not as pretty as Greybriar," Doone said, "but he's going to have speed that the old one never got even a smell of."

"He would do very well in the milk wagon," said Uncle Ledyard.

They were both looking at him now in the door of the horse barn where John Callant was combing the sweat off him with bright showers from the edge of the stick. And Doone looked bitter, for he loved the grey horse, and it hurt him not to have a good word for him from his father.

But the old man would never give it to him. Now he said, "You needn't think I've come over to look at the brute, Doone." He held up a blue letter in his fist. "Here's the devil to pay," he said.

"Is it from the admiral?" Doone asked.

"It is. He writes me he's coming up from Long Island," said Uncle Ledyard, "and he says he ought to get here tomorrow afternoon. And now he wants to know if it's going to be convenient, the damned old rip."

Doone sucked in his breath, and I knew why. They had just barely enough money to run the stable, and they let the house go, so when the admiral was coming for a visit everything had to be turned out, the silver polished, the house cleaned, the harness shined for the carriage team, and the wagonette waxed, for the admiral lived in a grand way and moved in the high society of Long Island, and Uncle Ledyard didn't like to be ashamed of anything that belonged to him.

"What train is he coming on?" asked Doone, and I knew he was calculating the time he would have.

Uncle Ledyard gave a snort that sounded like the snort of Ajax,

5

the black Percheron stud horse when little Ralph Amber led him into the horse barn on a business venture.

"Train! Train! The old devil has gotten beyond any trains. He writes me he's coming in his automobile!" His eye rolled murderously until it came over the paddock and he saw the colts pricking their ears at the sound of his voice. "The damned old jackass thinks he's going to drive in here and disturb the country with his dirty engine, roaring and spitting out his stinking smoke and sounding his horn at the hogs down at Meecher's crossing—and I wish to God he would run over them or I will myself someday and bring that crumby loafer Meecher into court for damage to my disposition."

Doone grinned at him, and seeing me with my eyes sticking out on sticks, Uncle Ledyard grinned himself and asked me whether I knew what a motor car was. I told him then that I had seen them in New York City in the winter, but I had never ridden in one.

"Well," said Uncle Ledyard, "I'll ask him to give you a ride in his, if he doesn't wreck the thing getting here."

I could see that he was mightily pleased at the notion of the admiral's visit. The admiral was one of the few friends he had left—they had gone to college together—and with Doone not caring for people around, or indeed anything but training the horses, the old man must have found the place lonesome, for though my father often came to see him, they could never agree on the matter of a Royal Coachman as against my father's favorite red and white fly, which was a trouble to them both.

"There's another thing, Doone," said Uncle Ledyard. "It'll give you something to think about. He's bringing the girl along."

Doone looked up.

"Kathy?" he asked.

"Yes," said Uncle Ledyard. "And you'll have to look out for her."

"I'm busy," said Doone. "Let her run around with Teddy."

"I'll not let her," said I. "I don't want any girls interfering with my business."

Uncle Ledyard grinned at the two of us.

"Maybe you'll find her changed, Doone."

"She used to be a damned nuisance," Doone said. "Running around the horses in her bare legs almost as dirty as Teddy is now."

Uncle Ledyard shrugged his shoulders.

"It's all a damned nuisance," he said. But he didn't mean it. He was thinking of the afternoons he would have with the admiral on the back verandah over their long glasses, both of them remembering the old days together. It was a pleasant place, that back verandah, for the flat land carried your eye out straight into the sky, with the paddock fence and the neat heads of the two year olds against it. Even under the shadow of the broad roof you had a feeling of the sky over you, the run of the clouds, the hot still heat of the sun with the bees drowsing in the weed-grown borders or the wrens in the lilac hedge, or the drumming of the colts' feet against the sod. I used to like lying in the old red and purple tasselled hammock and hearing the admiral swearing in the heat of the afternoon, his silver hair carefully combed, his mustache right to the last hair, the dew of Highland whiskey on his red cheeks and his stock white under his chin and his blue coat, cut by a tailor from London, outlandish opposite Uncle Ledyard's loose corduroy. I began to think about it with a kind of luxury in my nostrils for the admiral always brought with him the scent of a strange elegant world. But a slap on my rear brought me to.

"Wake up," said Doone. "Get over to John and tell him I want to have him in the house as soon as he's finished Blue Dandy."

They went off for the house side by side, Doone to get after Mrs. Callant who managed the housekeeping after a fashion that made all the women of our valley rail against her—maybe from envy, and Uncle Ledyard to frame a telegram to the admiral that the Telegraph Company would be willing to accept.

"John," I said, walking into Blue Dandy's stall and sitting down in the straw under the horse's nose, "Doone wants you in the house as soon as you're through here."

"He does, does he?" said John finishing off the quarters with a stick. Then he drew on the light burlap blanket and began rub-

7

bing down Blue Dandy's legs with his bare hands. The horse nibbled my hair with the tip of his tongue, a trick I never saw in any other horse, until I made a snatch for it and he tossed his head.

"So, there!" said John, but Blue Dandy paid no attention to him and began again to nibble me with his tongue tip. "What does he want me for now, annyway?"

"He's got some work for you."

"Don't I know that?" said John. "Well, he can wait till I finish the horse."

I shivered under the tongue tickle and then made another grab, and this time he let me catch it in my fingers. For some reason it pleased him, and he dropped his nose closer while I held the tongue and closed his eyes and drooped his ears, in a way that made John spit out his quid for disgust.

"The old mule," he said.

I sank back on my back, with the horse over me and looked up at the wet curve of his belly, seeing the clean way his legs were put into his body. The stall was right beside the door, and the door to the stall being open, the sun came in around me where I lay in the deep straw. I could see the motes lazy in the sunlight, and smell the fresh timothy overhead in the loft and listen to the teeth whistle of John on one note; and the fine hot smell of Blue Dandy covered us both.

"John," I said, "when do you suppose I'll be let to drive Blue Dandy?"

"Oh, I guess in a while. You've got some growing to do."

"I'm pretty stout, John."

"Not enough. I'll tell you, though. When you meet with a bee that has the thirteenth stripe on his back, come and ask me again."

"Oh," I said.

John picked up the nigh hind hoof and looked at the plate, tapped it with his finger nail and let it fall. I watched him lazily, my fingers mechanically twitching the warm tongue.

"John," I said. "What kind of a girl was Kathy?"

"The admiral's girl?" John asked absently.

"The same," said I (for when we were alone together, my tongue always followed the twists of John's speech.)

"Well," he said, "she used to be a coltish creature. A bit of a harridan in her I think, as is in the admiral, himself."

"What did she look like?"

"She was a lean little fidget, black as a Boyd, but her eyes grey. And she had good legs and a long black braid on her back, and she was always pestering Doone to take her in the sulky with him, to ride in his lap, with her hands on the reins behind his. She had some promise as a filly. . . ."

"John!" I said. "What are you talking about?"

John turned an impudent eye on me.

"Sure you was asking about her."

"She isn't a horse," I said.

"I didn't say she was. No doubt she's growed into a fine lady. I think Doone was partial to her some way. But she hasn't been back. And annyway he don't have no interest in girls at all."

"I haven't," I said, "why should he?"

"Well, well," said John. "Maybe he shouldn't. But if I was a handsome gentry and all the girls asking under their eyelids, I wouldn't be speaking to my horse alone when I saw a good looking piece bugging potatoes alone in the field, unless I said 'Whoa.'"

I looked at John for a while.

"But what was *Kathy* like?" I demanded.

"Ain't I telling you? She used to bedevil me all day long, running in among the horse barn in her bare legs and her pinafore up behind, and no decent sight, and sitting down in the straw under my feet, and asking John-this and John-that, till my poor noodle rocked with the blather, for all the world like yourself."

"Oh," said I, haughtily. "I was just asking because the admiral's coming tomorrow afternoon, and I think that's what Doone wants you for—to clean the silver."

John gave me a grim, hurt look, but I was not sorry for him. If there was one job he hated beyond ordinary work, it was cleaning the silver, for his wife put him out on the porch in plain view of the road, with an apron around his middle and eau de cologne in his hair to keep off the barn smell.

2

I had been asked to stay to lunch, so I stayed. In any other house even a twelve year old boy would have felt in the way; but Uncle Ledyard took me into the office with himself, and I sat down on the floor beside the gun case where Artemis, the Gordon setter bitch, had her bed, and looked up at the deer heads on the walls and the stuffed bass that had been caught in the big hole in the canal and that weighed six pounds and a quarter. Uncle Ledyard sat in his leather chair in front of the stove and lit his cigar and let the thunder of housecleaning racket over his head.

For like all dirty people, Mrs. Callant made a great noise about cleaning, and after she had served us our lunch we could hear her voice screeching from all parts of the house at once, for Minna, for Mrs. Toidy, who did the heavy cleaning, or for John. Her feet would bang down the stairs, her strong hands would shake the bedding from the windows, her impulsive fingers drop a glass with a crash. She was always asking what Mrs. Phoebe would say to this mopping, that dusting, for Mrs. Phoebe Boyd could not bear the dirt in Uncle Ledyard's house and made a yearly attempt with three pairs of white cotton gloves to show her she was a lazy slattern. But Mrs. Callant only succeeded in raising the dust and making an unholy turbulence. The trouble was that she was a born cook, and Uncle Ledyard took her food for the stuff of heaven it was and accepted her airs and her racket along with it as he was doing now.

I do not know what he was thinking about but he must have known I was looking at the bass for he said suddenly, "I caught him on a royal coachman. So the next time your father offers you one of his crazy red and white contraptions ask him for a royal coachman."

I looked up at the bass and grew cold, because that was a point

I knew my father was right on and it seemed an injustice in God for Uncle Ledyard to have caught the fish. But I said, "If Father had been fishing there that evening, he'd have caught him, too."

"Would he?" asked Uncle Ledyard, putting his hand in his beard and peering down at me, "And what does that prove, Teddy, since he wasn't?"

"Why," said I, "that bass would have weighed seven pounds instead of six."

The process of cleaning stopped over our heads while Uncle Ledyard laughed, and hearing it John Callant with a fork in his hand stuck his face in at the door to see what was up.

"And by God, Callant," Uncle Ledyard said to him, "do you know, I think the boy is right at that!"

Just then we heard Mrs. Callant clattering down the stairs and her voice on the edge of screeching, "Oh, Misther Boyd. . . ." Her red Hibernian face appeared in the door and she saw John.

"Get back to yer silver, you idle lazy loafer wasting your time in the house."

John gave her a dirty look and she lifted her damp cleaning cloth to slap him, when my Uncle Ledyard said, "Susanna!" with all the harshness of his heavy voice.

Immediately her hand dropped in front of her apron, and she put the other in it, and her bold eyes grew round and amazed. She jerked her heels for a curtsey and said, "Yes, your Honor."

There was a great silence in the house, with only the distant noise of the reaper in the oats.

"John," said Uncle Ledyard, "that's all."

John grinned at his wife as he went out and I could see her memorizing the dirty look she wanted to give him, but she stood there very meekly in front of Uncle Ledyard. He looked at her a while before he spoke.

"Haven't I told you time and again to come to my door gently, and to knock on it, and to come in if I say come in and to go away quietly if I don't?"

"Yes, your Honor."

"And if I say come in what are you to do?"

"I'm to come in quietlike, your Honor, and tell you what it is that's bedeviling me."

"And do you call this coming in quietly, you noisy sluttish roaring beasey?" thundered Uncle Ledyard. "Do I want to be screeched at by you to come running all over the house? By God I'd like to put my belt across your backside to make you remember your place."

"Yes, your Honor," Mrs. Callant said, curtseying again.

Uncle Ledyard breathed fiercely in his nose and stared at her from under his shaggy brows with a hard stare which seemed to me to please her unaccountably.

"Now tell me decently what it is that's on your brain, if you've got one."

"Oh sir," said Mrs. Callant in a desperate kind of whispering voice. "It's just that it's come into my head where we are to put Miss Kathy, now she's a fine lady."

"What's the matter with the room she used to have?"

"It was all right for a little girl," said Mrs. Callant. "But it doesn't seem daintyfied now, and besides it's all full of mice."

Uncle Ledyard swore.

"Why is it full of mice? Why haven't you cleared them out, you loafing Irishwoman? What do I hire you for to take care of my house if you let the mice eat it out from under my feet?"

Mrs. Callant seemed momentarily at a loss. Then her eyes fell on Artemis beside me on the floor and a glance of hatred was exchanged between them.

"Sure and I think it's that bitch has been killing the cat, your Honor."

Uncle Ledyard swore at her again and she seemed quite contented.

"You're right, Susanna," he said. "She's been to a finishing school and run the admiral's big house on Long Island for him and we must do better for her than her old room."

"Yes your Honor, that's just what was in my head too."

"Be quiet, can't you?"

"Yes sir, that's what I'm trying to do."

"Be still," roared Uncle Ledyard.

12

"Yes, your Honor."

"The admiral has the guest room next the withdrawing room, for he doesn't like the stairs."

"No, they're bothersome to a gentleman going to bed."

Uncle Ledyard gave her a glare.

"What's the matter with the other room downstairs?"

"It smells of the bats," said Mrs. Callant.

"Why does it?" asked Uncle Ledyard, scowling threateningly.

"Sure, it's the bats that smell, not the room," said Mrs. Callant, "And I can't be forever chasing them out, the nasty creatures."

"Then I don't see where we're going to put her," said Uncle Ledyard.

Both Mrs. Callant and I knew there was the room Doone's mother used to have, but the old man would let nobody into it from the day she died. It was a queer thing about him; but there it was, and nobody could decently suggest his giving it to Kathy.

There was a long pause.

"Haven't you any ideas at all?" asked Uncle Ledyard.

"No, Misther Boyd, unless it's yourself that has one. But I was just thinking couldn't we put her into Misther Doone's room?"

"What'll we do with Doone?"

"He won't be minding the bats."

"I don't think he'll like it," said Uncle Ledyard, "but call him."

Doone came in from the horsebarn in answer to the bell which Mrs. Callant swung brawnily from the back porch. He hardly seemed to be listening to Uncle Ledyard.

"It's a nuisance, Doone, but you see how it is."

Doone seemed annoyed, but he took it good naturedly.

"So long as I don't have to do the moving," he said. "I'm worried about Pansy, Dad. She looks to me as if she'd foal early."

"No," said Uncle Ledyard.

"She does."

"I'll ask John Callant."

"He doesn't know."

"Poor fool that he is," said Mrs. Callant. "Shall I change the rooms, then, your Honor?"

"Yes, yes."

Doone went out, and Mrs. Callant after him. She closed the door with great caution and then shrieked for Minna and Mrs. Toidy at the top of her lungs. We heard them come running, talk excitedly, and then all three mounted the stairs, to gather Doone's few clothes.

"I wish that Doone had something in his head besides the horses," Uncle Ledyard said, after a time.

"He likes fishing," I said.

"I know that, Teddy. But it's not what I'm thinking."

He lit his cigar again and puffed on it and under cover of the smoke I saw him eyeing the miniature of Doone's mother that hung under the picture of Greybriar over the mantel.

3

When I came over the river the next morning, I brought a letter for Uncle Ledyard from my mother. And as I approached Boyd House in the early morning sunlight, it seemed to me that the old house was wearing a new shine, for the light glistened on the warm old yellow of its clapboards, and the dew still lay on the shady side of the roof that came down from the peak of the house in a slow curve, clear out to the verandah eaves.

It was the oldest house in our part of the valley, and I always thought that the Boyd who built it must have been a shortish man because the rooms had such low ceilings that Doone always had to bend his head in going through a door. Title to the land was to Julian Boyd from the State of New York, and that Bounty Right together with a bill of sale signed by Mr. Boyd and five Indians in council and marking the transfer of two thousand acres for a rifle, a set of razors, a quilted dressing gown, and one barrel of whiskey, was all the title they needed to show so long as they kept up the back pages of the family Bible, that ended with Doone's name.

Minna was mopping the back porch, making a smell of suds

14

against the smell of asters, and I passed her with a nod, and went through the dining room.

It was a small room, as a dining room should be, so that a man could feel himself in close communion with his dinner, and the furniture was beautiful old Hepplewhite, in Domingan mahogany, almost golden with age, that made eating there a time of dignity. And I found Uncle Ledyard having a cup of coffee with the sun about his plate.

"Good morning, Teddy," he said, and accepted my mother's letter.

I watched him while he read it, his eyebrows drawn low, his eyes concentrated on my mother's even handwriting. Then he looked up at me and said, "I'm sorry your mother's sister is ill, Teddy. I hope it's not as bad as it sounds. Of course you can stay with us. We'll be glad to have you, for with the admiral here and Kathy, Doone will be needing an extra hand with the horses."

"I'm willing to help him out," I said as calmly as any man could, for all the way over it had seemed the most fortunate thing in the world that my aunt should be ill and my mother have to go to her, so that I could come over to Boyd House.

"Have you had breakfast, Teddy?"

"Yes, thanks," said I. "Where's Doone?"

"He's out with Pansy. He doesn't fancy the way she's behaving."

"I'll run over," I said.

"I wish you'd come back," he said, "and help me bring up some stuff from the cellar."

"I will."

But Doone was coming out of the stable and met me in the yard.

"How's Pansy?" I said.

"I guess I was wrong. She's all right for the time."

Pansy was a small black creature with a two-seven mile on the books. She was bred to The Earl, a horse that had done some great trotting the last year on the Grand Circuit.

"You'd better not go in now," said Doone. "I don't want her disturbed."

"How's Blue Dandy?" I asked.

15

"He's fine."

"Aren't you going to work him today?"

"I have. Before you came, Teddy. But now we'll have to make ready for the admiral."

"Well," I said, "I'm staying here now, so I'll be able to help you out. And if you want," I added, with my heart pumping up against my windpipe, "I can take Blue Dandy round for you now and then."

His hand dropped on my shoulder.

"I guess we'll make out together," he said.

"Can't I please drive him, Doone?"

"Do you know how old I was before Dad let me trot in the sulky?"

"No."

"Fifteen."

"But I'm big for my years."

He gave me a pat, but I wouldn't go into the house with him, for I was afraid I might cry, but instead I went out to the asters to see if there were any bees with thirteen stripes on their backs. I had never counted the stripes on a bee before, and after a while it looked hopeless, because I saw none with more than seven. But by twelve o'clock I was getting too hungry to keep to myself, and I found them at lunch together.

"When will they come, Dad?" Doone asked.

"About four o'clock," Uncle Ledyard said.

In spite of myself I was excited. And by three o'clock, with the fidgety waiting, I had forgotten all about Blue Dandy. For in our back country there had never been an automobile.

Doone had put on his black coat and Mrs. Callant had pressed Uncle Ledyard's pepper and salt and I had put on my stockings and shoes. There was a table on the verandah with bottles on it and glasses and mint in a white bowl with ice floating in the water, and raspberry vinegar for Kathy and myself. Uncle Ledyard looked hot as tomatoes and Doone was long-faced and I lay in the hammock, curled up, for there was a tickle in the bottom of my insides.

You couldn't hear a sound in the house behind us, except for

Minna's giggling now and then. The men were bringing the oats in from the eight acre piece, but their voices sounded far away and less articulate than the groans the reach made under the heavy load as the horses hauled from shock to shock.

I thought I couldn't bear sitting still another minute, when Doone lifted his head.

"Listen, Dad."

The old man threw up his chin. I held my breath. There was a clicking of toe nails through the withdrawing room, the screen door opened, and the thin black and red shape of Artemis toed over the porch. Her tail was stiff as a rod with a three pound bass making a long run and she growled softly.

"Quiet, girl," said Uncle Ledyard.

In the field the team stopped in a turn and Adam Fuess on the load shaded his eyes and looked toward where the road opened from the woods. Then one of the two year olds whinnied and there was a spatter of hoofs for the corner of the paddock, and then far away we heard the noise, like the noise a goose makes, flying in the fall against a high wind.

"Is it the horn?" asked Uncle Ledyard.

"It doesn't sound like cursing," said Doone.

"Then it isn't Jim," said Uncle Ledyard.

Doone got slowly to his feet. Artemis looked up at him and gave a wave of her tail and then stared out again and growled. Uncle Ledyard got up, too, and I followed him and Doone and the dog to the carriage circle, and we stood between the tubbed geraniums, myself on the carriage block, and stared at the woods.

Then we heard the engine running with a noise like firecrackers strung very tight together. The horn sounded again, like a man who has swallowed too large from his glass, and there it was, coming out of the woods with its brass front and the brass rails running down to it from the bit of glass and a great roll of dust hiding all its back end.

There was a chap in the front seat bending his belly over a wheel, with glasses over his eyes like the goggles you drive in a horse race with. And the admiral was standing up and leaning over the chap's shoulder with his hat in his hand and his white

17

hair shining and his face red from shouting. And beside him was a woman sitting very straight. I noticed even as far away as she was the straight graceful way she sat the jounces of the motor car. She had on a soft whitish yellow coat and a hat of the same color; but there was a bright green veil tied over it and round her neck and the ends reached straight out behind her like the tail of a flying bird.

We could hear the engine picking up in the noise it made and the dust rose higher, and then the car brayed like a jackass, and we saw that it was the admiral punching the horn. Uncle Ledyard caught me up on his shoulder and roared, "Hurray, boy, hurray!" Doone waved his hand, and I screamed, "Hurray, hurray!"

Mrs. Callant and John came running out of the house, and Minna sidled out behind them, and I caught a glimpse of Mrs. Toidy's face peering from the upstairs window. In the field Adam Fuess was waving his hat from the top of the load and the big team had their heads up and were lifting their feet and snorting. And we all shouted again for in truth it was a marvellous and heroic thing to think of that coughing contrivance travelling by itself all the two hundred and ninety miles from New York City to Boyd House.

The driving chap leaned over, turning the wheel in his hands, and the front wheels of the car turned towards us, and the car came after them, whirling round the corner, whirling back to make the circle, and, as the driver chap pulled at a rod outside the door, stopping right in front of the block as neatly as John Callant would have wheeled up the wagonette behind the bays. Then the driving chap pushed a button in front of him and the engine ceased coughing and the body shaking. There was a moment's silence and then there was a report like a twelve guage shotgun that has gone off in both barrels when nobody was expecting it.

I jumped, and Uncle Ledyard swore, and behind us Minna squealed and Mrs. Callant crossed herself with her hand over her apron. But the admiral was roaring with laughter.

"Only a backfire," he said off-hand. "How are you, my boy?"

He stood up in the tonneau and looked down at us, just a little condescending from his pride in his new car. But Uncle

18

Ledyard was grinning up at him and saying, "Get out of your bread box, Jim, and let me shake hands with you."

The driver chap had got out, looking rather cramped in the knees, and opened a door in the side of the car, and the admiral got down.

"By God, boy, it's good to see your old face again," he said, pumping Uncle Ledyard's hand and giving it the grip that I had always tried to see. But I never did, though I knew when they were giving it because they looked solemn and stiff and happy like two dogs at a new post. Then the admiral turned to Doone and shook hands with him saying "How are you, Doone?" And Doone thanked him. But I saw that he was looking past the admiral at the lady in the back seat, so I looked too.

The admiral and the driver chap were gritty beyond belief, but no dust showed on her whitish coat and the green of her scarf was too bright to be dimmed by it, and as she rose from the seat her cheeks looked fresh in the shade of her hat. Her color was high from the long drive. She was very lovely as she hesitated in the tonneau for she stood gracefully and easily, and the coat fitted her close, showing her slimness from the hem of her skirts to her eagerly lifted chin.

Then she got down through the door and came over to us, and she walked well with her feet sure of the ground. Uncle Ledyard took off his hat and so did the admiral. He said, "This is Kathy," with pride. But Doone was bareheaded. He took her hand and bowed. His voice sounded strange to me as he said, "Hello, Kathy."

"Hello, Doone."

Her voice was low, strong, and cordial, but there was hint of reserve in it, too, as there had been in Doone's, as if each had found a strength in the other they had not been looking to find, and they were surprised and on guard. But there was no mistaking the look in Doone's eyes. I had seen them once look like that when he first put his hands over a filly.

Then Uncle Ledyard was booming. "Well, well, Kathy," and she was giving a little cry and running into his arms, and his stiff short beard was bending against the fresh skin of her cheek; and Adam Fuess in the oat field might have heard his smacking kisses.

19

She stood back laughing softly and holding both his big hands in her slim gloved ones.

"Dear Uncle," she said.

He beamed all over, with his eyes, his mouth, his whole self seemed to be smiling at her.

"My lord, Kathy," he said. But her eyelids drooped in front of his stare and she made a curtsey as she held his hands, and then she rose with the most graceful gesture in the world, as if we were all of us in a play, and her eyelids swept up from her eyes and I saw the color of them for the first time under her thick black lashes.

John had said they were grey; but they were beyond any grey that I ever saw, for now they seemed blue, and now green, and now almost hazel, like the colors one finds in silver.

But now her eyes caught sight of him and she cried, "John!" and then, "Mrs. Callant!" And John came grinning up to her, his face like a frog, eyes popping and mouth going round his face like the hoop on a silo.

"Bedevil and all . . ." he began; but Mrs. Callant pushed him aside.

"Always a-swearing, you nasty fool," she said. Then she made a curtsey to Kathy and said, "Pleased and honored we are, Miss Kathy, and hope to entertain you comfortably. You're to have Misther Doone's room and he's to sleep with the bats."

Kathy laughed and turned to look gaily at Doone who was flushing a little, and the admiral roared and cursed and said with a laugh, "Hard bedding, Doone."

Uncle Ledyard said, "Stop the racket, you fool," to Mrs. Callant, and then to John, "Help with the bags, John. And dust them off carefully."

"That's right," said the admiral, his blue eyes sticking out boldly, "I'm dry as feathers with all the dirt of your dirty back roads, Leddy. Joe," and he spoke to the driver chap, "get out the bags. And then John Callant here can show you where to put the car and where you're to sleep."

"Put the car?" said John, turning a condescending eye on the driver.

"Do as you're told," said Uncle Ledyard.

"Sure and where am I told to put it?" asked John in the rhetorical voice he used when he was offended.

"You can put it in the barn," said the admiral, as though he were bestowing a favor.

"In the barn? Do you want to scare the living wits out of Pansy?"

"Who's Pansy?" Kathy asked.

"She's the black mare," I said. "She's going to foal."

That made Kathy look at me, and she smiled.

"Who are you?" she asked, for they were all tossing about with the bags of which there were more than you could believe possible, since the admiral never moved anywhere without all his forty pairs of shoes. "I'm Kathy O'Chelrie," she said.

"I know you're Kathy," said I. "But I thought your name was Porter like the admiral's."

She did not take offense, seeing how surprised I was.

"No," she said. "My father was O'Chelrie, and my mother married the admiral as a young widow."

"Oh, I see," I said. "Well, my name's Teddy Armond, and I've heard of you from Uncle Ledyard, and John Callant."

She gave me a little bow.

"May I call you Teddy, like the others?"

I do not know why, but her words put a small shiver in the hollow of my back and I felt that if she kissed me I shouldn't mind this time; but I respected her more for not doing it. And then I remembered something and I looked at her again.

"Haven't I seen you before, somewhere?"

"I don't believe so," she said. "The last time I was here, Teddy, you hadn't been born."

"I have, though," I said, getting more and more sure of myself. "I've seen a picture of you."

She smiled again. It was a lovely smile. She had a beautiful wide, generous mouth and her teeth were white and strong. She looked like a person who had never been tired in her whole life. And then I remembered, and the little chill went all over, and in the quiet sunlight with the bustle of getting out the bags all round us, I caught a vague and sweet scent from her. It was not like

21

perfume such as ladies put on their handkerchiefs, it was light and bright and a little intoxicating, and it lay between us like our understanding. I forgot even my excitement about the automobile, for Kathy was Kathy O'Chelrie, of New York, who was in the play that had had the whole city agog.

Then Doone came over to us and I said, "Do you know who she *is*, Doone?"

"What do you mean?"

The admiral looked up at me, red in the face, with his white mustache stiff as a bull's horns, but I didn't heed his annoyance. And I would have told Doone if Kathy had not met my eyes again. The corners of her mouth twitched to a smile, but her eyes were serious and made me feel great pride in myself.

"I've promised not to tell," I said. "You'll have to find it out for yourself."

"What is he talking about, Kathy?" asked Doone.

She looked at him, and smiled. I think even then she was in love with him, and I thought, if I were Doone, I would be with her.

"Don't you know?" she said. "I'm Kathy. You used to call me a damned nuisance, Doone. I remember once I stole your trousers and you had to chase me for them." The devil in her eyes made me laugh. Doone flushed.

"I remember," he said. "And I gave you a proper lambasting."

The color waved in her cheeks. She had plenty of temper. And they stared at each other a quick hard meeting of eyes.

Then the admiral swore.

"A damned nuisance is right. Ledyard, do you realize we've come three hundred miles in the last two days and you haven't offered me a drink yet?"

4

It was the strangest thing in the world how Kathy's entrance changed the very breath in that old, man's house. It was something I noticed when she passed over the threshold. The sunlight seemed to come with her.

She stood in the living room that occupied the center of the house and drew herself up with a deep breath.

"It hasn't changed. It hasn't changed at all. I love it."

Uncle Ledyard's voice sounded hoarser than usual as he put his arm round her slim long waist. "It hasn't looked the way it does now for a good many years, Kathy."

"What'll I do with that damned engine, Misther Ledyard?" John Callant whispered.

"Put it in the woodshed, John," whispered my uncle.

But the admiral heard him.

"You can't treat it that way, Leddy. Good God, you old coper, don't you realize that automobile cost more than three of your horses put together!"

"Did it, Jim? You'd do better to deal with me then, I think."

The admiral drew a shivering breath and his eyes swelled. And I waited expectantly for the bursting dams of his profanity. But John said, "The lad out there wants a garridge for it."

"Put it there," said the admiral quite calmly.

"But there isn't anny such thing," said John, scratching his head. "I can put a rick cover over it, if you like."

"No," roared the admiral.

"Would it take cold, then?" asked John.

"You blasted impudent rogue!" said the admiral.

"Sure the reaper's out. Maybe we could put it alongside the manure cart."

"Get out of here," said Uncle Ledyard. "And take care of it properly."

John went out grumbling and we heard him say to the chauffeur, "Wind up the trinket, me boy, and bring it along after me." He wasn't taking any chances of a ride.

The car coughed and roared and then went off.

Kathy smiled.

"Nothing's changed."

"It'll seem a rough place," said Uncle Ledyard.

"No it won't. It's lovely. I don't think I've been in real country since I was here—oh, years and years ago."

"There's no other real country," said Uncle Ledyard. "Maybe you'll want to get washed. Mrs. Callant'll show you Doone's room."

We four men went out on the porch and the admiral sat down in the high backed rocker as if he hadn't come farther than a trip to the village, and he and Doone and Uncle Ledyard fixed their own glasses and drank good health to each other. I poured myself some raspberry vinegar and put in the mint and went over to the hammock. Then Doone excused himself to go look at Pansy, and the two old men sat still for a long moment smiling at each other.

It was then that I knew really of the change in the house. It wasn't dead behind us the way it was when the admiral and Uncle Ledyard used to sit on the verandah. Then everything about it seemed to look out, at the men in the fields, or the colts in the paddock, at Doone on the track with John Callant and the sulky behind one of the racers, at Artemis coming in from a stroll. Now the house had an inward life, and it had a voice.

It was the light quick feet of Kathy I heard, moving back and forth in Doone's room over our heads. The splash of the water into the basin. Her voice humming on the edge of song. The noise her slippers made as she took them from the bag and dropped them on the floor. They were delicate sounds, and hearing them made me sink lower in the old tasselled hammock and wonder at the way I felt my hands at the ends of my wrists, and tightened the muscles in my legs.

"Well, Jim," said Uncle Ledyard. "You look pretty hearty."

"I'm all right, Leddy," said the admiral, combing the Bourbon out of his mustache. "I can't run around as fast as maybe. But thank God my digestion's all right."

24

"It's a pleasure to have you, then," said Uncle Ledyard. "You and Kathy. Do you realize, you damned sailor, that she's a beautiful piece of it?"

"Why shouldn't I, being a damned sailor? And with a hundred people a day to tell me if I couldn't see it for myself. Even Teddy has eye enough for that."

"I hope she won't get bored here, grown up as she is. It's different from your place."

"A hell of a lot she sees of that," snorted the admiral.

"What do you mean, Jim?"

"Well she's gone on the stage now. That's what I brought her up here for. To get her away from all the puppies that paw around after her. They'd follow her to hell, but they wouldn't come here. I wouldn't myself, if you weren't here and didn't have the best whiskey in America."

"There's plenty of that," said Uncle Ledyard. "Why don't you marry her off?"

"I could marry her in a minute to Rowland Atterbury or any other man you'd care to name," said the admiral. "But she won't stand for them. Girls have got their heads now-a-days, and ten to one she'd make me a scandal. Now in France they do it decently. A father can see to breeding his own line. You keep them at home and marry them off and they have a child and that's the end of the contract. After that there's nobody responsible."

Uncle Ledyard tilted back his chair.

"I wish Doone would get married."

The admiral cocked his eye.

"Do you mean him and Kathy?"

"Well, I wouldn't say no."

"Lord," said the admiral. "Doone couldn't get her."

"Damn it, Jim, it's the other way round. He won't look at a girl."

The admiral stuck his nose into his glass.

"He was looking at her pretty hard when we got here. Ten to one she turns him down."

"All right," said Uncle Ledyard. "Fifty dollars."

"Good," said the admiral. "That's easy money for me."

25

"He won't do it," said Uncle Ledyard, "but if he did go after her, I'll bet a hundred dollars he'll bag her."

"You poor fool," said the admiral, "I'll take it." He took a long drink from his glass. "I like Doone, you know. Even though he's a queer solitary man like yourself, I've nothing against him. They won't think he's much of a match at home, for he hasn't the money. And that's one thing she has to have or she'll die."

"He's better blooded than any of your Long Island pups," said Uncle Ledyard.

"I won't say yes or no," said the admiral. "But she has money enough for the two of them in her own name, and she'll have more from me."

"What's money got to do with it?" demanded my uncle.

"Well, I won't try to stop it."

"You'd be cheating on our bet if you did."

The admiral opened his mouth.

"So I would, you old fox."

"Have a drink," suggested Uncle Ledyard.

"Thanks, I will. I'll drink against my possible expenses. And I've bought a new boat."

"Curse your boats," said Uncle Ledyard. "I'm expecting a foal by The Earl out of Pansy. He's by Circumstance out of Fancy Girl. I'll show her to you tomorrow."

"Tomorrow," said the admiral, "you're going to have the thrill of your life, Ledyard. I'm taking you out in the car."

5

We heard Kathy coming down the stairs, and in a moment she was walking through the withdrawing room and at the door, and we were all on our feet.

She didn't want anything to drink.

"Minna brought me some water fresh from the spring," she said. "It's made me feel clean."

Uncle Ledyard smiled at her with his eyes from under the long hairs of his eyebrows and the admiral nodded. "I believe it is good water," he said, "though I've never tasted it myself."

"Don't stand up for me," she said. "Please."

We all sat down again and watched her. She had leaned against a verandah post with her hands holding it behind her. Her back rested against it so straight that there was no daylight showing between, and she had thrown back her head to rest her cheek against the white paint. The afternoon sunlight slanted across her, leaving one shoulder in the shadow and making a sculpture of the fine bones in her face. She seemed half asleep there, with her eyes veiled, as if she would never move again, as if her body was drinking the secrets of the house and the meadows.

The two old men sat solemnly looking at her and not saying a word through her silence, though the admiral's breath was beginning to rasp at the edges of his nostrils.

As the sun sank the light warmed on her face, showing the details that I did not know at that time a woman had, the down under the brows and on the upper cheeks, like a bloom on fruit it was so fine, the small way her nostrils were set, and the sensitiveness of her upper lip. It was short and curling, a light and beautiful thing. But the lower lip was strong and round and full, and her mouth in the sunlight was dark red. She was so completely withdrawn from us that when she suddenly drew in her breath, she seemed like a person waking. Her breast sprang and she opened her eyes. I was startled to find them looking straight at me.

"It's so good," she said to Uncle Ledyard. "I feel the way I used to the first day I got here. I can't sit down with you. I must see it all."

"Shall I take you around?" asked Uncle Ledyard.

"No, you stay here with Jim. I've got to go round everything till it's dark. I've got to get tired. All tired out tonight, or I won't sleep."

Uncle Ledyard smiled.

"Run along then," he said, "and mind you come in when Mrs. Callant rings the supper bell."

"I will, I promise I will."

They smiled at each other. Then she was looking at me again.

"Will you come with me, Teddy?"

"If you like."

"Come on then."

She swung away from the post as if her feet were released and I scrambled out of the hammock. I was surprised when she went into the withdrawing parlor, and more so when she stopped in it for a minute. For it was a strange, and to me a disagreeable room.

It had rose pink walls and fine old lyre-backed chairs, and brass lamps with etched glass globes. The seats of the chairs were of brocade so faded that they were snuff color. There was a stove with corinthian columns and much brass, and a harpsichord with rosewood inlay, and a small grand piano, of which I had never heard the voice, and a lady's secretary the glass doors of which were lined with old rose silk. It was a room half dead in which there was an old scent that might be forgotten perfume, or decaying hopes. And there was only one picture on the walls, an engraving of a picture called "Sacred and Profane Love". Some former Boyd lady must have bought it for that room and her successors must have approved of it. Though you could scarcely see it in the shadows, Kathy stopped in front of it. When I stopped next to her, she took my hand. And I felt her touch to be the only warm living thing in the room. Then she tilted her head and looked up at the ceiling.

There was a small trap door just over her head.

"Do you know what that is, Teddy?"

"No. I've never bothered to notice it," I said.

"Doone's mother had it made, so after dinner she could come in here and he could say his prayers to her through it. She was a delicate lady, I believe. She was very beautiful. I wonder if she was happy."

"Why shouldn't she be?"

"That's what a man would ask, Teddy." Then she seemed to forget me for a while. I tried to think of Doone, as a little boy, with the candle on the floor in his room while he knelt and his dark face like a gypsy's saying, "Our Father." I must have said it aloud, for suddenly Kathy squeezed my hand tighter and looked down at me. I could not see her face in the shadow, but the bend of her neck was so gracious that my heart stopped. Then she laughed.

"Come along, Teddy. Let's go outdoors."

"Where?" I asked.

"Everywhere."

We went out, and we went everywhere.

The sky was vast and crimson, there were fleece clouds overhead that caught the light against their breasts and turned it down. The two of us walking through it were like small things caught in a great flame. The buildings looked stiff and square and the trees were like black torches.

We went to the garden where the rose beds of Doone's mother lifted pale globes of fragrance over the pig weed and the white phlox shone like drifting silver. We skirted the glen, looking down at the pool from which the house water was pumped, and in which, when Uncle Ledyard had it dug, the men found two skeletons, a dozen silver buttons, and an Indian tomahawk. He had had them buried together in the burying ground, for he said there was no way of telling which was the Indian—a matter much better left for God to decide for Himself. We went over to the dairy barn where Adam Fuess was weighing the last milk and pouring it into the cheese factory cans for hauling in the morning. And we stood by the door as the cattle came out, with their bells and their warm grass breaths in our faces. We went up into the haymow and Kathy listened to see if there were any kittens and when we heard them and found them, yellow and white with their eyes not open, she nearly cried. She caught up her skirts and jumped with me clean to the mow floor and we laughed breathlessly and ran outdoors.

It was darker now. The light was nearly off the flat land and the valley was in shadow. I pointed out to her the lights from our own place. And we heard a boat horn sounding from the canal towpath. Then we came to the back of the horse barn and heard Doone saying something to John Callant and the rumble of trolleys on the door. I showed Kathy how I had learned to lift the hook on the manure door and we went in. It was almost dark, but Pansy was standing in her box stall at the back and she did not seem afraid of Kathy. Then we stopped while Blue Dandy put out his head and I showed Kathy how to tickle his tongue for him. Maidy and Arrogance wouldn't speak to us, so we came back to him. He looked fine and tall in the dark, like the ghost of a horse.

No one saw us come out, and we went down by the canal with the bridge over us and saw the boat's light at the bend and heard the horn. I put out my hand in the dark and touched Kathy. She was trembling a little.

"It looks cool, doesn't it, Teddy?"

Then we heard the clang of the housebell and we went back up the glen. And at the top we met Doone.

"I was looking all over for you," he said. "Where have you been?"

"All over," I said, as Kathy did not answer. "We found kittens and looked at Pansy . . ."

"You're not supposed to go in there," he said.

"Why not?" It was Kathy that asked.

"She's due to foal soon and she's nervous."

"We didn't disturb her," said Kathy.

"She was quiet, Doone," I said. "I showed Kathy Blue Dandy. He gave her his tongue."

"Did he?" Doone sounded pleased, though I expected him to be jealous, as I should have felt if it had been my horse, and he said nothing more as we walked back to the lights of the house.

6

We had dinner that night as I had never seen it in the old house. The heavy silver was out on the sideboard and there were candles all over, and Minna in a clean dress, looked quite smart. We had a soup made of green beans, light and creamy, and broiled small trout, and a saddle of lamb, and two kinds of wine, and a salad of cucumbers and icicle radishes, and a currant pastry.

It was a fine sight to see the admiral eating of everything and looking over the top of his glass and then into the bottom of it and smoothing his white mustache. Uncle Ledyard was stiff and broad at the end of the table as he carved the saddle, and Doone looked handsome in his black coat with his black hair and dark face. And Kathy at the end of the table laughed with them all and talked to Doone and sometimes to me. She made him tell her about the horses, about Blue Dandy in particular, till the admiral grunted and wanted to know how anybody could have a liking for horse racing now that automobiles were to be bought for money.

"You can travel all day."

"And walk up the hills," said Uncle Ledyard.

"You needn't in a Packard," said the admiral. "They'll take you thirty five miles an hour on a decent road and swoop you up the hill like a sloop on a wave. I could mount to Heaven's gates and make it in top gear, or maybe second, and you with your Blue Dandies would be eating my dust."

"I shouldn't think of that," said Uncle Ledyard. "I'd look to your brakes, if I were you, Jim. You might make the wrong turn at that speed."

The admiral growled.

In the living room John Callant opened the cellar trap and a smell of hams and bacon hanging there, and taragon in vinegar, and lavender, came up about us. And then John Callant came up again with a bottle of the old port and put it on the table.

"Oil your machinery with that, my boy," said Uncle Ledyard, "and maybe you'll convince me with your talk."

"I will," said the admiral.

So we all rose and Kathy went out of the room, and because I couldn't have the port, Uncle Ledyard sent me after her. I thought she would stop in the living room where the fire was crackling, and sit on the great red leather couch, but she went on into the withdrawing room, and when I had followed her there I was amazed. The candles were lighted in the lamps and the room was glowing softly, and Kathy was sitting at the old yellow keys of the piano. She began to play.

31

It needed tuning, but she did simple things with it so that there were just a few notes to come through her voice, and she sang for me very softly. I do not know what the song was, because I did not catch the words, she was so near to humming it, but her voice was soft and almost small. I looked at her with her dark hair and her red dress and her round slim bare arms.

And she said through her humming, "It's a queer old room, Teddy. It's rather pathetic. It's full of Boyd women. Here's their piano I'm playing on, and its voice is small; and the harpsichord has lost all its voice. Outside the door of this room is their big living room with its big furniture and its smell of men and to-bacco. And on the other side is their verandah where the men drink. The roof throws a shadow on the light in this room. They are all surrounded by the Boyd men—all big black men. I wonder if they were afraid of them. But the most pathetic thing of all, Teddy, is that there are no more Boyd men but Doone. Have you ever thought of that?"

"What's the matter with Doone?" I asked.

But she did not hear me.

"All around this room is the talk of horses. The men went all around this room, and if they came into it it was to go to the verandah or to come in from it to the living room. They were always passing through it with their strong voices and the smell of horses on their trousers. But, Teddy, you could smell everyone of those chair-seats and you wouldn't find the smell of horse on any one of them."

Her voice was deeper and it made me shiver and feel sorry for the Boyd women, though I did not see why, and angry against them, too—though I did not see why for that either.

"The Boyds have always married fair haired women. Pale crea-tures, I should believe. I don't know why. They were very good to them and treated them like ladies. And there's no lady for Doone."

Her fingers flashed on the keys, and a mocking trillet came from the piano. *And there's no lady for Doone,* it said.

"And there's no place for a lady in this house," continued

32

Kathy in her strangely electric voice, "no place except this room. Be damned to it. I want a drink!"

"What for?"

But she had swung off the stool and stepped out on the porch. I heard the bottle click once against the tumbler rim and I saw her outside down a swallow of Bourbon. She looked at me in the door, and I suppose I looked afraid, and white.

"Come out of there, Teddy. Let's not feel sorry for the Boyd ladies in their little rose colored room, or glad for the Boyd women in the countryside anywhere you fancy. The room is pathetic, it seems to me, because it was built by the men for their ladies and preserved. It's the Boyd mausoleum, though they don't know it. Tell me, does Doone ever run after the country girls?"

I was shocked. But I tried not to show it. My voice must have been stiff as I answered, "John Callant says not," for she laughed and kissed me, holding me tight against her, and as I wriggled I smelled the perfume in the lace yoke of her dress.

She put me down again, saying, "Poor Doone, it's a curse on him. He's lost even that. All his heart is in the horses. Damn them. Damn them!"

"Wait till you see Blue Dandy," I said, "and you won't damn them anymore."

"Let's go into the living room."

She looked almost hoydenish as we passed through the rose room now. All the sweet sadness was out of her. Her voice was ready to laugh. Her color was high. And she moved with scorn in her hips, as if with her skirts she stirred aside the ghosts.

She leaned against the hearth, supple as a wild vine, and I lay down in a corner of the red leather couch. Then, as swift as a seed dropping, she was herself again, and the men were coming into the room.

The admiral looked redder than ever behind his white mustache, and his eyes were bulging a little, like blue marbles, and he was tremendously polite in calling John Callant to place a chair for Kathy. Doone looked solemn and ready to laugh at him. Uncle Ledyard said to Kathy with that smile he had for her only, "Did I hear you singing in the rose room, Kathy?"

33

"Not a tune," she said laughing. "The piano's too far off."
He looked wounded.
"I'll have the tuner tomorrow," he said.

And suddenly Kathy's lip trembled and her silver eyes flashed towards me and I saw they were full of tears. She put her arm over his shoulder and kissed him.

"That would be lovely, Uncle. I'll play to you then."

"Will you, Kathy?"

"Whatever song you like."

She was looking at Doone now, and her eyes were a challenge even I could read.

But the admiral, who had fallen into a doze, jumped and swore at a knot bursting in the fire.

"A clean miss," he roared. "My God, Mister, this isn't target practice!"

7

August is apt to bring us fine weather. The meadows are sultry, but there is a wind in the sky and the clouds are great and dignified as they march against the mountains. It was clear the next morning when we sat at breakfast with the farm sounds spreading into the fields. And as we finished, John Callant put his nose against the screen door and said, "Misther Ledyard."

"Yes," said Uncle Ledyard.

"It's this feller that says he's a shoffer wants to ask the admiral does he want the car?"

"Yes I do," said the admiral. "I want it in half an hour."

"And what shall I tell him?"

"What I said," said the admiral, staring up coldly.

"Very well," said John. "But he's a queer chap."

"What do you mean?" Kathy asked.

"Well, Miss Kathy, he said he couldn't sleep at all last night."

34

"What did you do with him?" Uncle Ledyard asked threateningly.

"Sure we gave him the corner room. It wasn't the bedding, I'm sure. And my missus was keeping her eye on Minna that's taken a fancy to his elegance. He said it was the silence kept him awake."

"Silence?"

"That's what I said. He said it kept dinging in his ears all night. It's very queer," said John, shaking his head. "I wouldn't trust a man like that, myself."

"Never mind," said the admiral. "Tell him to be prompt. We'll have a spin before it gets hot. You're coming, Leddy. It'll show you what the world's doing while you stifle up here. How about you, Kathy?"

Kathy glanced at Doone.

"I think I won't, Jim."

"Nor I," said Doone. "I'm busy this morning with Blue Dandy."

"All right," said the admiral. "Then Leddy and I will go. I'll take you the loop round Hawkinsville."

"Let's arrange to come down the hill," suggested Uncle Ledyard.

"No, by God, we'll go up," said the admiral. "With just three aboard she'll do it easy. We'll go down by Meecher's crossing and get a good run at it."

Uncle Ledyard was silent. He didn't like the notion, that was plain, but he had the look of a man who has made up his mind to die game.

The car came rattling over from the machine shed on the minute and whirled round the carriage circle on its little wheels. The chauffeur had polished off all the dust, but I could see the admiral sniffing at it when he got in to see if John had put it beside the dung cart. Uncle Ledyard got in and closed the door and said, "Good morning," to the chauffeur like a man saying good morning to Charon. Then the chauffeur got into the front seat and sat still, waiting for orders. I thought he did look like a man who hasn't slept well—there was an edgy expression about the eyes.

"Drive ahead," said the admiral, "and when we come to the turns I'll tell you which way to put her."

The chauffeur yanked at some rods and the car started. The admiral waved his hat very gallantly and the dust rose up and they turned down the glen. We did not see them again all morning.

"It's a wonderful sight, to be sure," said John.

I agreed.

"I'd like to drive it myself," I said.

Doone threw me a hard look, but Kathy smiled.

"I'll show you if you like, someday, Teddy."

"Can you drive it?"

"Yes, but Jim won't let me."

I thought about it for a moment and then I said, "I won't do it though till after I've driven Blue Dandy."

I thought that would be a long time off.

Kathy and I went over to the track and watched Doone bring out the grey horse. He was going to travel again, you could see it in his eye. As he entered the track, Kathy drew her breath in.

"He is beautiful!"

Doone heard her and his smile flashed for her. But he didn't speak, except to the horse, and Kathy might have been myself for all the attention he paid her till he had finished the first heat. He made it in 2:10. I have never seen a horse come along so quickly as Blue Dandy did once he started to really trot—but then he was three years old.

As he went under the wire, I asked Kathy, "Can your automobile move like that?"

"It isn't a comparison," she said with a small smile. "That's a machine and this is a horse."

"Just the same," Doone said, as he swung off the sulky. "I would bet that Blue Dandy could run down that motor."

Kathy flashed.

"What would you be willing to bet, Doone?"

"Anything in the world."

"Would you really?" she asked.

He said, "Yes," but his eyes were on Maidy coming out with John. "Put her round," he said, and he held the watch.

The mare was a leggy black thing, with a racking stride. You could see she was fast, but she hadn't the thrust of Blue Dandy. We watched the colt again, and then Kathy went back to the house, to wait the mailman. Inside the rose room sounded the slow tinkle of the piano as the tuner worked over it. Mrs. Callant was scolding Mrs. Toidy in the kitchen and Minna was making the beds.

There was a letter for Kathy which she read twice over before she said to me, "I'm offered a new part in the fall. A leading part."

She was leaning her chin on her hand and staring out at Doone on the track behind Arrogance.

"Does he do that all day, Teddy?"

"He has to bring them into shape for Syracuse," I said. "He hasn't too much time."

"What would he make if he won, I wonder?"

"I don't know," I said. "But he needs the money."

"And what will he do if he doesn't make it?"

"Oh, I don't know. He'll get along, I guess."

Mrs. Callant came out on the porch behind us hiding her floury hands in her apron.

"Good morning, Miss Kathy. It's sorry I am to disturb you, but it's the piano man wants to know would you run your hand over the keys."

"Yes, of course."

The rose room had a faint musty morning smell, as it always did. With the lights gone out of it it seemed just a place again. But Kathy sat down at the piano and ran off the scales.

"It's fine," she said to the tuner.

He bowed, and knelt down to pick up his tools. He fumbled a little, to find the fork.

"It's right there beside you," said Kathy, impatienty. "At your right hand."

He said thank you, found it, and picked it up.

"It costs five dollars," he said.

"The fork?"

"No the tuning. And there's five dollars for the last time."

"You'll have to see Mr. Ledyard," Kathy began. Then she asked, "When was the last one?"

"I tuned it for Mrs. Boyd a week before she died," he said.
"Hasn't my uncle paid you yet?"

"He wouldn't speak to me."

Kathy's color flared up. Her hands pulled a single harsh chord
from the keys, she rose and swept out of the room. When she
came back, she had ten dollars in her hand.

"Thank you," said the tuner.

"Don't thank me," she said sharply.

He picked up his bag and bumped against a chair. She didn't
say anything at his clumsiness, but she was breathing angrily.

"What makes him so clumsy?" she asked when he was gone.

"He's nearly blind," I said.

"Then why didn't you help him, Teddy. Aren't you ashamed?
Haven't any of you any feeling for people?"

Her anger swept over me, then she went out of the room.

"I'm sorry," I said. "Aren't you going to play some music?"

"I couldn't touch it," she said.

She watched Doone from the porch and her eyes looked at me
as if she wanted to hurt him. I could not understand her at all.
She was fidgeting. She couldn't be still. She came in again with
long angry steps and sat down in the cool dark living room. The
windows seemed to make a visible barrier against the sunlight. It
lay just outside the frames, but it would not come in; and yet the
sounds of the horse's hoofs came in, and the steady "So-o-o,
so-o-o," of Doone's voice.

As she listened to it, stiffness seemed to slip out of her. She
quivered under it. She was like a horse afraid of the whip. Then
she said, "For God's sake shut that window."

I closed it.

"Please go away, Teddy."

I went out of the room. I went onto the porch, but Doone was
through. He was walking with easy strides across the grass, and
the scent of sweat was on the knees of his trousers and his hair
was tangled from the wind. He nodded to me and went into the
house to the bathroom, and I heard him washing. I stayed outside
wondering what was the matter with Kathy and feeling lonesome
and shut off both from her and from Doone. After a while I let

myself quietly into the office and sat down beside Artemis on the rug in front of the gun case.

The living room door was open and the house was still. I could not hear a sound.

Then I heard Doone coming through the dining room, and a faint smell of horse reached me. He stopped in the shadow of the door as if he were looking. Then he came forward into the middle of the room. I knew in some way that he was not looking for me and I did not move.

Kathy's voice said, "Aren't you going to speak to me, Doone?" and I guessed she must be lying on the red leather sofa. He didn't answer her. In the dining room the clock could be heard ticktocking and Mrs. Callant's feet moved about in the kitchen.

"Have you ever wanted to kiss a girl, Doone?"

I cannot describe the note there was in her voice. I know it made me go cold and I dropped my hand on Artemis' nose and it felt cold as my hand.

"Why?" he said. And there was something strange in his voice, also.

She waited a while before she spoke.

"Because," she said, "the way you were standing there wondering if I was asleep made me wonder."

"It's a queer question, anyway."

"It's a queer question for me to ask a man," Kathy said.

"I don't doubt that, Kathy."

It seemed to me as if they were speaking with swords.

"Doone, what was your mother like?"

"To people, or to me?"

"Oh to you, Doone."

"She was a very lovely person, to me. I don't think I ever loved anyone in the world like her. That's all I can tell you, or will tell you, Kathy."

"Were you sorry for her?"

"Why do you ask that?"

"I've felt sorry for her," Kathy said.

"I think other people were, too. I used to hate my father before she died. But there was no reason for it."

39

"Was he so good to her?"

"He gave her everything he had."

"What was that?" Kathy asked. And when he did not answer, she went on, "I suppose he saw that she didn't take cold, and brought her dress goods, and took her driving on Sunday, and kept her in her fine room out of the sun."

"Yes, he did all that," Doone said slowly. "I never heard him curse in front of her."

"Oh lord!" Kathy fell silent. "She must have been pretty."

"She was," said Doone. "But she was a sad person. There was something, I think, not right about her life."

I heard Kathy sit up on the sofa.

"Doone, why do you keep yourself like an anchorite?"

"I don't know. I keep myself busy. I like my horses. There is nothing like a horse in the world. And there'll be no horse like Blue Dandy, when I'm done with him." His voice warmed. It was like his own again. But Kathy said something.

"What's that, Kathy?"

"I was saying that horses had taken the soul out of you Boyds."

"I don't see what cause you have to say that," he said seriously. "There is no better friend than an honest horse, or an honest mare, either. They give you all there is in them. They teach you to use your hands and your eyes, and to govern your temper."

"You poor fools. Govern your tempers like Ledyard! Doone, are you blind?"

"No, Kathy, not quite blind."

"If you treated your women the way you do your horses, they'd give you something, Doone. 'All there is in them'. Poor things, they've never had the chance. By not hurting them you've never let them hurt you, but you've tortured them to death. I know it. Every last one. Wake up, Doone, for God's sake wake up. Look at me!"

"I've been looking at you, Kathy."

"For a while you used to be friends with me. We used to pretend we were married, barelegged little devils that we were. And you were twice the man then than you are now." Her voice softened. "Look at me, Doone? Why do you suppose I came up here?"

"I don't know."

"Kiss me, Doone."

I heard Doone breathing in the quiet of the house.

"Kiss me, you poor blind boy."

I held quite still, not drawing a breath. It was not a kiss I heard, only silence.

Then Kathy's voice was very low.

"Do you see now?"

"Yes," he said harshly. "How can I marry you?"

"Don't bother about that Doone."

"Do you think I'm a fool. Do you want to be like the girls in the fields that they're always whispering about behind our backs?"

"Why not? I'm alive, Doone."

"By God, so am I! Kathy, you wouldn't stand it a week, living here. You'd be lonesome for your friends, all your glad friends in their glad clothes. You'd miss the hand clapping."

"Oh, so you know about that?"

"Yes I do."

"So you think I'm not the proper wife for a Boyd. You want them like flowers; bleeding hearts, I suppose."

"I think you are rich, and on the way to be famous."

"Damn you, Doone. Then why did you kiss me?"

He chuckled, suddenly, and I let out my breath, knowing he was all right. And he rolled a brogue like John Callant.

"Sure and didn't you ask for it?" He turned to the window. "What do you suppose has happened to Dad and the admiral, Kathy?"

Then we heard the admiral swearing.

I slipped in behind them and I saw Kathy standing up at his side, and her face was fiery and her eyes cold and she was trembling.

"You've no heart in you, Doone."

8

We all looked out of the window, and Doone began to laugh. I laughed too, and then Kathy could not stop herself from joining us.

For the swearing was coming round the corner of the Glen. It came behind a gaunt brown farm-team.

"That's Meecher's," said Doone, and there was Meecher walking beside them, his face solemn, and virtue in his walk as if he were the twelve apostles. He had a rope hitched from his team's eveners to the front axle of the car. And sitting on the front seat, the sweat rolling off his brow and the profanity rolling under his mustache was Admiral Porter, doing his damndest to keep the front wheels of the car behind the horses. My uncle Ledyard was sitting back against the cushions of the back seat as solemn as a circuit judge. But of the chauffeur there wasn't a sign at all. They drove up to the carriage block and the admiral put on the brake before the team stopped and the car slid along like a stone bolt. Then the admiral got out.

"Here's your ten dollars salvage," he said, and paid Meecher. "Now go home and be damned to you and your dirty pigs."

He yanked off his hat and stamped into the house. He stopped in the dining room.

"John," he shouted in his fog horn voice. "John, John, John Callant! Come here."

There was a great to-do in the kitchen and John looked through the door.

"For God's sake, John, bring me some hot whiskey and lemon to my room."

"Is it your Honor's had an accident?" said John.

"Blast your impudence! Do what I tell you!"

"Sure and is it sick you are, sir?"

The admiral paused and put his hand on his waistcoat.

His voice became hollow.

"Yes," he said. "I'm sick. Hurry up, John."

"What is it, Jim?" Kathy asked.

"Shut up, girl. Teddy come and untie my shoes. I'm tired and I want to sleep."

He went to bed, drank his toddy, closed his eyes.

Uncle Ledyard came in laughing.

"We got to Meecher's, and coming round the corner," he said, "we ran into the white sow. She was farrowing right in the road. We couldn't get by her. We couldn't back up out of the ditch. We had to wait until she was through."

He began to rumble.

"Do you know how many pigs she had?"

John, passing through with the pitcher of toddy making him a trail of steam, said over his shoulder, "She's the grand old sow, and I'll believe there was twenty-four of the babies."

Uncle Ledyard took hold of the point of his beard.

"Twenty-seven," he burst out. "We arrived at the first and when he hit her the second was born. Jim had been talking about the wonders of science and I had almost begun to believe him. But after the fourth had come into the daylight, he cursed. He would curse at each next one. By the tenth his cursing was overlapping the eleventh, and by the fifteenth he was roaring like a bull caught in a bog. And when the old sow got to the twentieth he was so tangled up in his speech he couldn't make out whether he was speaking to me or to the driver chap or to the sow, and she was quiet as the mother of earth, beyond grunting now and then and having another piglet."

Uncle Ledyard fell back on the sofa and called weakly for a glass. John, grinning all over, had it ready for him.

"I have never looked at a man like Jim. He was beyond the power of speech but he still made a noise. I suppose he had been cursing for forty minutes, and the sun shining down on his face had heated him a little. I think he had got into Portuguese swearing, for I couldn't understand him at all. Then the sow had the twenty-sixth and she lifted her chin at him and shut her eyes and grunted.

" 'What are you doing there sitting and doing nothing you lazy pup?' " said Jim to the driver chap. 'Get out and move those pigs.'

" 'I'll not,' said the driver, 'I hired on for a shoffer, and not to be moving your pigs.'

" '*My* pigs,' roared Jim, and he went on for a while. 'Get out before I throw you out.'

" 'I will not,' said the driver.

" 'Do you know this is mutiny?' asks Jim, sitting stiff as a ramrod.

" 'For two cents I'd spit in the eye of the whole damned navy,' said the driver, 'and as for you, you old billy goat, if you come out here in the road, I'll knock you down.'

"I think the driver was a city fellow and he didn't like the look of this country from the first. But Jim wasn't waiting. He got out of the car so fast I could hardly keep up with him, and I thought I'd better be handy."

Kathy and Doone threw up their chins and howled, and I laughed too, seeing in my own mind the two old gentlemen scrambling out into the dusty white road to trample the driver together. But Uncle Ledyard went on, with a drink and a long breath:

"I don't think the driver chap had his stomach in it. 'I'll not fight two old roosters like you,' he said. 'I'm through with you.'

" 'You're not, you're fired,' yelled Jim, and he started at him across the sow. But she popped like one of these new small gauge shotguns and there was the runt and she got up between us. The driver looked at the runt and I thought he was going to be sick. Instead he turned his back on us and walked off for Boonville, and I don't doubt he's made the twelve o'clock train for New York. And we had to get Meecher and hire him to draw us back because Jim didn't know what to do with the engine, and I'm glad he didn't for he was in a mood to drown us all."

"Poor Jim," said Kathy, bubbling with laughter. "He won't be able to tour in his car because he won't let me drive him."

"I'm glad of that," said Uncle Ledyard. "I think I got a touch of the sun. It was a very hot place for a while."

We sat still at last, listening to the admiral groaning in his sleep. But he got up for luncheon and beyond a little excursion into the breeding of the chauffeur, he seemed fairly normal. After the meal he and Uncle Ledyard were very companionable on the verandah, and about four o'clock they collected some men and had the car pushed into the machine shed and the door closed upon it. It didn't move again till the night Kathy took it out on her flight for New York and we went after her. . . .

When we had dinner that night I felt a strange tension in the room. And yet it was all soft with candlelight and the reflections of them in the wax on the mahogany and Minna dropped only a fork. Nor was there anything the matter with Uncle Ledyard. He cut into the Tamwyth ham as if it were butter against the edge of his knife and his big hands cut slices fine as paper. The admiral wasn't saying a great deal, to be sure, but his hot whiskey, and the whiskey he'd had in the afternoon, were making him sleepy. And I don't think there was anything wrong with Doone—at least he didn't show it.

But Kathy had been late in coming down stairs. Whether she did it on purpose, I don't know, but there was mischief in her that night. She had put on a dress of a strange burning orange, and she stopped on the stairs as she came down, so that the candle lamp on the newell post shone up against her and put reflections of the dress in her black hair. Doone stopped in a sentence to John Callant who had come in from the barn and he never took it up again. And John's lower jaw gapped enough to show his missing teeth and I saw that against explicit orders he had his quid stowed away in the gap. It came loose while he stared and he had to leave the room.

"I'm sorry I kept you waiting," said Kathy in her deep voice, and it was so natural that it shocked us.

As she moved the light played over the orange dress making flame of it. It was cut very low and square in front, and fitted her tightly and her skin looked so white that I couldn't take my eyes off it. She came over the dark floor with the little toes of her black shoes moving as light as apple seeds and her body like a gypsy dancer's. And Uncle Ledyard bowed to her and offered his arm.

"The lads must wait a while longer, Kathy."

She tilted her chin to him as they swept into the dining room, but out of the tail of her eye she looked back at Doone. He was like an amazed man before the fire and he did not move until the admiral struggled with the arms of his chair.

All through dinner, she was bright at talking. She spoke about the stage, and of the contract she had been offered that morning by the mail. She described dressing in the windy dark rooms back of the stage when snow was whistling outside, and hearing the sound of it on the other side of the wall and the sound of the audience clapping their hands. It was peculiar how vividly she brought another phase of life through the faint horse smell in that old house. Glasses tinkled through her words when she described after theatre suppers, and the young gentlemen attending her stiff with eagerness or weak with too much wine.

She was talking at Doone; the admiral never heard a word; and Uncle Ledyard was always too fond of his food. But Doone talked back at her so naturally and seemed so polite in wanting to know what she had to tell, that I took no notice of him. I could not take my eyes off her. For tonight truly she had the scent of the other world in her.

And she wasn't through with it at dinner. Whatever she was trying to get out of Doone and had so far failed to get, she would not give up her game yet.

She went into the rose room when they stayed for their port, and she sat down at the piano. As she passed the door and her orange dress came against the rose walls it was as if someone had screamed. But there wasn't a sound except the arrogant tapping of her heels and the swift scrape of the bench as she drew it up under her. Then she played.

I do not come from a musical family, and I do not know whose was the music. But it was strong stormy stuff, with long rolls like thunder, and swift sharp petulant dancing of the trebles. The small room she played in was too small to hold the vastness of a sound that seemed to set the candle lights swimming. It flowed in waves through the door until it filled the living room and it went on into the dining room. I heard the cautious feet on gravel and saw the servants standing out on the drive in the moonlight.

Doone could not stand it sitting in the dining room. He came into the living room and sat beside me. He would not go to the door of the rose room and she would not stop her playing. It was not until the admiral stamped uncertainly in upon us and roared, "For God's sake, Kathy, stop that noise," that she banged to a stop.

We were dizzy with the silence. Then she stood in the door, one hand against the lintel by her cheek, and smiled sweetly at us.

Uncle Ledyard's voice said, "Now play us something simple Kathy. Please."

She smiled at him sadly and disappeared, and the piano began to sing little tunes—of Tom Moore's: "I knew by the smoke that so gracefully curled. . . ."

And her voice was small and low and Uncle Ledyard looked very much moved, like a man dreaming on his good digestion, but Doone's face became haggard.

She played on for a little while, then she stopped altogether, and we saw that the admiral had fallen asleep.

"Perhaps," said Kathy, coming softly into the room, "I'd better follow his example."

She said good night and went slowly up the stairs, and as she rose from sight the beam cut off the orange dress. I never saw it again, after that, except once.

We called John Callant, who took the admiral away with a kind of pity. Uncle Ledyard climbed heavily to his room. Doone disappeared through his door, and I went up to the little room that had been Kathy's. I tried to sleep, but the music was swinging my bed. And finally I heard John Callant returning from the admiral, and his voice talking to Mrs. Callant.

"Stand over, Susie."

The springs creaked.

9

The moon was well on in the sky when I woke again. And I was broad awake. I knew something was happening.

The night was warm and still and the crickets were making a tremendous threeping out in the oat stubble. When I went to the window my first look was toward the horse barn, and sure enough there was John with a lantern, running for the house. His bare feet slapped onto the porch and he went through the dining room. I pulled on a sweater, opened my door stealthily, and stood in the hall.

I could hear him knocking gently on Doone's door.

The back hall was dark except for the crack of light coming from the Callants' room and I stepped over that. The kitchen was still thick with the dinner scents as I went through it. In the dining room a dim sheen of moonglow lay on the mahogany.

I could see Doone's door open and John Callant standing in it with the lantern.

"She's coming, Misther Doone. She's been at it awhile, I'm thinking, but it's a bad position. It's the front feet and her head turned, surely."

"I'll want my bag," Doone said. "Get it out of the office."

John slipped like a bat across the living room and rummaged through the office. Then he returned empty handed.

"It's not there, Misther Doone. I can't find it. Oh glory, what have you been doing with it?"

"Be still, you fool. I haven't been doing anything with it. I told Mrs. Callant to put it there when she moved the things out of my room."

"That woman," hissed John.

"Go ask her," said Doone.

John scurried past me with righteousness glaring from his eye.

48

The lantern light he carried was sucked up the stairway and he went to his bedroom door.

"What have you been doing with Misther Doone's case?" he demanded.

Mrs. Callant creaked the bed.

"What do you mean? Blathering at me. Sure I don't know which case it is you're racketing over."

"The case with the tools in it," said John. "Pansy's took now, and if it's dying she is because you've lost the tools with the case in it, it's skinning the hide off your back Misther Ledyard will be if I don't myself."

"I don't know," began his wife shrilly.

"And be still, can't you? Would you be waking the house? Now tell me where it is or I'll put my own belt acrosst you."

"Where would it be but in Misther Doone's room where it always is?" demanded Mrs. Callant. "Sure isn't he always telling me not to handle his dirty things?"

"Bring me my pants to the kitchen," said John severely, "so I can spring into them as I pass. It's the straw in the stall that bothers me."

He came hurrying by me again with a breath of the stable and Doone met him in the living room.

"Where is it?"

"It's in your room," said John. "I'm ashamed of her myself, the idle loafer, too lazy to touch it as yourself told her."

Doone swore.

"Get me a pan of hot water. *Hot*, John."

John passed me once more, this time for the kitchen, where his wife met him rubbing the sleep from her eyes with the leg of his trousers.

"Give them here," he ordered, "and heat me a pan of water, quick. And hot, me girl, or Misther Doone will be enraged with us both."

As they stuffed the stove with kindling, I stole into the living room and lay down on the deep sofa. Doone was standing undecidedly by the door to the rose room when his voice was called

49

softly. He hesitated, then went into the room, and the walls shone pink in the lanternlight.

"What is it, Doone?" Kathy whispered.

"Pansy's foal," he said softly. "I'm sorry to have waked you, Kathy, but Mrs. Callant has left my case of instruments in your room. Can you find it for me?"

"Yes. Where is it, Doone?"

"It ought to be in the wash stand back of the crockery."

I could see him standing still and dark in his shirt and trousers and his bare feet in slippers. He was in front of the picture of Sacred and Profane Love and looking up at the little prayer-door. Kathy's feet made no sound, but I heard the chink of crockery, and then I saw the bag being lowered. Her bare arm gleamed white in the lanternlight, slim and quick.

"Can I help, Doone?"

"No. No thanks. Just drop the bag."

Her fingers were reluctant in unbending. He caught the bag in one hand and tucked it under his arm.

"I wish you'd let me help."

"It's no place for you Kathy."

He came past me swiftly, without looking left or right. As the lantern swung through the dining room door, an eddy of darkness flowed over the living room, and in it I smelled the cigar smoke of the evening, and a bit of wood smoke from the fireplace, and the faint dew-damp grass smell. Then I heard John Callant saying on the porch, "Sure and I think it's hot enough. The kettle was steaming."

Their feet and their voices died over the grass. . . .

As my eyes became accustomed to the darkness, I saw that the light in the rose room had not quite gone. Color had left, but the shapes of the stairs and the piano were dimly visible, and the brass candle brackets on the music rack had threads of gold. I got up softly to look in the door.

The light came from the prayer-door which was still open. Kathy was kneeling beside it. She must have had the candle on the floor for there was a soft upward luminance on her face. I had

never seen her so. She seemed hushed. Her lips were fuller and
the eyelids were darkened. Her dark hair was hanging all around
her, but one shoulder broke through. It was white and curved
from the limpness of her hands.

Though my heart was bursting to call her name, I did not even
stir until her eyelids lifted. A slight shiver possessed her, and she
said, "Oh, it's you, Teddy."

The clock ticking in the dining room measured time from a great
distance.

She said again, "What are you doing up, Teddy?"

"I'm going out to the horse barn," I whispered. "Do you want to
come with me?"

She said, "Yes," at once, and I went back into the living room
to wait for her. She was like a ghost coming down the stairs; her
feet seemed timid of the stair-treads. All I could see of her was
the white of her nightgown, and, as she passed the door, a touch
of moonglow on her breast.

"You aren't coming out that way, are you?"

"I forgot," she said. I thought she was still asleep. "I'll get a coat,
Teddy."

"Here," I said. "Take Doone's."

I was in a hurry, and Doone's long driving coat hung behind
the door. She slipped it on without a word; it hung loosely from
her shoulders, enclosing the nightgown. It made her seem smaller
as she stepped with me onto the damp grass.

We did not speak as we went along the drive. The threeping of
crickets seemed to accompany our steps. A few fireflies were playing patterns among the trees of the glen. And before us, the hay-
scented door of the barn loomed with a nebule of brown light
far in.

Kathy's hand dropped to my shoulder as we stole through the
door, and through our slippers we felt the knots and splinters of
the rough planks. Pansy's stall was at the back, and there, against
the wall, we saw the black shadows of Doone and John bending
their heads together.

There wasn't a sound in the barn but their muttering voices
and the soft breathing of the horses as they stood with their heads

over the doors. Then John grunted and Doone said, "It's all right now," in a deep, strong voice. And at the sound of it, the pricked ears of the horses relaxed.

Kathy and I stole forward together. We stood at the edge of the door looking into the stall. And we saw Doone kneeling, and the black mare still lying in the mussed straw, with John Callant squatting at her loins, his lumpy hand resting lightly on her side. They were both looking down at the foal.

"A fine foal," Doone was saying. "He shows his bone already."

He gave the mare a pat and drew himself erect on his knees.

"He's the incarnate spit of The Earl," said John. "He'll be a fine horse, I'm telling you."

Doone turned suddenly to the pan and rinsed his hands. He washed them with entire preoccupation, taking each finger in turn, cleaning between them. When he was satisfied he dried them on a meal sack.

"You'd better sit up with her a while, John. And I'll take the pan back to the kitchen. Tell Susanna to boil it in the morning."

"Yes, Misther Doone."

I felt Kathy's hand draw at my shoulder, and together we slipped out of the barn with only the eyes of the horses following our passage.

We did not speak at all, going back to the house, but in the dining room, Kathy pressed my shoulder again.

"Good night, Teddy," she said. "You'd better go to bed, now."

"Good night, Kathy."

I went upstairs slowly. At the landing I looked back. She was hanging up Doone's coat behind the door. I listened to her feet gently passing into the living room, then I heard the faint creak of the sofa. And I knew she was going to wait for Doone.

But I was sleepy. As soon as my head touched the pillow, I forgot everything in the wide world.

What Kathy said to Doone when he found her waiting for him, or what he said to her, or whether they said anything at all, they know best themselves. But that she had waited for him, I discovered at breakfast when Uncle Ledyard said:

52

"We'll have to go out and look at the foal."

"Did Pansy foal last night?" I asked as innocently as I knew how.

"Yes, Teddy. And Doone says he's a beauty."

I glanced at Doone and found him staring sternly at me across the table. But when he did not give me away, I knew that he had found Kathy, and I glanced quickly at her.

She was eating her raspberries so naturally, and she looked so fresh in her green dress, with its short puffy sleeves, and she seemed so peaceful and contented, that I could hardly believe she had been up at all the night before. But when she smiled at me she gave me a pleasant feeling of secrets shared between us.

We finished breakfast leisurely, and then the four of us went out to the barn. The admiral was not interested. Horses were nothing in his life. I don't think he ever took notice of an animal before the morning he met Meecher's sow.

John Callant had cleaned out the stall and Pansy was standing in the far corner with her nostrils flaring gently in the fresh straw. Doone went in to her and stood her over and we looked together at the foal.

He was black as she and still shining and he lay with his chin out and his eyes closed.

We stood together a moment without speaking and then moved off and Doone came out and closed the stall door. John Callant came out of the harness room with the harness slung on his arms and went in to Blue Dandy. Uncle Ledyard watched him.

"That new boy's going to show you something real, Doone. I fancy his breeding."

Doone laughed.

"I'll keep my money on Dandy," he said.

And he wheeled out the sulky.

Kathy stood by as they put in the grey horse, but she did not say anything. And Doone scarcely noticed her. Her face showed nothing of her thoughts. She seemed very still, and reserved; but she watched him till he had gone through the gate to the track. Then she went quietly back to the house. Later in the morning, when Doone had brought Blue Dandy out for his third

mile, I heard the piano faintly from the open window of the rose
room.

10

With the automobile out of action, the old familiar life of the
farm laid its hand on us all. The cowbells passed back and forth
from the pasture at sunrise and sunset, Doone trained his horses
morning and afternoon, the mailman came at ten o'clock behind
the old white horse, we ate breakfast and lunch and dinner, and
the admiral and Uncle Ledyard sat together on the deep verandah at the back of the house and talked about their college
days, and Mister McKinley, in whom the country should con-
fidently put its trust instead of listening to that wild man Bryan,
who held out a cloven silver hoof with the innocent smile of an
angel. It was wonderful to hear the admiral mention Bryan.

But in the dusk of the evening, before dinner, Doone and Kathy
began to take walks together. Sometimes they would meet at the
verandah steps, or sometimes they would wander off separately,
and now and then Doone would take his rod and Kathy would
carry the landing net and they would go down by the canal to try
for a big one in the shallows.

When the admiral saw that for the first time, he opened his
eyes, set down his glass, and took hold of both ends of his
mustache.

"By the Lord, Leddy, did you see that?"

"I've been expecting to see that," said Uncle Ledyard.

"I'm shocked," said the admiral. "As long as she showed her
mother's wild Irish I wasn't afraid. But this business makes me
feel five hundred dollars fluttering to get out of my pocket."

"Don't get too worried yet, my boy," said Uncle Ledyard. "She
always did go fishing when she was little."

The admiral snorted.

"You can't tell me that when a woman offers to carry a man's net

54

for him and sit by the shore and be bitten with bugs just to watch him do a namby-pamby business like that that she isn't in love with him."

Uncle Ledyard looked thoughtful.

"I never thought of it that way," he said.

"She's sold her soul to him," said the admiral. "He's got her in his hip pocket. If she was just for making love with him, she wouldn't be hampered with flyfishing outfits. Not Kathy."

He took a long drink.

"Maybe," he said, "the poor fool won't be able to see his chance."

I wasn't invited on these evenings strolls of Kathy's and Doone's, and when I invited myself, I was firmly discouraged. And I wouldn't have gone at all, if Doone had not come home one night with the story of a big bass rising. I made up my mind to catch that bass. And the next evening I was on the other side of the canal casting with my own rod and one of my father's red and white flies.

It was nearly dusk when they came along the towpath, and they came so quietly that I had no chance to reel in or to do more then flop down in the grass and let my fly trail in the currents, praying that Doone wouldn't see it.

He was out to do business that night. He didn't linger an instant on the bank, but whipped the fly from his reel and waded in to cast. By parting the grass with my hand I could see him fifty feet from where I lay, getting a beautiful length, his mind lost in the water and the black current collaring at his knees. Kathy was sitting on the steep bank with the handle of the net between her feet and the hoop over her shoulder. There was thoughtfulness in the level black line of her brows and a strange sort of wistfulness in her mouth.

It seemed a perfect evening for bass—the moon not yet up and the water grey with a very slight ripple; but bass are a queer fish, and not one broke the water.

Twilight surrounded us, and the occasional whine of the reel as Boone stripped off some line, the suck of the water at his legs as he gradually worked down to the edge of the shoal, and the rhythmic rising of the line, looping and shooting, seemed only a

55

part of its stillness. It was a long while before Kathy said: "You won't catch any fish tonight, Doone."

"It looks that way," he said, but he went on casting.

She drew a little breath, and it was so still that I could hear the quiver of it plainly.

"Doone," she asked, "when are we going to get married?"

His line faltered in the back cast, and his fly splashed heavily. I thought he would swear at her for disturbing him so, but he acted as if he had not heard her at all or noticed his own bad cast. Only he seemed to put viciousness into the next cast or two, and the rod whistled to itself.

"I don't know," he said over his shoulder.

His fishing changed entirely as he spoke. It wasn't a sport any more; the rod was like a whip in his hands that he was using mercilessly against her. But she would not allow it.

Her voice was full and vibrant and compelling.

"Can you doubt after this week that I'm in love with you?"

"How can I answer that?" he asked.

"I've done my best to prove it to you, Doone." Her voice had dropped and I saw her as I never saw her again. Humble before him.

He wasn't entirely graceless. He said, "I'll always thank you for that, Kathy."

It seemed to me that she leaped against his words.

"I don't want thanks, Doone."

"Do you claim a debt?" There was something in his voice that made me think of Uncle Ledyard.

"No," she said, throwing up her chin. "It's a debt I've paid to myself."

She rose to her feet, dangerously swift, and her voice was stormy.

"Do you think I would come dunning you, Doone? Like a country girl. I wouldn't dun a Boyd—it wouldn't pay."

I could almost see her trembling. But she had got what she was after. He dropped the point of his rod, letting his line trail, and turned to her.

"Kathy?"

"Curse you and your thanks, Doone Boyd, and be damned to you."

She lifted the net over her shoulder and threw it as far as she could into the canal. It dove in with a splash just beyond him, stood upright for an instant, and teetered slowly into the current. Before he could snatch it it was out of his reach and settling in the deep water.

Bass are a queer fish. The big one took that moment to rise. He rolled like a whale and the sound of his splash was as if a sack of potatoes had gone over the side of a boat. The line sang through my fingers and the rod bucked. I yanked up the tip and jumped up in the grass like a wild Indian.

"Doone," I yelled. "I've got him!"

I did not look to see how he took my appearance. But I heard the splash of his legs. Then in a moment he was beside me, and his voice was steadying.

"Easy, Teddy. Keep up the tip of that rod. That's it. Use both your hands. Don't be ashamed of it. You've got a man's bass at the end of your line. Now begin wading out with me. You've got to fetch him into the current. Down with the tip, he's breaking!"

I had lost all thought, but my hand did as he said, and true enough, the bass came out, the whole length of him, a black shape in the middle of foam and he fell back on his side like a cannon bursting.

My little rod pumped like my heart and I waded out along with Doone into the cold water and braced my back to fight him.

Doone was saying, "Oh God, Kathy! Why did you have to throw in that net?"

"I'll lose him without a net," I cried.

"We'll beach him someway," said Doone. "Start backing up the current, Teddy. There's a bad log out there. We'll get him into the current and tire him. Put down that tip for God's sake!"

The fish leaped again, turned over on his nose and came up stream like an express. I stripped in my line as hard as I could.

Then Kathy said from the shore close to us, "Will he stay up there for a minute, Doone?"

"He will for a minute."

I heard a soft splashing, like an otter sliding into a brook, but I didn't dare lift my eyes from the faint white spot of froth where my line cut into the water. He jumped high in the black shadow.

"He's turned again," said Doone, and again I began pulling the line in. Then we heard Kathy draw a gasping breath, and she splashed up beside us.

"Here's the net."

My heart sang at her words, but Doone said, "Give it to me, quick."

And he had it in his right hand and was dousing the mud from it. He seemed to reach over a mile of water, and as the bass came down past us he thrust it like a sword. It was a beautiful piece of judgment, perfectly calm, and I knew he wouldn't miss. As he lifted the net I saw his wrist buck to the flopping of the bass.

"He's a dandy, Teddy," he said quietly.

I sighed, and the rod seemed to ache in my hand. I turned around then and saw Kathy. She was standing between us and she was bare as the fish. Strings of water were dripping out of her black hair and making a silvery sheen on her skin in the grey twilight.

"He is a beauty, Teddy, you played him well."

"It was Doone," I said, as modestly as I could.

He was thumping the bass with the back of his knife and now he dropped him on the grass. I reeled in towards him and looked down.

"That's the biggest one I've caught, Doone. Will he weigh as much as the one in the office?"

"I'm afraid not, but he's over four pounds or John Callant is a Frenchman. We'd never have got him without the net. Good girl, Kathy."

She was slipping into her clothes on the bank above us.

"You needn't say that, Doone. I'm glad you got it, Teddy."

I paid no attention to her, for the fish was filling me, and Doone was cutting a forked stick for me to carry it by. When we picked up our things to start back to dinner, Kathy had gone. But as we walked along the towpath, Doone seemed to me to be unkindly silent about the fish.

We had a great to-do weighing the fish before dinner and Uncle Ledyard poured me a glass of port after dinner and I had to tell how he jumped, how he ran up the current, and how Doone got him with the net. I said that the net had been dropped in the current and I made a story of Kathy's diving for it in the darkness in the black water; and she smiled to me; but both she and Doone were very still. And after that I had to go out on the kitchen porch while John skinned the fish and we opened his stomach to see what a fish of that size might have been eating.

"It looks like a crayfish," said John, poking the bit with the point of his knife. "There's two of them in it."

"Glory be," exclaimed Mrs. Callant, "who would suppose a living creature could eat such a thing?"

"It's the powers of their digestion," said John.

So I saw the fish put into the ice chest on a white kitchen plate, a trivial remnant of the fierce thing I'd caught, and I went back to the living room and catalogued his contents. It made a grand evening for me.

I was sleepy with the port, sleepy and comfortable through and through, so that as my voice petered out, I became aware of the silence of the others, and particularly of Kathy who had curled herself in a corner of the red leather sofa and stared steadily into the fire. She would not play, when Uncle Ledyard asked her. She said it was my evening and that a woman should not butt into it. Even when I said I didn't mind her music, she wouldn't play. And Doone sat at the side of the hearth, and he too looked into the fire.

They sent me to bed when the admiral went, but I woke up again in a dream of the fish and remembered that I had left the fly that had caught him on the mantel piece. I had a thought that it would be comforting to have that fly stuck in the frame of the mirror against the wall, and once I'd thought of it, it seemed to me that I couldn't possibly sleep unless I had it there. So I slipped out of my room and went downstairs.

I stopped in the door, for the lights were burning, and I saw Kathy standing on the stairs.

"Good night, Doone," she was saying lightly. "I am going to bed."

"Why do you go so soon?"

" 'You used to come at ten o'clock.' "

I thought she seemed silly. Her voice was brittle.

"It's past for us both. I'll forget all about it, Doone, and so will you. Good night."

"I shan't forget it, Kathy."

"You don't need me anymore than I need you. As you say we're different. I'm not a Boyd lady by instinct, though apparently I've made another Boyd woman. But you shan't have my name to rust in your Bible. Put me in the Apocrypha if you must put me down somewhere, again. I'd rather be there."

"You've lost your temper, Kathy. It'll be different tomorrow."

"I have not lost my temper. I don't even feel hurt any more. If you put my money before me, that's your prerogative—or your taste. As you please."

"Oh, can't you see, Kathy?"

"Or is it because you've had enough of me now?"

"That's a cruel speech."

"You didn't hesitate to take it when I offered it to you," she said, and she bent for a moment over the rail. "Perhaps you are wise, Doone, at that. You thought you knew what you wanted. But you don't know," she added. "None of you Boyds ever did. Poor devils."

She smiled very sweetly and genuinely when she said that, and kissed her hand to him so debonairly that he had nothing to say.

"Good night, Doone."

Her skirts rustled lightly as she went out of sight.

I heard Doone poking the logs, and then sitting down, and I slipped back to my room, knowing he might stay that way for an hour.

A thunderstorm was brewing beyond the flats. When I looked from my window I saw its head rising black in the moonlight. It had a heavy voice, and the old house shivered under it. I got into bed and lay still to listen to the gathering of wind. The curtains over my window lifted when it came with its cool breath. And then the rain was on the roofs, the gutters ran full, and the lightning danced on the plaster of my wall, with the thunder bearing down upon us, blow after blow.

I could not sleep till it was over, and as it died beyond the valley half an hour later, I decided that I might as well get my fly anyhow.

11

In the living room I found Doone. He was just coming down the stairs from Kathy's room, and his face was troubled.

"Hello," he said to me, and I saw that he was still dressed. "What are you doing down here?"

"I was after the fly, Doone."

"What fly?" he asked irritably.

"The one I caught the fish on."

"Oh, that one." He stood still for a moment by the fire, with his head cocked towards Kathy's room. "Have you seen Kathy in your midnight wanderings?" he asked.

"No," I said. "Isn't she in bed?"

He gave me a black look. But at that instant, John Callant came in to us.

"Misther Doone," he said. "What's up?"

"What do you mean?"

"Is the admiral all right?" asked John.

"What do you mean?"

"I heard a racket in the storm," said John, "and I went out to see if it was the horses, but what it was was the engine."

"What are you talking about?"

"The Packyard, the automile, to be sure," said John, with the wind whistling in his teeth. "It's gone!"

61

"By God, that's it!" cried Doone. "She's jumped off the porch roof and taken it out."

"What's that about my motor?" demanded a sepulchral voice.

"Motor!" exclaimed John. "The words was in me mouth."

The admiral's door opened and he stood there in his flannel gown and carpet slippers with the blue night cap's tassel dancing first over one eye and then over the other.

"Kathy's skipped in the motor," said Doone.

"God damn it," roared the admiral, "she'll kill herself and smash it to bits. She drives like the devil."

By this time Uncle Ledyard had waked and come to the head of the stairs.

"What's the racket for?"

"Kathy's stolen my motor," roared the admiral.

"Where's she going?" asked Uncle Ledyard, hurrying down with his night shirt open to show the black hair on his chest, curly as the forehead of a bull.

"To New York, I suppose. She got another letter from that manager chap who's always after her. I suppose she got bored."

Doone turned on John.

"Put Blue Dandy in the runabout."

"Yes, your Honor."

John scurried away like a rabbit.

"Where are you going, boy?" asked Uncle Ledyard.

"I'm going to catch her," said Doone.

"Catch her?" scoffed the admiral. "With a horse?"

"With Blue Dandy," Doone corrected him.

"How long is she gone?" asked Uncle Ledyard.

"She can't have more than half an hour's start."

Uncle Ledyard grasped his beard.

"Half hour's handicap. Twenty-five miles to Deerfield Hill. You'll have to catch her on that, Doone."

"I will," said Doone.

"The devil you will," cried the admiral.

"The devil he won't," said Uncle Ledyard. "That horse is my own breeding. He's the stuff of a king in him."

"He might if it wasn't Kathy in the Packard," said the admiral stubbornly.

"We made a bet on it," cried Uncle Ledyard. "Remember, Jim?"

"A hundred dollars," said the admiral.

"I'll double it," said Uncle Ledyard.

"You poor fool," said the admiral.

I could hear them talking back and forth as I ran to my room and yanked on some clothes. I hadn't been asked to go, but I was going anyhow. In two minutes I was down again, crouching in the shadow of the carriage block. John was bringing Blue Dandy along the drive, at a walk, as if going to chase a girl in an auto in the middle of a black night were the most natural thing in the world. The big grey pricked his ears at me, his nostrils flared, but John was watching the windows of the office, through which he saw Doone taking money from the desk. He stopped the runabout just beyond the block, sprang out and stood to Blue Dandy's head. I could just see the red shine of his bat ears between me and the light; and I took that chance to climb over the back and crawl under the seat.

Then Doone came with his long strides and jumped over the wheel. I saw the two old gentlemen crowding through the door in their night shirts, and stand together, the admiral holding the tassel of his night cap from his eyes with a steady hand.

"Bring her back, boy," roared my Uncle Ledyard.

Doone gathered the reins and John sprang back from the horse's head.

"Hold him down to his wind, Misther Doone."

"He's off," cried Uncle Ledyard as the wheels turned deliberately out of the circle.

"Make it three hundred dollars," suggested the admiral.

Then the wheels swung into the high road, and I dared raise my head over the side to take a last view of the flat lights of the house. I saw the two old gentlemen standing with John on the lawn. Uncle Ledyard was waving his hand. And I saw Mrs. Callant leaning from an upstairs window. She was screeching, something I think about wanting to know was it the house was on fire.

Over my head, Doone spoke to Blue Dandy.

I have no very clear idea about those first three miles and a half. For though we spun along easily and smoothly through the Boyd woods, Doone swung off the Forestport road at the Corners and took the lane short-cut to Alder Creek, and through the lane the runabout bucked like a mule and I was sore before we had gone a hundred yards. But I didn't dare crawl out until we had come onto the Utica road, for I knew that Doone would send me home afoot.

I lay on my side with my head toward the back and watched the tree tops sweep the stars, and saw the lantern light travel along the bushes, and listened to the steady mushy thud of Blue Dandy's hoofs in the muddy road. The rubber tires made no sound, even in striking the stones, but the water ran off the spokes when we slid through a puddle and the brown roil of it sprayed from the tire level with my own eyes.

It was a good thought of Doone's to take the lane; he wanted to go slow anyway at that early stage and the roughness of the narrow track need not steal from his pace. And as Kathy must have gone round by Forestport we gained nearly a mile and cut her lead several minutes.

But it was a painful journey for me, and as soon as the wheels spun out on the smooth hard surface of the main highway, I kicked round and stuck my head under the seat flap and said, "Doone."

He did not speak, but his hand closed on my neck and he lifted me out like a rat.

"Don't make me walk back, Doone. Please."

"You have the god damndest way of turning up, Teddy," he said. His voice was perfectly calm. He wasn't angry with me. He was surprised and he was thinking. But he never stopped driving, and that, I thought, was a good sign for me.

"Please, Doone," I said. "I want to come along with you."

"You're that much extra for the horse to drag," he said grimly.

"Only seventy-five pounds," I said. "And he doesn't know I'm here."

"You little fool. You may make just the difference."

"Not to Blue Dandy," I said, with complete confidence. "And besides, Doone, I love her just as much as you do."

He didn't answer that. He was still holding me by the neck and steadying me on the short foot board. Then he pushed me into the seat.

"Sit down," he said.

I knew it was all right, then. I braced myself against the backrest and put my eye on Blue Dandy.

Something, whether it was Doone's hand on the reins, or the new road, or a word from John Callant, must have told the horse that he had a long trip before him, for he had settled himself in a long stride. He wasn't straining himself. He was just trotting, and the lantern on my left sent a glimmer forward along his side and I saw his head up and his ears pricked against the stars. His head swayed a little to the trotting, but his withers went straight as an arrow away from us and his quarters drove his hind hoofs against the road with the smooth strokes of pistons. No matter how you looked at that horse, he gave you a sense of his power and his great heart.

"Aren't we going a bit too fast?" I asked Doone.

His eyes were dark under his hatbrim, but the lantern put a faint gleam on his closed lips and his chin.

"Do you think so, Teddy?" he said. And he considered it. His voice was full of passion as he made up his own mind; "I think the boy knows what's up. He's got his eye on the road ahead of him. He's not after Kathy, or anything alive. It's the Packard he's chasing. It's his own race, really, and he knows it."

After that we didn't say anything; but I watched the road coming back at us through the light, a running ribbon, with the wet of the rain still on it. There was little mud, for the road was shouldered and ditched and beaten hard with the summer's travel. But it must have felt cool and welcome to Blue Dandy's hoofs.

The air was cool, too, and fresh from the storm, and there wasn't any wind. I could see the stars clearly, a great arch of them over the open fields. They did not move; nor did we seem to move, either, when my eye was on them; only the trees marched backward against us and the breast of the earth rose and fell with the grade of the road as if it were breathing.

The farms lay silent on each side, lightless and sleeping. The cows in the lower pastures stood knee deep in mist, black shapes like floating black boats. The oat shocks were like tepees on the hillside lots. But the fields were still for the crickets were yet knuckled down in their shapes after the heavy rain. There were only three sounds in the world as we crossed it: the clink of a cowbell as the cow lifted her head to see us go past; the barking of a dog as he ran to the road and watched our lantern come down on his property; and the fast, unbroken thudding of Blue Dandy's hoofs.

We had passed the high ground by the Hurley House and were coming down the long grades when Doone suggested a little more speed, and we made the run into Remsen in under the hour. The village was dark and had a little cold wind of its own against our faces, and the walls of the houses beat back the sound of our passage, so that long after we had rolled by the smithy, I thought I could hear the sound of hoofs behind us bouncing back and forth between the houses.

Doone slowed Dandy on the two short hills between there and Barneveld, but we made the downward curve into that town flying and in that run the lather came out on the horse and the scent of him was strong against our faces. He was lifting his hoofs and setting them down as if he flung the road back on his calks.

But Doone stopped him at the water trough and wet his handkerchief and cleaned his head and took him out at a walk.

In all that time we had seen no living man. And in Barneveld only the doctor lifted his window. Maybe he was expecting a call that night. But a curious bitch trotted along the sidewalk abreast of us with four paramours in her wake.

Then we went through the underpass of the railroad and had the long level stretches ahead of us to Nine Mile Creek. Blue Dandy took up his speed again, and I began to nod sleepily to the shuttle of the wheels. I scarcely noticed Doone's arm pulling me

66

over to him, but I leaned against his coat and smelled the tobacco smell of it and closed my eyes.

His body was still and hard as a rock. His wrist took up the play of Blue Dandy against the reins. But it seemed to me as I fell asleep that I heard his heart beating, though it might have been the steady drumming of the horse's hoofs.

12

It was the sudden leap of his chest that woke me.

"There she is," he said, quietly.

And I sat up and rubbed at my eyelids. For a time I could make out nothing but the fences flying back at me and the surge of the grey quarters of the horse. Then far away ahead, coming out from some trees I saw two short beams of light. They went on for a way and then vanished. But they came out again and I saw that they had passed behind a barn.

"She's on the edge of the hill," said Doone.

And as he said that, the lights dipped over.

"How far ahead is she, Doone?"

He glanced aside for a bearing and said, "Half a mile, maybe."

He lifted the reins and felt of the horse.

"We're going fine. He's seen the lights, I think, and marked them down."

In truth the horse was travelling now. The wheels of the runabout were humming in their pointed boxes, the whiffle tree cheeped hungrily, the tires whimpered against the road. The sound of speed was in them, and to me it seemed that a wind was freshening from the south.

"She won't see us yet a while," Doone said. "She's been over the road only once and her eyes will be stuck to it."

We went over the hill like a breaking wave and swept down so fast that I thought Blue Dandy was bound to break and gallop.

Doone was talking, "So-o-o-o, boy, so-o-o-o," over and over, a steadying sound. And the horse laid back his ears to it and kept his breast up to the collar and his head high. He blew out a great blast from his nostrils that shuddered the runabout under us, and it seemed to me that his deep even panting was a sound to smother the noise of a hundred autos.

I could not see that we lost any pace as we drew out of the shallow valley and took the level to the first dip before the road climbs the back side of Deerfield Hill. But Doone had the reins in both hands. He was not watching for the lights of the car; his eyes were on the horse with his heart. I think for that last wild stretch he forgot all about Kathy, and his soul like the horse's was in beating the automobile.

It was I who saw the lights turn on the sharp bend ahead and made out Kathy's head bent back to us. Her hat had come off or she had thrown it away and her hair was loose on the back of her neck. She saw us. She must have guessed who we were. Maybe she could make out the grey shine of the horse's hide. But she didn't falter. Her eyes returned to the road, and the car picked up speed.

I felt Doone crowding me over to the left. Then he was on his feet and leaning across me, and Blue Dandy was taking the curve, and the trees tilted away from us, and a barn wall leaned back from the road like an old woman lifting her hands for horror. Our off wheels slewed clear to the edge of the ditch and the tires squeaked frantically against a patch of broken stone, and then we had the straight ahead of us and Doone sat down.

Kathy was going like lightning. We could see the head lights pulling farther and farther off. But Doone laughed.

"There's the hill," he shouted. "She'll have to change her gears and we haven't got to bother about that."

Blue Dandy snorted again as we took the right curve to the dell. The car had gained a hundred yards going down there and was rocketing up the beginning of the grade.

"She'll not make those turns," cried Doone.

As we came to each of them I stared ahead expecting to see the

68

car on its back with its wheels spinning. But each turn of the woods unfolded and swam back and the road was bare, and we came to the long straight upward slant and saw the car.

It was marvellous courage in the horse, feeling the ground rising against his feet, but his stride never faltered. The wind was coming out of him at each breath, and his hide was black with his sweat. His head was out against the bit hard. And even I could see he was slowing. But I saw that the auto was slowing also. And the auto had no heart—only a kind of oil. For a moment it almost stopped and I saw Kathy pushing desperately against the brass rod. The gears grunted and ground. We gained so fast for an instant that it seemed that the auto was rolling back down the hill to us. But then a cloud of smoke burst from it, and it picked up again noisily, and for a long time we held even, not gaining, not losing.

But at last as we saw the road stretching out of the trees to the sky at the crest of the hill, Doone gave a shout.

"Now, boy!"

He did not reach for his whip, because he had no need of a whip; and besides the race was Blue Dandy's. I felt a last burst of power in the traces, and then the auto began to come back to us.

Doone swung the horse left. We crawled up abreast and I saw Blue Dandy putting his eye on the auto. The engine missed a beat. Kathy's chin dropped, and all of a sudden she threw out the gear and yanked at the brake. The car stopped swiftly, and Blue Dandy hauled up so they stood side by side—auto and horse. The auto was quivering from the idling engine, but the horse shook from the beating of his great heart. And anyone could have seen which was the better.

Doone passed me the reins.

He climbed down over the wheel slowly and walked up to her. She didn't get out of the car but leaned her chin on her hand and her elbow on the edge of the seat and bent down to him.

"Doone!" she exclaimed prettily. "What on earth brings you here?"

"Can you ask, Kathy?"

Deliberately she turned her eyes to the horse, and I saw that they were still shining.

"He is a beauty, Doone! No wonder you're proud of him."

"He's the finest horse in the Universe," I said.

"Don't butt in," Doone said to me. And now I saw he had forgotten the horse entirely. "Do you think I'd let you go off like a thief, Kathy? Without a word to me? In the middle of the night?"

"Thief, Doone!"

"You know very well. You've got my pride in your hand, and Lord knows what you've done with my heart."

"Have I?" asked Kathy.

"It was gone, and that's how I found you missing."

"What shall we do about it, Doone?"

She had folded both hands on the edge of the seat and was leaning far out to him, and her eyes were soft for him.

"I've brought along the stable money," said Doone. "Are you going to New York?"

"I was," she said soberly.

"I'll get in with you then," said Doone. "We'll get married in Utica. Let people talk if they want to. I've lost my pride, but I don't give a damn."

"Maybe," said Kathy, and her eyes twinkled, "maybe you've found it."

"Can I have it then?"

"You've had it all the time, Doone. But if you want legal title, I don't mind."

Doone said no more. But his face was sober as he passed through the lights of the auto lamps. And Kathy turned round as he got in and lifted her chin at him and smiled.

"Aren't you going to kiss each other?" I asked, for I had my own proper ideas on such subjects.

But they did not need to kiss each other. They smiled at me rather vaguely. And Kathy said in a low voice, "We'll get married in Utica; but I don't want to go to New York. We'll go to the hotel—I think it's exciting for new married people to go to a hotel, probably, and sign Mr. and Mrs. in public, don't you, Doone?"

"I think," said Doone, "anything I do with you now will be exciting."

She gave a little husky laugh.

"We've got to pretend, you see, Teddy?"

"I see," I said.

"We'll spend the night there and tomorrow we'll come home in the evening."

"Don't you want to go home to New York?" Doone asked.

"I want to go home," she said. "I've wanted to for a long time now. But, Doone, I thought you were putting me out of Boyd House."

"Let's get on, then," said Doone.

Kathy bent her head obediently and put in the gears. Then she looked up in dismay.

"But Blue Dandy, Doone!"

"Oh," I said. "Don't bother about him! I'll get him home all right. That's what I came along for."

My heart was in my mouth, as I said that, but I looked straight at Doone. And he looked back.

"Of course," he said. "Teddy can take care of him."

He put his hand on her arm, and still looking at him, she put in the gear and started the car. It made a great noise of moving, but it went. I thought Blue Dandy might put up a show at it, but he merely eyed the thing and pricked his ears once at Doone. Then I turned him.

I walked him all the way back to Barneveld and put him up at the livery for a feed which I charged to Uncle Ledyard. I slept for an hour in the next stall and then took him on. It was the grandest day of my life. The horse was tired and we took it very easy, and it was nearly noon when we got through the Boyd woods. But Blue Dandy put on a fine show in that last half mile. We came home at a ringing trot, and I held the whip on my knee and said, "So, boy, so," as deep as I could. They saw us coming.

Uncle Ledyard came out to meet me and the admiral was with him and John Callant ran over from the barn. I tossed the reins to him as I got out.

"You'd better take him in, John."

His mouth gaped at me.

"Where did you catch them, Teddy?" Uncle Ledyard asked.

"On Deerfield Hill," I said. "We took our time."

"Where are they now?" demanded the admiral.

"I should think," I said, "that they're getting married."

The admiral did not swear very long, but it was handsomely loud.

"You'd better have a drink, Jim," said Uncle Ledyard.

"I'm all right. But it beats me how she cranked the car in the first place," he said.

"Sure I did that for her," said John. "I wound it up myself in the dark."

"You dog," said Uncle Ledyard. "Why didn't you tell us sooner?"

"Sure she needed a sporting chance," said John. "A girl against that horse."

"John," I said sternly. "You'd better take him in right away."

"Yes, your Honor," said John.

II

1

I was a proud boy that morning, marching up the lane with the bull terrier at my heels. Every spring when my family returned to the Black River from our winter in New York, I could hardly wait to get over to Boyd House to check up on the events that had taken place in my absence, to inspect the colts that had been foaled and find out how the horses were training, and to hear all the news of the family. But I had never had anything of my own to offer in return, for the city seemed to me a dull place where nothing of interest ever happened—or never had happened till March of that year when out of a clear sky a friend of my father's had given me the dog.

There had been dogs in our family of course, like my father's pointer and the farm collie, with whom I had always been on close terms; but this was the first dog that had been given to me for my own, and I was bursting to show him to Uncle Ledyard and Doone, and Kathy; but above all I wanted to show him to John Callant. John Callant, I thought, had known something of fighting dogs in the ring and would for that reason be really fitted to appreciate the fine points of a bull terrier. But first, as a matter of politeness, I would stop at the big house.

There were still a few wake robins blooming at the head of the lane. The farm team were plowing the eight-acre piece beyond the paddock, with a group of plover, well spaced behind them, prospecting the furrows. The colts whinneyed at sight of the strange dog, and I saw his shoulders stiffen at the sound, as though it were new to him; but he did not break pace with me but kept close at heel as we walked down the drive towards the old low house.

"Stay there," I commanded when we came to the office door, for he was well trained, and I wanted to show him off. He sat down with great dignity, a statue of white marble on the block of limestone, and pricked his ears toward the training track where John Callant was jogging one of the mares. His nose worked quietly. I don't believe he had ever been in real country before.

I went into the office to find Uncle Ledyard going over the records of the horses Blue Dandy might be racing that August at Syracuse. But he dropped everything when he heard me and swung round on his chair and got up. His bold eyes smiled at me and he said in his heavy voice, "How are you, Teddy? I heard you got back last night. How's your mother? And father?" And he went through the family politely and gravely. "Kathy will want to see you right away."

We went into the living room and he shouted for Kathy. She entered from the dining room, tall, graciously welcoming, and I looked at her curiously, for my mother had told me that Kathy was going to have a baby this summer. But there was no change in her manner, except that her eyes were quieter.

"Hello, Misther Teddy!" Mrs. Callant cried from the dining-room door. "How you've grown, to be sure!"

And I said with dignity, "Hello, Mrs. Callant." And she made me a sign which meant she had fried doughnuts that morning.

Then Doone came down from his bedroom with his overalls on, ready to take the horses onto the track, and we shook hands. I felt that I was back in my own country. But I was holding my breath with excitement too.

"It's time I was going out," Doone said. "Want to come along, Teddy?"

"I think I will," I said. And then Doone looked out of the window and saw the dog, and said, "Hello, there! Who's that?"

74

"Oh," I said, "that's my dog. He generally tags me around. And I left him outside. He stays where I tell him to."

"Bring him in," said Uncle Ledyard.

So I went to the office door and whistled, and the dog turned and gravely entered the house. He had great dignity, greeting Uncle Ledyard and Doone, and he put his nose gently into Kathy's lap.

"Oh, Teddy," she said. "He's a beauty! . . . You beautiful dog!"

His ears flattened a little and his tail waved gently. And Uncle Ledyard said, "He's a fine dog."

And Doone said, "He looks like a good one." And my heart was stuffed with pride.

"What's his name?" said Kathy.

"Leonidas," I said. "For the Spartan."

"That's a fine name for him," said Uncle Ledyard, and Kathy stroked the flat head and said, "My, he's handsome."

Then Artemis, Uncle Ledyard's Gordon setter, entered and we watched the two dogs greet each other. Leonidas was dignified. He had a grand manner of reserve. And after a minute Artemis lost her stiffness and we saw that they were friends.

We went out to the stable, Doone and I and Leonidas, and John Callant had Blue Dandy harnessed to the sulky, ready to go. He gave me a grin and held the reins while Doone got onto the seat, and we watched him from the doors as he jogged the horse out. Leonidas sat on the ramp, taking the sight of the great grey horse without comment.

"What do you think of him, John?" I asked.

John Callant spat and put his quid back in his cheek and squatted.

"Come here," he said to the dog.

Leonidas looked at me and I nodded proudly, and he came stiffly up to John and they looked at each other—the stubby small Irishman and the fine white dog with his pointed ears and his deep chest and his steady eyes. The dog posed as if he were on the show bench, and for a moment John stared at him and whistled softly. Then he held out the back of his hand for the dog to sniff,

75

which the dog did, delicately. Then he put his hand under the dog's jaw and drew him gently forward.

John's hands were broad and coarse and stub-fingered, but his touch was like a sculptor's on the white body. It was light and firm and sure with his knowledge of anatomy. The dog closed his eyes and I saw his muscles playing under the touch.

"He's a brave, handsome beast," said John. "How old is he and where did you get him, Misther Teddy?"

"He's four years old, and Mr. Freeman, a friend of father's, gave him to me last winter," I said. "He's pedigreed."

"I've got hands and eyes," said John Callant, "so you needn't be telling me that, Misther Teddy."

There was great respect in John's voice, as if ownership of Leonidas had made me a man's stature.

"There's blood in him to build the finest kingdom in the world," said John, the tone of his speech almost biblical. "And the bull terrier is the king of dogs, the way the lion is the king of beasts."

I squatted down beside him. The morning sun came in upon us, putting a gold gleam on the short, even white hairs of the dog's coat.

"He's a fighting dog," said John.

"He's got good manners," I said. "He hasn't been any trouble."

"He's no roaring brawler," said John. "But he's fought. You needn't tell me, Misther Teddy. I've handled dogs in me time. He's got the lifting muscles at the back of his head like a bull. Pass your hands down his loin, back of mine. . . . Now over his neck. . . . And now take his jaw in the soft of your hand."

I did as he showed me, and I felt the hard muscles, half asleep, barely stirring at the touch, and my hand thrilled.

"He could whip any dog in the country," said John, "and himself chewing tobacco and a treadmill tied to his tail."

I stiffened, and I looked at Leonidas with a new respect; for if John Callant said so much, I knew he meant it. The little man had told me stories of the dog fights on Long Island. And now and then he told stories of the small fights that took place in our valley. And I had heard Uncle Ledyard tell, too, about George Beirne, who was now a white-haired gentleman of sixty-five, but who in the days of his young manhood always had the best dog in the county. He would drive the roads with his dog tailing his cart and stop for any barnyard challenger. And if his own dog was whipped he would buy the winner from the farmer, or fight him if he wouldn't sell. But when Leonidas came into my hands, dog fighting was become an undercover business, and though some of the gentry, as John called them, sometimes attended, they kept the matter to themselves.

And looking at Leonidas now, standing so quietly, it was hard to imagine him in the fury of battle.

"I'm not going to fight him," I said to John Callant. "Father's set against dog fighting."

"To be sure," said John. "You don't want him to be killing all the dogs around here."

I felt virtuously adult, but at the same time a shiver passed over me at his words.

Then Doone called to us from the track to come and hold the watch on Blue Dandy.

2

The spring went quietly with the voices of the peepers; and I left off fishing for trout and turned my attention to bass. Fishing, that year, gave me new pleasure; for everywhere I went, Leonidas followed me.

He wasn't a dog given to rough-housing or any form of play. But he walked along beside me on the towpath and lay down in the grass where the fish wouldn't see him, never moving except for his knowledgeful eyes that followed the fly, and the occasional prick of his ears toward a rising fish.

But as soon as I struck, he would be on his feet, tense-bodied, his tail trembling stiff, and a low, soft, murmuring growl of excitement in his deep chest. And he would be as pleased as I was when the fish was landed.

Or we would depart over the meadows after woodchucks, which he liked better, and he would creep up toward the hole with me and lie flat beside me in the grass—and he had far more patience than I at the waiting game—and the moment the woodchuck put his head out and I shot, he would launch himself like a white spear.

But I think best of all, like myself, he enjoyed going over to Boyd House and watching the horses training, and lying around the cool stalls afterward while John Callant cleaned the horses of sweat with the smooth strokes of his stick. He seemed to feel at home in the hot horse smell, with the fresh, golden straw wadded between his forepaws for his chin to rest on; and John Callant would talk to us as if we were both friends of his.

He was a fine companion for a boy of thirteen, and he taught me that many things I had been afraid of were not things to fear at all. . . .

Secret news in our valley travels in a strange way. Long before the haying, word came of the drummer and his dog. He hadn't even crossed the border of Oneida County, but one morning as John was sponging Blue Dandy's ears and nostrils, after he had turned in his first 2:07 heat for Doone, he said to me, "Jenkins, the new drummer for Loftus Company, has got a dog, Misther Teddy."

"Yes?" I said drowsily, for I was lying on my back under Blue Dandy's nose and he was playing with my hand with his tongue.

"Yes," said John Callant, through his hissing breath. "I've not heard much about him, but he's whipped the Belcher dog in Martinsburg."

I didn't answer.

"It means he's pretty good," said John Callant.

There was a rustle in the straw beside me, and Leonidas dropped his chin into my free hand.

"Well," I said, "I'll bet Leonidas could lick the stuffing out of him."

"I don't doubt it," said John. And the topic lapsed.

But a week later, Adam Fuess, Uncle Ledyard's farmer, dropped into the stable at noon with his after-dinner pipe in his teeth, and said, "Well, John, I've just heard the drummer's dog has fixed another."

"Did you?" said John. "He seems to be pretty good."

"Henderson quit before his dog, I heard tell," said Adam. "It took three buckets to get them loose in time."

"He must be a holy terror," said John. And he didn't look at me. Neither man did. They were passing information back and forth.

"Leonidas," I said, annoyed, "could trim him easy."

"Could he?" asked Adam. "This drummer's dog is a trained fighter, I guess."

"John Callant says he could," I said.

John Callant bent down to buckle the belly tab of the blanket. "He ought to," he said, "but I don't know."

"Of course he could," I said, and got up and walked over to the house for my own dinner.

And, as I walked, Leonidas came quietly along beside me, his clean head at my knee and his tail swaying gently. I looked down at him.

"You could lick the tar out of him, couldn't you?"

He raised his eyes and pricked his ears, but he didn't lose stride.

During the next week we heard of two dogs beaten, one in Lowville and one in Turin.

The mailman stopped at the barn on his way in and talked to Adam Fuess about it as Adam was cleaning out the manure, and Adam told John, and John told me.

"He killed the second one. They couldn't get him off," said John. "He must be the champion of the world."

The blood rose in my face.

"You said yourself Leonidas could beat him!" I cried.

"I said so," said John Callant. "But I don't know, Misther Teddy."

"You do know," I said. "I know, anyway."

"You can't ever tell," said John—"not outside of a ring, that is."

"I won't fight him," I said. "I don't need to. I know."

"Sure and he's your dog entirely," said John placatingly. "But

79

it's a pity there isn't a dog in the valley to stand up to a city slicker."

I don't suppose they knew that they were working on me. To John it was the most natural thing in the world to put one good dog against another.

But he had planted his seed carefully the first time he saw the dog, and what he had said since had been no more than careful watering. If you had accused him of putting pressure on me, he would have been hurt. The dog was my dog, and he said so.

But the drummer reached Boonville on the sixteenth of June and made his contacts and got his orders, and John asked for the evening off, and I knew he was going over to the North American Bar to have a look at the dog. And in spite of myself, I turned up early next morning at Boyd House to hear what he was like.

John Callant was whistling a jig as he cleaned out the stalls and swept the floor. But the rhythm he put into it was speculative and sad.

"Hello, Misther Teddy," he said. "Hello, Leonidas, me boy. It's a fine morning."

I sat down on the water bucket and watched the stiff strokes of his broom. He wasn't paying any more attention to us that morning, and he worked harder than usual. He raised the chaff dust in clouds, and the horses had their heads over the doors with a look in their eyes that was very close to amusement.

"Stand over, will you, you great bison!" he roared when Blue Dandy made a pass at his hat. I laughed. And he whirled round at me and the dog, who was by my feet, staring outdoors.

"Oh," said John Callant, "you're there, are you? I thought you had gone."

"Did you see the drummer's dog?" I asked.

"Yes, I saw him. And a fine animal he is too. But I forget, you aren't interested in him."

"You know that's a lie," I said.

"Oh, it's a liar I am now! Well, you aren't the first one to miscall me on this place."

"That's another," I said.

John grinned and leaned on his broom.

"Well, there's plenty of others besides yourself, Misther Teddy."

"What was the dog like?"

"Sure and he's a bull terrier like yours," said John. "Only he has one half a black saddle on his back and one black ear. And he's bigger than yours, and a handsome dog. I don't know that he's handsomer, for he has some scars. But the breeding's in him. I've nothing against the dog," said John Callant, poking his broom at a straw, "but the drummer's not to my taste at all."

"What's the matter with him?"

"Oh, he's kind of a high and mighty cuss, with a mean look, like sweat in his eye. He stood up to the bar among us and said it was too bad there wasn't anny more good dogs to be had in the country parts at all."

"He hasn't seen Leonidas," I said complacently.

John won me by saying, "I told him that meself, Misther Teddy."

"What did he say to that?"

"Oh, he laughed. He said he was hearing that in considerable towns nowadays, but he wasn't getting a look at the dogs it was said of. He laughed a little, and the boys weren't feeling very friendly about it. 'Talk,' he says. 'I'm a man that knows me manners,' he says, 'but I'm not saying I'll believe it till I see the puppy and the money in his teeth,' he says. 'Well,' he says, 'I suppose the cows are holding out on you boys and the money's hard to give away.' "

John began to sweep again, slowly, and now and then casting a surreptitious glance at Leonidas.

"The trouble, according to the drummer, was that there wasn't anny more decent-bred dogs in the country parts," said John. "Or if there was, their owners was too cowardly to let the brave dogs fight."

"I'm not," I said. "It's just I don't want to."

"That's what I told the drummer," said John. "But he laughed at me, and some of the boys laughed too."

"You know Leonidas could lick him!" I cried, feeling my fists get hot and the tears in my head.

"Sure, I do. And sometimes I've thought, why not let him? It's the honor of the county is in it," said John, "and he's the grand dog, surely. But he isn't mine, after all, and it isn't my business," said John with a great air of virtue.

"John," I said, "did the boys feel unhappy about it?"

"I wouldn't say yes or no," said John carefully. "But they did mention your dog. They've most of them seen him. And they all say he's a grand dog and wished George Beirne had had him so he could fight, the way it used to be in the old days."

"John," I said, "I'll let him fight."

And when I had said that, I knew I had been wanting to all along.

"Will you?" said John.

"Yes."

John grinned and then grew serious.

"Misther Teddy," he said, and offered his hand, "you're a credit to the county."

I felt very proud as I shook John's hand; and I looked down at Leonidas, and I felt confident and excited.

John was practical.

"Of course, you can't handle him yourself, and it's no discredit to you, either, Misther Teddy. It takes years to make a man handle a dog properly. If you want, though, I'll handle him for you."

"Yes," I said, feeling my ignorance.

"He's in fine shape," said John. "Running the country all summer like the conqueror he is. I've got to go to Boonville on an errand for Miss Kathy, and I'll stop in to the bar and let the boys know. We'll make the arrangements and I'll tell you tomorrow morning."

"Do you think he'll win, John?" I asked, for it seemed a matter of form to me.

"Sure he will," said John. "I'll be having my own money on him. And so will the boys. But, Misther Teddy," he added, "I wouldn't be talking about it. It's you that's doing this for the honor of the county, but there's some wouldn't rightly understand."

"I won't," I said.

But walking home that afternoon with the white dog placidly

82

keeping me company, I asked him if he was afraid, and if he minded, and I talked to him as if he understood every word. And perhaps he did. For there was no fear in his walk, and I felt so proud of him that it was on the tip of my tongue twenty times to tell my mother that Leonidas was fighting for Oneida County against the drummer's dog of Loftus Company.

3

For three days I moved in what seemed a haze of glory. John Callant was making excursions at night and holding rendezvous with all the "boys" in our valley, and during the daytime one or another would turn up at Uncle Ledyard's stable for a word with John about this, that, or the other, and the fulfillment of the simple errand would require them to step out back with Leonidas while I watched from the stable door, and then they would come in again, and the "boy" would shake hands with me solemnly and wish me and my dog luck; so that I felt that the days of youth had passed for me and that I had entered man's estate.

And the only thing that troubled me was the dignity of my dog in letting them feel his muscles or look at his teeth.

"He isn't a savage one with people," said John Callant. "He doesn't waste himself with growling. But I tell you he will fight, Adam. Just as a good horse is quiet in the barn."

They would nod and estimate weights and go away, and John Callant would tell me afterward that they had decided to bet this much or that much on my dog.

"The boys are all cheering for you, Misther Teddy. You and the fine dog. It's a great thing for them, to be sure."

And he made it seem a great thing, in fact.

The wonder of it was that with all the greatness of the fact, no word of it got to my family. It was as if a palisade had been secretly erected round my father's place. Nor did any word of it get to Boyd House, for, as John said, Doone wasn't friendly to the fighting of dogs and he wasn't sure about Uncle Ledyard any more.

When he said that, my first doubt rose in me, but he smothered it by telling me that George Beirne had been approached and had been agreed on by the drummer and himself as referee.

"It isn't just a catch match," said John. "It's a great fight for the world. He's said he'd referee it, and he's coming down this morning to look at the dog."

George Beirne was Uncle Ledyard's cousin. He was almost as tall, but more slender, and his features were more finely cut. He looked very handsome walking into the barn in his immaculate muslin driving coat, with his white hat tilted sidewise and his blue eyes shrewdly estimating the dog. As I watched I felt they were of a kind. If George Beirne was in it, I had nothing to worry about.

He passed his hand over the dog's back and down his legs.

"He's a magnificent specimen," he said. "Teddy, you're a stouthearted lad."

He shook hands, nodded at John, and walked out.

John gazed admiringly after him.

"He's one of the real gentry for you, Misther Teddy. Of course, he couldn't wish you luck, being the referee."

Before George Beirne left, he had a word alone with John Callant in the barn. And directly after, John came up to me as I sat on the rails of the track and said sidewise out of the corner of his mouth, "The fight's tomorrow night."

"Where, John?"

"In Bender's barn, at nine o'clock."

"Bender's?" I asked. For Bender ran a modern dairy on the Boonville road.

"The old barn," said John. "The one back down the cattle lane."

"Oh," I said. "The one with the hole in the roof."

John nodded.

I thought for a moment.

"John," I said, "how are you going to get Leonidas down?"

"Sure, I'll lead him along the lane and Adam Fuess' brother'll pick us up by the spring box."

"I'll meet you there," I said.

John's chewing froze in mid-swing.

"You're not coming, surely?"

"I'm coming, John."

"But your mother won't let you out."

"I'll say I'm coming over to Boyd House, or I want to go fishing, or something."

"Sure and if she finds out, I'll be murdered entirely," said John. "First her and then Misther Ledyard, not to mention Misther Doone."

"I don't care," I said. "I want to be there."

"You'd better be letting me take the dog," said John after a while. "I'm to handle him, annyway."

He had to run off then to take in Maidy, but in a minute he rejoined me while Doone was limbering Arrogance up.

"You can take Leonidas, John," I said, after a while.

"It's best," said John.

4

It was one of those hot nights when the mist lies close to the river bottom and the voices of the old bullfrogs are heavy. As I walked along the river by myself in the dark, the road seemed lonesome to me, and I noticed the shadows of stumps as I had not noticed them for a long time. I missed the white shape of Leonidas that should be walking evenly at my knee. And I was half afraid to go on.

But then I began to think of him standing up for the county against the big city dog, and I felt that I had to go on. He had looked very dubious as I tied him to the wall ring in the empty box stall, and I had done my best to explain to him. When I looked over the wall a moment later, he was sitting as I had tied him, very still, with his ears pointed, and his face to the door through which I had gone. Then he had become aware of me, and his tail had rustled the straw gently. He looked lonely as marble there, and all the way home to my supper I seemed to feel him sitting there looking into the empty blankness above the stall wall. And when at last he heard feet, it would be John Callant's he heard—not mine. John Callant would take him away in the darkness, and I seemed to be able to see him, walking beside John's bowed legs, with his dignity upon him like white armor, unquestioning, affable, and strong with his own courage. The thought of that made me walk on more sturdily. John Callant would handle him right.

Luckily, my mother had gone away to Lyons Falls for dinner that evening, and she would not be back till past midnight. I had nothing to trouble me there, and my whole mind was on the dog.

When I came out of the woods, it was easier walking, for there was star-light on the mist, and shapes assumed their natural form. I could make out the cows grazing through the mist in the night pasture, the silver wet of dew on their horns, their muzzles glistening. By Hawkinsville I heard a rig rattle over the long bridge and knew that a wagon was going toward the fight. There were only men's voices aboard.

And I pressed on through the village, climbing the hill and crossing the canal at the top of it. A couple of boats had tied up in front of Amos'. I could see their cabin lights reflected on the water, and I heard Art Maybe's voice talking to the two boaters.

"Yeah," he was saying. "It's little Teddy Armond's dog. John Callant says he's a dinger, but I've got my money on the drummer's. It stands to reason, a dog that wins in seven fights in a row must have the grit in him."

I never liked Art Maybe before, and I never liked him afterward.

"What do you say, Pete?" said one of the boaters. "Might as well have a look at it."

"Might as well," said the other.

"I'll give you a lift over," said Maybe; but I hurried on.

I was afraid. It was the first time it had occurred to me that there might be any doubt of the result. John Callant had said the boys all had their money on my dog, yet here was Art Maybe, notoriously close with cash, putting his money on the drummer's dog. Perhaps the others were all betting against Leonidas.

86

It seemed to me suddenly as if I were alone in the world, and that Leonidas was by himself, and we were separated, and the one thing we both needed was for both of us to get a sight of each other.

I ran for a while. But when a rig rattled up behind me, instead of hailing it, I climbed over the stone wall and lay down on the far side. A second wagon was overtaking the first, and the second driver hailed, "Hey, there!"

The first wagon hauled up.

"Where's the fight?"

The driver of the first wagon bawled back, "Bender's barn."

"Whereabouts is that?"

"I guess likely if you foller me you'll come pretty close to it."

The men laughed, and the second driver blew his nose and said, "I've come clear from Port Leyden and I feared I wasn't going to get there."

"Say, have you seen this drummer's dog fighting?"

"He's a slasher," said the Port Leyden man. "That's his name."

"Well," said the Hawkinsville man, "I've got a dollar on our dog and I've got another loose in here."

"That's fine," said the Port Leyden man. "It's going to get a lot looser. Not but what I'd like to see that drummer licked. But a man has to make money where he can. Boys, you ain't seen that slasher in action yet, but you're going to see a lot."

He laughed and the man in the first wagon laughed, and one said, "I calculate it'll be a close mix. I ain't seen a real fight since Mr. Beirne was pitting his dogs. But John Callant says that Teddy Armond's dog is all right."

Their voices faded out ahead of me.

I got back into the road and ran.

I was afraid then I would be too late. I could see more rigs coming down on the corners from Boonville, and still more coming from Forestport. I was appalled to think how many rigs there were. I had thought that there would be only a small crowd, but the rigs and the men in them measured like hundreds against the sky. And as I cut across Bender's day pasture, their voices came to me as they talked back and forth, laughing a little loosely. And Art

Maybe's wagon with the two boaters in it trailed their hoarse voices in a canaller's song.

I felt wildly resentful against them. I began to understand that it didn't mean fighting a dog for the honor of the county at all. For there was whiskey in their voices; the sound of them was like a breath in the night sky, and the shapes of their heads above the hedges made ugly blots against the stars. And I ran with all my might.

Long before I reached Bender's old barn, I saw the lantern light making threads between the warped boards of the walls. Its old, sway-backed roof stood against the sky all alone. And it had the smell of old wood and dust and cobwebs, the mingled smell of dry rot in the rafters and the moldy, unsunned earth under the rotting cowstable floor. It was as if the ancient walls had shut in a section of the world's air long ago when the oldest Bender built them, so long ago that the air had died there and become like a grey body. The voices of the gathered crowd were heavy against it.

As I stood on the far side of the barn by the old caved-in cellar hole of the first Bender house, I was afraid to go in. It seemed to me that a metamorphosis had taken place with the gathering of those men's voices. And though I could recognize a voice here and a voice there, I was not sure of knowing it, for the tones were rampant with the ease of men in their own company. The horses hitched to the railings of the old barnyard lifted their heads from time to time and pointed their ears toward the barn.

I didn't want to be in among the men now. I was afraid of them. But I couldn't stop myself from going close to the walls. And finally I crept in through the cow door and stood under the mow floor.

Their feet were just over my head, but their voices now sounded far above me, and they echoed with a strange cavernlike quality in the hollow of the roof. I went down the length of the decaying wooden stanchions until I came to the hay drop, and there I found a series of cleats mounting a studding, ladderwise. I put my hands on one and found it solid, and I began to climb in the dark. I got to the top and found myself at the height of the eaves with the darkness of the roof peak over me and to my left the warm shine of the lanterns making a haze in the moted air. A straw rack ran from my hands out to the edge of the wagon run, and I climbed out on it and crawled along it on my belly, making no noise, until I could look down.

There must have been thirty or forty men clustered round an open space in the middle of the wagon run. The smoke from their pipes mounted lethargically past my face and drifted out into the shadows of the empty mows. The lanterns they carried showed me every detail of their faces, but even the faces I recognized I did not seem to know. Some were eager, some tense with the money involved, some inane from the whiskey their wearers had passed down, some were openly savage, and one of two were cool and taking stock. But all wore a strange masklike quality, as if it had been painted on by the lantern light. And their voices were lustful, and as I listened to the bandied estimations of the dogs, and to the bets going one way and another, it seemed to me that I was losing my hold on the world, and that the valley I lived in wasn't the Black River Valley I had always thought it was, but an alien place, and I a stranger in it.

For the voices had no meaning in my ears.

And then the crowd parted by the door and George Beirne walked in. He was cool and neat in his light coat, and the lantern shone silver on his white hair, and he greeted the men he knew. He stood in the middle of the floor and examined the footing in the ring.

The wave of voices that had met him died, and men began moving their heads to see out of the door, and a man directly under me pulled out a thick silver watch and said, "It's just lacking a minute of nine," and I recognized the watch as Adam Fuess' and felt a brief wonder that I had not recognized him.

Then the men below me seemed to stiffen and the quick, dry sound of their breathing infected me and I felt my own back grow stiff as I lay on my belly. And the drummer walked in out of the dark. He walked in with the dog short-leashed and shook hands with George Beirne. He was a pasty-skinned man, with pinched city clothes and yellow shoes, and his eyes were black and sharp, and he had a cigarette stuck to his underlip, and when he talked, the cigarette pointed his words like a small white finger.

His voice was flat. He said, "Any corner suits me, mister. Me and Slasher ain't interested in corners. All we want is a little dog," and he grinned thinly round the staring faces, and the cigarette drooped in his face and a faint tremor vibrated the slender blue ribbon trailing from it.

He turned round, and I saw the dog.

He was a good bull terrier, but he had a tendency to stand out at the elbows too far. And he was coarser through the chest than Leonidas, and one of his ears was chewed and torn from an old fight, and there were thin welts of scars along his throat. But he faced the door with his feet braced and his good ear cocked, and the black spots on his hide lay dark as ink.

The heads of the men moved this way and that to see him, but he stood quite still, and after a moment we all waited again. And we did not hear John Callant arriving. We did not know he had come until the throat of the drummer's dog rippled and his low growl came out of him. Then his hair rose in a short, stiff roach over his shoulders and his feet seemed to plant themselves to the floor. Though he hadn't moved at all.

And I saw Leonidas. John Callant had a thong on him, but he walked in beside the little man coolly and stopped on the edge of the ring with the deliberate slowness of perfectly made muscles. A cry rose in my throat and hung in my mouth at the sight of him. He wasn't as heavy as the other dog; he didn't look cocky. But the poised, white perfection of his body was clean as a new sword among those men.

John Callant walked forward to George Beirne and shook hands, and he nodded to the drummer, but the two dogs had forgotten the crowd, and their eyes saw only each other. And the crowd went through its inane moving of heads again, and its words were a hoarse murmuring in my ears, and I didn't hear at all what George Beirne was saying in his cool, clipped speech.

I could see only Leonidas. I saw him back slowly under John's urging until he was opposite the drummer's dog on the other side of the ring. I saw John Callant crouch over him, taking him between his knees. I saw John's hands, with the dirty, scarred nails, moving over his white body and loosening the thong around his neck. And I jumped up on the platform and shouted down on them to stop it.

Their faces turned toward me with a weird slowness, first one and then another and another, until all of them were staring up at me.

"I won't let him fight!" I cried.

I saw John's mouth gaping and George Beirne came under the platform and looked up at me.

He was perfectly cool.

"I thought you'd agreed to this, Teddy."

"I did. But I don't want to now."

He said, "But you said you would, Teddy"—very quietly. "John Callant told me so."

"I did," I repeated, my voice a dry pain in my throat. "But I don't care. He's my dog."

The drummer looked up from his crouch and his lips sneered. The cigarette was short on his lip now and he had to squint his eyes against the smoke.

"I might have known it," he said in his flat voice. "There ain't anybody here has got a decent dog with guts."

He laughed shortly.

A hoarse growl rose out of the men, and one or two I knew stepped out under me and looked up with George Beirne.

"Come on, Teddy," they said. "You go home and we'll look out for things."

"I won't!" I cried.

"You said you'd put him against the Slasher," they said.

"He's my dog!" I shouted desperately. "I won't let him!"

Joe Miller stepped up with the others. He was a hand on our own farm.

"I'm here, ain't I, Teddy?" he said. "You know me."

"I don't care who's here!" I felt the tears coming out of my eyes but I couldn't stop them. "He won't fight!" I yelled.

"Look at him," said Joe Miller. "He ain't scared, Teddy."

And he pointed a bent hand at Leonidas.

The dog hadn't moved. His head might have dropped a little, but his muzzle was pointed straight at the drummer's dog. And his throat fluttered gently.

"I don't care!" I shouted again, helplessly.

It was like a dream, myself battering against those red faces with my small, repeated words, and the faces rising at me, growing larger in my sight, great bowlders of flesh I couldn't stop or even close my eyes against.

Then a man swore and another cried, "Hear that!"

I heard a rig coming rapidly through the Bender yard and swinging into the cow lane. The horse was a trotter, and a fast one. The wheels bucketed over the stony piece and into the old barnyard, and over the heads of the rest, I saw Uncle Ledyard tramping up the ramp to the mow doors.

He shouldered the men aside until he stood in the middle of the ring beside George Beirne. He paid no attention to the men. He just glanced at the dogs, the drummer and John, and he looked up at me with his eyes hard and his mouth shut tight in his beard, and he said to George Beirne, "What's going on, George?"

George Beirne said coolly, "A match has been made of Teddy's dog against this drummer's."

"I didn't know, Uncle Ledyard!" I cried.

Uncle Ledyard's face grew dark.

George Beirne said, "He gave permission," and shrugged his shoulders.

Uncle Ledyard turned on John Callant. "Did he?"

"Yes, your Honor," said John, with terror all over him.

"Did you, Teddy?" Uncle Ledyard asked me quietly.

"Yes," I blubbered, "but I didn't know how it would be."

"Stop sniveling." Uncle Ledyard said harshly.

Then Doone came in with his face black with passion. He spoke shortly to Uncle Ledyard.

"Naturally, he didn't," he said. "Probably they've all been working on him. You did, John?"

"Indeed and I didn't," John Callant said indignantly. "Would I be corrupting a lad? I said it was his own dog all the time. Didn't I, Misther Teddy?"

Uncle Ledyard looked up at me again.

"Yes," I said. "But I didn't know."

"George," said Uncle Ledyard, "I think you might have told me about it."

"I was promised to secrecy before I knew which dog it was," said George Beirne. "Besides, what of it, Ledyard?"

"It's a dirty business that no decent man would dirty his hands on," said Uncle Ledyard. "Persuading a child to put his pet up to be slaughtered."

"Slaughtered is it?" cried John Callant. "I'll bet my next month's salary he won't, Misther Ledyard!"

"Be damned to you, John, and keep your mouth shut till I speak to you!" roared Uncle Ledyard.

"Say," said the drummer in his flat voice, "is this a church benefit or a dog fight?"

"You keep quiet, too," said Uncle Ledyard, "if you want to get out of here with your hide whole."

But the crowd was beginning to get up their courage.

"How about our money?" they said.

Uncle Ledyard spoke to George Beirne.

"It's the biggest match there's been around here since the old days," said George Beirne. "There's a lot of money outside this crowd, Ledyard."

"Wait a minute, then," said Uncle Ledyard. "Teddy, jump down."

He held out his thick arms and I jumped and he caught me under the armpits.

"George," he said, "I put you on your honor not to let any fight start for five minutes. . . . Come with me, Teddy."

His big hand fell on my shoulder, and he walked me outdoors and round the barn out of hearing.

He sat down on an old beam and told me to sit beside him.

"Teddy," he said, "it's a bad business."

I could hear him breathing deeply beside me.

There was something comforting about the familiar scent of

93

him, the strong tobacco smell and the flavor of his clean stables. I felt my nerves slipping. And I tried hard not to cry.

"They said it was for the honor of the county, Uncle Ledyard. It sounded fine. But I didn't know."

His breath roughened a moment. Then his thick arm passed over my shoulders.

"Teddy," he said quietly, "you ought to have known that if the honor of the county was involved, Doone and I would be in it?"

"I didn't think."

"Lots of us don't think, Teddy. It makes us do mean, senseless things. If there was anything worth fighting for, don't you see we'd do the fighting ourselves. We don't ask our friends to go out and knock down a man that needs it, do we? And we don't send our dogs."

"I know."

"But, Teddy, you've said your dog would fight. You've given your word, and, right or wrong, a lot of men have taken it as good. Right or wrong, they've put money—many of them more than they can afford, probably—on this fight, I don't like it. I don't like it so much that I'd pay off all the money out of my own pocket if I could. But I think you'd be ashamed if I did that."

I nodded.

"I think, if you want to know, Teddy—"

"Yes," I said.

"I think you've got to put it through. It's the only thing to do now."

I drew in my breath miserably.

"All right, Uncle Ledyard."

"And I think you ought to tell them yourself. Tell them you've decided to go through with it, but that, win or lose, it's the last time you'll fight your dog in a match."

"I'm afraid, Uncle Ledyard."

He didn't speak, but put his hand on my shoulder again and pulled me up. We walked slowly up the dark ramp to the lighted door, and we walked side by side into the ring. I tried to speak, but I think Uncle Ledyard relented when he looked at me.

"Gentlemen," he said, "Mr. Armond has asked me to say to you

94

that he has decided to let his dog fight, but win or lose, he'll not fight him again."

They cheered. They weren't cheering his speech. They were yelling for the fight they had been waiting for.

Uncle Ledyard leaned over me.

"Do you want to stay, Teddy?"

I felt sick, but his hand on my shoulder gave me a kind of courage and I nodded.

"Good lad," he said, and drew me back to the edge of the ring. Doone came over to my other side and put his hand on my other shoulder. And I stood between them staring straight across the ring at Leonidas. There was a buzzing in my ears so that I didn't hear, and my eyes could not clearly follow what happened.

5

All I saw was his white shape walking out slowly from John's hands. Stiff-legged, he looked, as if he were walking on his toes. And his head was high.

And then his head dropped and I saw the muscles swelling behind his ears, and his lip lifted from his teeth. There was a deep snarling and I turned my eyes to see the other dog charge. He was more like a bull than a dog, with his overheavy chest, and his crooked forelegs, and his torn ear drooping like a broken horn. He came like a shot, and behind him I saw the drummer still crouched, his mouth a little open to show one gold front tooth, and his hands spread.

It was a trick some dogs learn, John told me afterward, for fighting inexperienced dogs, using the shoulder and his weight to knock the other off balance. And John held his breath, for a fight could be lost right there.

But I did not know that. All I saw was the savagery in the drummer's dog. The tips of froth along his lips and his strong teeth. And it seemed to me that Leonidas would be knocked over. I did not see how he turned, but his tail lifted like a sword, and when the drummer's dog whirled with claws rasping on the old plank floor, Leonidas was facing him, and in the same instant sprang. It seemed to me he fought cleanly and honestly, without tricks and without feinting. That time he missed his strike on the drummer's dog's throat, but his teeth caught just before the shoulder and a thin ribbon of red slashed the other's white front. And the drummer's dog's teeth clicked sharply as he missed the hold he had expected.

And then they moved so fast my eyes could not follow them, but saw them in quick poses, held for an infinitesimal space in time, and lost again in the fluid interchange of posture. I saw the head of Leonidas come up, the ears clean and white and flat against his neck and a red streak against his shoulder and a grey patch of slaver on his back. And I saw him go down before a sudden charge and the flash of his feet as he kicked himself free and he came up under a second charge, looking white hot, and a yellow fire in his eyes. He made no sound, though the drummer's dog snarled, like a dog singing to himself, and the men behind pushed against us and shouted.

But the drummer's dog was panting as he sprang again, and I felt sick. My eyes swung desperately away, round the men's faces, and they were blurred red spots I could not see. I closed my eyes and prayed I would not shame Uncle Ledyard and Doone by being sick.

I heard a sudden desperate clutching of toenails in the rough boards, and the sudden letting out of breath from the men's throats, and then a great shout, and I opened my eyes and saw the drummer's dog rolling free and a great slash on him, and Leonidas was standing with his head down and his lips red. I saw his loins gather as he sprang and their jaws clashed teeth to teeth like the meeting of bucks' horns; and I looked away once more.

I saw the drummer, still crouching, with his eyes slits and his mouth unsneering. And I saw George Beirne tense, with a kind of fire in his eyes, and a sadness, too, as if in his breast he felt the breath of long-lost times. And I saw John Callant squatting on his hams and his mouth grinning like a frog's.

96

I turned again to the dogs with my heart feeling bigger than my chest, and I saw Leonidas poised again, and his tail was up and his ears flat as he sprang in.

The drummer's dog went down.

They made no sound now, for Leonidas had found the hold and he had the throat. The other dog kicked under him. But Leonidas' muscles made a hump in front of his shoulders and he bore him back.

George Beirne moved over to the drummer.

"He's beaten."

The drummer cursed.

"No, he ain't."

"He's beaten," said George Beirne. "He made a good fight."

"He's gone under," said the drummer. There was a strange kind of agony on his pasty face. "Let him lay."

"I'm going to break them," said George Beirne.

"For God's sake, then," said the drummer, and his knees trembled as he rose.

I did not see any more. I heard them sloshing water buckets over the dogs, and then Uncle Ledyard had me by the shoulder, and he marched me out of the barn. I looked back once. And Doone was coming behind me. He had Leonidas on leash, and the dog made a pale, fine marble at his side. He was walking quietly, and his dignity was on him.

When Uncle Ledyard boosted me into the rig, I was crying. I did not dare to look at Leonidas as Doone lifted him in beside me. I did not help him up on the seat. I only dimly felt the lurch of the wagon as Uncle Ledyard climbed on and then Doone. They sat together on the front seat and Doone turned Arrogance into the lane.

Leonidas got up on the seat beside me and lay down. His head was bent to lick the slash in his flank. He licked it quietly with his eyes closed.

Uncle Ledyard and Doone were silent.

And I looked at Leonidas, as he was not looking at me, and dared not touch him. And then he lifted his head to sniff the air running past us and put his head to my hand and licked it.

97

III

1

Blue Dandy's introduction to the racing public had caused Uncle Ledyard and Doone considerable pondering. Often and often they would spend most of the evening in the office; and Kathy, left in the living room, a bride of months only, said they did not hear her sometimes when she said good night to them. When I had visited Boyd House the Thanksgiving before, I had seen them that way once: Uncle Ledyard talking round the butt of his cigar, and Doone with his legs wound into the legs of the accounting stool and a whole ledger of racing times clipped from newspapers, as well as course records and year books, spread out on the desk in front of him. Oddly enough, it was Doone who wanted to start the horse easily. Uncle Ledyard was for landing him in the midst of the racing world like a bomb.

He had never had any use for the grey colt till he ran down the admiral's car, but now he was in love with him.

"I won't have him paddling round with a lot of hoptoads, Doone," Uncle Ledyard said. "I'll put him up against the best of his age in the country."

"Then you'll have to race him against McGinnis' Pascha and that mare of Crocker's—what's her name?"

"Amber Girl," said Uncle Ledyard oracularly. "All right, why shouldn't we do just that? Blue Dandy can take them. Ask John

Callant. Though I don't know whether you'd want to drive on the same track with a man like McGinnis, the old bearded son. I remember him cutting in on me the first time I brought Greybriar up against his Hambletonian Duke. I yelled to him to pull over, and if he didn't I'd hook him; and if he didn't think I had the speed to move up on him, he could have eight posts to reconsider his opinion."

"Did you?" asked Kathy, smiling at him as if she were hearing the story for the first time in her life.

Uncle Ledyard grinned sheepishly.

"I'm getting talkative in my old age, Kathy. But it isn't every man that has the luck to own one of the great horses in his day and then see his great-great-grandson becoming just as good."

Doone chuckled.

"It's a pity you didn't recognize Blue Dandy the minute he came along."

"Never mind," Uncle Ledyard refused to be riled. "I'll write McGinnis and Crocker tomorrow and offer to post two thousand dollars against each of them."

He leaned back and looked at us.

"Dad, are you crazy?"

"I am not," said Uncle Ledyard. "I'm not going to live so much longer that I can afford to lose the chance of a little excitement."

His hard veined hands laid hold of his knees, and his eyes seemed a little vague as he stared through the red grate of the stove.

"Four thousand dollars," Doone said softly.

Uncle Ledyard's head lifted sharply.

"Well, why not?" he demanded harshly. "Blue Dandy can take them."

Kathy laughed gently, but Doone shook his head.

"It's taking a long chance," he said. "Blue Dandy's never had a real race. But with luck, we'll beat one of the horses and break even."

"Break even!" roared Uncle Ledyard. "That's not the way McGinnis and Crocker and I are used to doing business. The winner takes the lot."

His bold eyes stared into Doone's, and suddenly Doone grinned at him, so that you saw how much alike they were.

"We'll have to mortgage Blue Dandy if he loses, just to buy feed for him," Doone said.

"You can sell him to me," Kathy said.

Uncle Ledyard grinned at her and put out his arm.

"You're a proper daughter in this house, Kathy. Come and give me a kiss."

He kissed her loudly and went on with his arm round her waist:

"It will be a great match. Just the three of us, and plenty of room. We can leave it to Crocker to get us the track. Syracuse most likely. He's on the committee. Blue Dandy will think he's having a brush with Maidy and Arrogance at his tail."

We were silent awhile. Then I wanted to hear what happened to McGinnis.

"Uncle Ledyard, what happened when you told McGinnis to pull over with Hambletonian Duke?"

Uncle Ledyard passed his hand down the side of his head with reminiscent fingers.

"It was a very slow heat," he said. "Crocker's horse took it. His driver had to pull him down damned near to a walk and take him along on the outside, and even then he got his foot through a wheel for a minute." He sucked at his cigar. "I can't exactly remember whether it was McGinnis' wheel or my own, Teddy."

The news of Uncle Ledyard's match against McGinnis and Crocker was the biggest thing that had happened in the north country since Greybriar trotted his two-minute mile at Goshen. But for the Boyd family it was the event of two lifetimes. It didn't matter to them that they thought Uncle Ledyard had lost his mind. They were back in the news. Land poor though they were, they had a horse to be started against the best trotters on the Grand Circuit. And it wasn't just a sweepstake. It was a match for four thousand dollars a side.

It brought them flocking to Boyd House for word of Blue Dandy. They came with their dilapidated cars or their ancient horses, or they asked to be met at the Boonville station. Even Mrs. Roger

Bourbon Castle stirred in her old Utica house, and one day a basket arrived for Uncle Ledyard. It contained a bottle of sherry so old that no member of the family could remember the name. There was her card, tied with a blue ribbon round the neck, and on the card, in her infinitesimal, spidery writing, a message:

My dear Ledyard: I have heard that sherry is sometimes given to race horses.

"Do you realize, Jim," Uncle Ledyard said to the admiral as they opened the bottle together, "that the old girl must have gone down cellar herself? She never let poor old Roger touch a drop from their bridal night, and he the biggest toper Oneida County ever produced. . . . I am not counting our naval visitors," said Uncle Ledyard. "How does it strike you, my boy?"

The dew formed visibly on the admiral's eyeballs.

"Ledyard," he said, breathing hard. "I wouldn't refuse the offer of the key to that cellar."

"Roger used to talk about it when he was dying," Uncle Ledyard nodded soberly.

They were great days, and I reveled in their excitement. I turned up every morning for the morning trots, to sit on the rail beside John Callant, with Leonidas in the grass at my feet, and watch Blue Dandy put to in the cool of the day. Tuesdays and Fridays, when the Boyds came to watch, were only shows. Only a few of us saw him at his real work. And when Doone sat behind the horse in the morning, and the night's shower had made good footing, he lost his doubts, and even Kathy, who walked out from the house, smiled. For the power of the great horse at his full stride was enough to shake the track. I could feel his thunder coming up through the rails against my hams, and Leonidas would lift his nose from the grass as he passed. He trained well. He would finish his time heats, breathing easily, and as light on his pasterns, jouncing back down the track, as though he stepped on feather beds.

Those were good moments, when Doone handed the reins to John Callant and we stood together by the rails, looking after the horse on his way to the barn. There were no doubts for any of us then. Uncle Ledyard would be reconsulting his stop watch, as though he might have made a mistake after all; and then entering the time of the heat in a small red leather notebook he kept for the record; and Kathy's eyes would be shining with a happiness I had not seen in her before; and Doone, for all his preoccupation in the horse, would see it and smile in return. The baby she was carrying had begun to show by now; but it seemed to make no difference in her vigor or the way she moved, and she kept pace with the rest of us when we took off after the horse for the barn. It seemed to me then, that all of us were in the thing together.

On those mornings, George Beirne was apt to turn up in his dog cart, a natty figure in his muslin coat and gray top hat. Sometimes he brought his nephew Peter with him, though generally he came alone; but whichever way it was, he always looked as fresh, emerging from the woods road, as if he had just stepped out of his tailor's shop in Boston. He would go all over the horse with Doone and Uncle Ledyard and John and myself, and we would listen to his words.

One day he came back from a tour Uncle Ledyard had sent him on, and there was a long session in the office. He was smoking a thin cheroot and his finger was curled to the glass the admiral had poured out for him; and there was a long silence as we waited for him to begin. But his beautifully chiseled face was calm and he spoke with great confidence.

"You can put the mare out of your mind, Ledyard," he said. "You will have to give her one heat. She goes like a swallow, but she hasn't the reach. But McGinnis has a real horse."

Uncle Ledyard nodded.

"He's a slow starter," said George Beirne. "But the way he'll roll into the stretch is nobody's business. Or yours in particular, I'd better say. He's likely to touch his best time on the fourth. So I think you'll want to gun for the second and third."

Uncle Ledyard nodded, and John Callant, leaning against the screen door with his hands like blinkers beside his eyes to let him see in, said, "True for you, Mr. Beirne."

Doone said, "It's the third heat, then, we're afraid of."

And young Peter Beirne lifted his voice and turned from staring at Kathy, and said, "If you think you can really win it."

The silence fell on us so suddenly that we all heard John Callant breathing, and I turned and stared at Peter Beirne.

I had remembered him as a ragged boy who sometimes used to stay at Boyd House when I was four or five. But I had not seen him for years. George Beirne had unashamedly collected money from Uncle Ledyard and anyone else who would contribute for his education, and had sent him to college.

"What do you mean?" asked Uncle Ledyard in his heavy voice.

Peter smiled at us. He didn't show the Boyd stamp as his uncle, George Beirne, did. His nose was short and straight and a trifle broad at the base of the nostrils. He had the curving mouth that might have been his mother's, for none of us had ever seen her. His father, Ralph, had gone off with her at eighteen; they had both died, and the boy had come back on the family in his infancy. And he had curling red hair.

He looked at Kathy now, with a touch of impudence in his blue eyes that made Doone look dour.

"I mean," he said, with a slight gesture of his hand, "that Blue Dandy, though he looks fine, is a green horse. Both the others have raced a full season against first-class horses. How do you know he can win, then?"

It was all right for Uncle Ledyard to admit that to himself, but to have somebody else say so was heresy. I saw the veins swell at his temples. But Doone's voice was dry.

"I've held the reins on him," he said.

The young man flushed.

"Yes, yes," he said. "But you haven't held them over the other two."

George Beirne said nothing. His pale face seemed slightly amused as he watched his nephew. But Uncle Ledyard scowled.

"Listen, Peter. It isn't a question of what anyone knows about Blue Dandy. Even if he didn't have the speed to take the universe, he'd have to win the race. And it isn't just because I'll be damned if I'll have McGinnis and Crocker laughing at the old

103

man from up north who has a soft spot under his hair. You've seen the crowd here this morning?"

Peter nodded, but he was smiling at Kathy as if he only half heard.

Uncle Ledyard struck his desk with his fist.

"Well, they've taken my word my horse is going to win. Every last one of them. And half of them are taking the bread out of their mouths to do it." His face flushed through his beard. "He's going to win!"

His bold eyes were menacing, but Peter let the menace run off his back. He did not smile with his mouth, but he conveyed a smile with his eyes, and as they passed mine they stopped as if to see whether the boy didn't get an idea of the drollery he had created. There had always been a kind of aloofness in the Beirnes, but the cross in him had added impudence. I felt my own cheeks stinging under it, and I saw Uncle Ledyard seething at his own inability to put his finger on it. Doone only looked contemptuous. And then Kathy rose.

"Horses!" she said. "Even the universe is full of horses here. This office hasn't room left for a woman."

"I'm sorry," Peter was saying. He walked out behind her into the living room. She paused in the door. Her head was tilted back against the jamb of the door; her eyes, silvery in the duskiness of the low-ceilinged room, had the aspect of drowsing, and her mouth was tender with the half smile that shaped it so beautifully that my heart ached whenever I saw it so.

Peter Beirne stood quite still, looking down over her shoulder. Her feet in narrow orange slippers stood in a pool of sunlight, and leaf shadows from the vines that laced the window stirred gently on her skirt.

Doone was saying, "No. Jim's staying with her. She ought to be quiet."

Peter lifted his eyes to her face. She had turned back. But she wasn't looking at him. I knew what he didn't. Behind the open door, her eyes were seeing the print of a picture. I wondered why she turned to it then.

His eyes favored her profile for a moment. Then, as the men stirred in the office, he touched her hand.

"Mayn't I come again sometime?"

"This house is always open," Kathy said. "I'll be pleased if you do. Jim's a dear, but his interests are limited." Her voice was gay with a kind of excitement I could not understand. "Doone and Uncle leave next week with the horses."

She moved as the men came through the door. Peter made his good-bys with civility. They all went out to the carriage block.

But I slipped into the rose room to make sure, to look behind the door. The picture was there, as I supposed. The old print of Sacred and Profane Love. But all I saw in it was two women. One was naked and one was dressed in a strange way, and neither of them seemed to me as lovely as Kathy.

2

For the first week after the horses had gone I felt ill at ease in Boyd House. There was nothing to hear on the broad verandah but the small sounds of the haymakers and the everlasting, hot cry of the locusts. The admiral was surly from a touch of gout, but I didn't mind him. It was the constant stretching of the senses for a sign of life from the track. The place seemed dead, as if, with the ceasing of hoofs on the track, the low sounds of Doone's voice, even John Callant calling a quarter, the pulse of life had died for us. The stable entombed a musty silence where cobwebs came.

And Kathy showed it. A kind of apathy lay over her so that she seldom spoke, and then with a strange note of vagueness. Her face was relaxed almost to heaviness, and for hours she sat still with her hands in her lap, as if all her senses had turned inward.

It was a strange, long time of waiting—the week became a month; the month, six weeks—with only bulletins from Doone or Uncle Ledyard—terse listings of Blue Dandy's miles. Now and then George Beirne, with some slight personal comment; twice Peter came, and during his visits, while Kathy entertained him in the rose room, my misery was bitter. The race went out of reach, then; even out of mind.

And yet, oddly, it was Peter Beirne himself who brought it back to us.

I had come over that day with a note from my mother asking if I might stay while she and my father went off on their summer visiting.

We had been for a walk, Kathy and I and Leonidas, and we had stopped for a while in the barn, and sitting in Blue Dandy's empty stall, with Doone's driving gloves in sight on the shelf, we had missed the dinner bell and had sat on silently there till lantern light put its finger round the corner of the door.

"Miss Kathy?" It was Mrs. Callant's voice.

"In here, Susanna."

Mrs. Callant stamped in and looked down at us with wonder in the upturned shadows the lantern put on her face.

"Sure and we've wondered and wondered where you was. The admiral's been wondering too."

Kathy's lips twitched.

"And here's that Peter Beirne come back from the track, and him and the admiral staring at each other across the dining table as if I'd baked murder itself in my pie."

"He is?" said Kathy. "Come, Teddy, we'd better go in. . . . Susanna, Mr. Teddy is staying here awhile."

"I'll tell Minna at once," said Mrs. Callant, and she gave me an odd, obvious stare. She had certain expressions that everyone knew who knew her at all, and that she prided herself were subtle, secret things. This one meant, "There's something for you in the kitchen."

But she said nothing as she lighted us up to the verandah.

Peter Beirne flushed with pleasure at Kathy's entrance, but the admiral glared.

"I'm glad you didn't wait, Jim."

"I did for a while," he said.

He took the decanter and his glass to the office. Peter lifted his eyebrows comically at the admiral's back. Then he turned to Kathy.

"Business first," he said, handing her a letter from Doone.

"Thank you," said Kathy. She put the letter in her dress and sat down. She smiled at Peter. She was lovely.

Peter Beirne had a fund of talk.

"They're all three fine horses. It'll be a close thing, though the mare's pretty generally ruled out. But Blue Dandy's done a two-flat mile. . . . You'll be glad to hear that, young fellow," he said to me; and to Kathy, "No doubt it's in your letter, quarter for quarter. All the Boyds but yourself are down there, and they're getting out their last pennies. You could rake in their money with a hayrake." He smiled to himself.

I left them to themselves when I finished my piece of the pie that so shortly before might have held "murder itself." I pushed open the kitchen door.

Mrs. Callant and Minna were sitting together, waiting for the pie to come back to them. At my entrance, Mrs. Callant turned on Minna.

"Have you fixed Misther Teddy's room?" she demanded. . . . "No, you haven't. Well, then, why don't you run along between now and the pie, and fix the beds? The way they're sitting at dinner, we'll be half the night clearing up."

Minna grimaced and went out, and Mrs. Callant turned to me.

She bent her full bosom downward and thrust a red hand into the privacy under her apron. She fumbled a while and then drew out a piece of folded paper pinned shut.

"I've got a letther from John. It's got this inside it for you. If he was drunk I'll have the hide off him," she said.

But I took my letter away.

The admiral was snoring softly in the study while Artemis and Leonidas, side by side, watched the glass in his hand. In the rose room, Kathy was playing softly while she talked with Peter Beirne. I shivered as I heard her laugh, and stealthily opened the letter from John. It said:

Dear Teddy: There is monkey business happening here. I

don't know what it is but there is a lot of people hanging around and offering me drinks till I can't trust myself at all. Last night I had something in it and I never heard a thing all night. McGinnis' man found me as if I was drunk entirely. He stayed all night. His name is Amberjack which is a queer name for a friendly man and he promised not to tell Mr. Ledyard. I would tell him only things seem very queer to me. Someone is covering all the Boyd money and I think it is the same man, but I don't know who he is. If it is it means something against Blue Dandy. What I want is can you bring down Leonidas? If he was here it would be all right with us all. McGinnis slept with his horse. He is a good fellow too. I can't tell Mr. Ledyard and Doone, because there is something queer and I can't write you because I don't know but I will tell you when you come down. I hope you are well as this leaves me.

Your friend,
John Callant.

The grain of the board he had written on showed through the laborious pencilings. I could see him in my mind's eye, even as his words sank in, bent over in private and sucking the pencil. Every fourth or fifth word showed where he had sucked the lead.

In the rose room, Peter Beirne laughed softly. I didn't hear what he said, I didn't hear what Kathy said in return. I lay back on the deep red-leather sofa with the letter tight in my hand. I seemed to see Blue Dandy lying in his stall, and John asleep on the bunk next to him as if he was drunk, and by the door of the stable a man with a small knife in his fist. John had told me tales of horses being nobbled before a race. "Drugs, knife, or a sponge," he would say. "It depends on the man entirely." I must have fallen asleep. For in the darkness I seemed to see the moon come out, and the man with the knife in his hand was Peter Beirne. I tried to shout to John, but he would not waken.

And then Kathy was bending over me and the admiral was swearing in the doorway, and I looked up and saw Peter Beirne with laughter on his mouth, and I felt the cold touch of Leonidas' nose on my hand.

Kathy said, "It's all right, Teddy. It's a dream."

"No, it isn't!" I cried, staring at Peter. He looked at me and laughed again.

"Teddy's tired," Kathy said. "He's run down and overwrought. You'd better go to bed, Teddy."

She looked at me, and I went up.

I did not undress, but lay on my bed with Leonidas beside me on the floor. For a long time I listened to the faint notes of the piano, until finally the admiral stamped through the living room to bed and the wheels crunched over the gravel drive and took Peter away. I held my breath, waiting till Kathy's candlelight bloomed in the stairwell and went into her room.

I waited for her to come to me, and when she did not, I went to her room and tapped.

"Who is it?" she asked.

"Teddy."

"Come in."

She was sitting before her dressing table. Her black hair was down and she had on only her nightgown. I was caught speechless with a whelming of my senses.

"What is it, Teddy?"

She turned round at me.

"Something's happened?" she said.

I nodded, holding out John's letter.

She read it through quickly.

Then she looked at me.

"You think it's Peter?"

I nodded again.

"I wish I could tell," she said.

She sat still with her hands on the edge of the dressing table. Then she turned on me. "Will you go, Teddy?"

"Yes."

Her eyes shone.

"I wish I were going with you." Her eyes went back to the letter. "I see what John means, I think. He'll tell you. Ledyard and Doone aren't to know. You'll understand, maybe. I must get hold of Adam."

She came down with me and slipped on one of Doone's coats.

109

We walked together down to the farmhouse, and there, after some effort, we roused Adam.

He came out hugely embarrassed, with his trousers clutched up in one hand.

"Adam," said Kathy, "Teddy has to go down to the track. We don't want anybody to know."

Adam rubbed his head as his eyes brightened.

"He's taking the dog?"

"Yes."

"I guess so. John wished he could take the dog when he went."

"I'd have sent him," I said.

"Doone wouldn't allow him to ask," Kathy said.

I understood. My heart was full of love for Doone.

Adam said, "My cousin's conductor of the milk train. He'll stretch a point for the Boyds. He can take them as far as Utica. Then Teddy can get on the western train there in the morning."

"When does the milk train go?" asked Kathy.

"Four o'clock," said Adam. "I'll take him over then."

We went back to the house together.

"I'll wake you, Teddy," Kathy promised. As she sat on my bed, her eyes were like silver. She leaned over to kiss me.

"Give my love to Doone," she said. "Remember."

3

As soon as the train stopped, I ran up to the baggage car and asked for Leonidas; and a moment after, I saw the dog's fine white head leaning out at me.

"Let him jump," I said, and the baggage man let go of the leash, and the dog landed at my feet as if his legs were made of spring steel.

"Pahdon me," said a voice beside me. "Is yo' name Mistuh A'mond?"

A Negro, cap in hand, was standing at my shoulder. When I looked up he smiled widely, showing an avenue of gold teeth. I suppose I looked doubtful, for he said immediately, "John Callant said fo' me to fin' a young gen'leman with a white dog, and dat surely is de whites' dog I evah saw."

"Where is John?" I asked.

"He said fo' me to fetch you to him," he said. "John's waitin' outside de groun's."

I wasn't used to Negroes then, but this one smelled reassuringly of horses.

"Who are you?" I asked.

"I'm workin' fo' Mistuh Boyd. I ten' de mares. My name's Benjamin Daniel."

Though his hat was still in his hand, he gave the impression of taking it off to bow, and his gold teeth sparkled.

Leonidas sniffed at the floppy cuffs of his trousers and dropped his tail and looked at me. "All right, Benjamin," I said.

"I got de trap right outside de station," said Benjamin Daniel.

An old horse with broken knees was being held by a tiny darky at the end of a cab stand.

Benjamin helped me up with a grand air and boosted Leonidas in, his black hands closing on the white body with a sensuous touch. Then he got up himself, picked up the reins and whip with a flourish, and shouted to the little boy to let go. The ancient horse lifted his head and roused sleepily. But the touch of the whip sent him into a rattling trot. . . .

"Dere's de groun's," said Benjamin, "and dere's John Callant hisse'f."

I shouted to see John running toward us.

The Negro drew up the old horse with a magnificent stylishness and cramped the wheel. He took off his hat as I climbed down.

"I got to get back," he said, "or Mistuh Doone will fairly flay de hide off'n my back."

He went off, leaving John shaking me by the hand, and then crouching down before Leonidas.

"The train was late," he said over the dog's head, "and I'll be late myself getting back, and Misther Ledyard won't like it. But it's worth a roarin' to have you and the dog, Misther Teddy. I've been watchin' so long I can't trust myself from sleeping anny more. But have you had anny dinner?"

I nodded. "I had sandwiches on the train."

"That's all right, then," said John. He got up, his hand on Leonidas' head. "How is Miss Kathy?"

"She's fine," I said. "She'd be down here, only the admiral has promised to keep her home." And then I added, for form's sake: "Susanna sent you her love."

"Did she?" said John. "But maybe we'd betther be getting inside. Misther Ledyard may get to considering I'm late."

As we turned the corner of the grandstand together and looked down the slope from the bank of the track at the long, low lines of the racing stables, we saw Uncle Ledyard walking up and down before the farthest stalls. His wide hat was back on his head and his short, grizzled beard was stuck out and his face was red in the sunlight. His massive legs put his feet hard against the ground. I did not need John's sharp-drawn breath to tell me Uncle Ledyard was raging.

"For the love of God," whispered John. "He's going to murder me entirely."

He would have drawn back, but at that instant Uncle Ledyard's bold eyes turned to us and saw us.

"John," he roared, "where the devil have you been?"

"Where's Benjamin?" demanded John, with high indignation. "Ain't he come back?"

"Of course he's come back!" roared Uncle Ledyard. "But he isn't minding Blue Dandy, you damned Irish rascal! He's hired to help with the mares! What the devil have you been doing?"

"Fetching Misther Teddy, to be sure," said John. "Ask him if you don't believe me."

"Hold your impudent tongue," said Uncle Ledyard. And he confronted me and Leonidas. "Hello, Teddy. What brought you down?"

"I came down to see the race," I said. "And I brought Leonidas along. I thought Blue Dandy might like seeing him."

But I felt myself flushing, and it was hard to meet Uncle Ledyard's eye. At that moment, Doone came out of a stall.

"Hello, Teddy. Want to see the horse?"

"Yes," I said, and I followed him gratefully.

The sunlight beat hot upon our shoulders, but the stall was cool as twilight. There was a window at the back, and like a miracle the leaves of a small willow, soft and green, showed through it. With his head silhouetted against the window, Blue Dandy was staring out past us through the door as if he were staring at the posts of the track. My heart swelled as I saw him. He looked enormous there. His head was up and his ears pricked. He took no notice of us, but his nostrils opened and closed softly. And though he stood easily, to my eye he seemed on fire.

Doone's hand dropped to my shoulder.

"I'm glad you've come, Teddy," he said. "We were getting lonesome here." I felt my heart grow still. "How's Kathy?" he asked.

"She's fine," I said. "She sent her love. She told me to remember."

He didn't say anything for a while, but his dark face was narrow and fine, like the horse's.

"I wish she were here to see him," he said.

I wished so, too, suddenly and poignantly. It seemed to me then that as the horse needed Doone and Uncle Ledyard, they needed her to take care of them.

But outside, Uncle Ledyard was roaring again:

"I've got to get out in a hurry, Doone, now John's back. That blasted harness maker's sent the wrong boot!"

He caught Doone's arm and they started off up the slope to the track. As they disappeared, a stall door opened farther down the line and Benjamin Daniel stuck out an anxious black face.

"Dey gone?" he asked.

John wiped his forehead.

"Praise God," he said, "he's going to murder the harness maker instead of me. He's always this way before a race, Misther Ledyard is. Roaring and hollering and stamping around like hell and bedamned itself—and no peace for a man's nerves."

But his voice was oddly proud, and Benjamin gave a confirmatory nod.

"Jes' like de ol' times," he said. "My meat's been fairly squealin' fo' de pas' half hour."

I felt very important that afternoon, sitting on a box before Blue Dandy's stall after his easy limbering up around the track. There had been a knot of people in the grandstand, watching. And even from the paddock gate I could recognize the Boyds among them as clearly as if they wore a family uniform. For there was something old-fashioned about even their best clothes, a shabby gentility in the black silks of the women and a country cut to the men's coats. And they kept all together, and they didn't talk like the backers of the two other horses, but sat silently, their eyes moving in unison as the grey horse circled the track.

Among them, the white, caped dust coat of George Beirne and his grey high hat stood out like the essence of fashion. And as Blue Dandy went by us the second time, I saw that George Beirne had seen me. He came down out of the grandstand at his cool, leisurely walk, following the outside rail of the track until he came to where John Callant and I squatted side by side.

"Hello, Teddy," he said. "Ledyard told me you'd come, and that you'd brought the dog." He glanced down at Leonidas, who was patting the dust with his tail. "He's mightily pleased."

I looked up at his fine face and flushed.

But he was looking back at the grand stand. "Half the family's here already," he went on. "And the other half will turn out tomorrow." He gave a short laugh. "You understand, John. It isn't just Ledyard's horse, it's all the Boyds'. Don't take any chances."

The sweat was on John's forehead.

"I wrote for the dog, Misther George. That's why Teddy's come down."

George Beirne smiled at me.

"I had lunch today with Ledyard. He'd picked up something at the harness maker's. But it's up to you, John."

John swore loudly.

"There ain't nobody going to get at him at all, now, Misther George."

George Beirne nodded again, and went away back to the grandstand, leaving John Callant aglow with admiration.

"He's one of the old gentry," he said to me. "Quiet spoke and no roarin'."

I understood, but my eyes were following Doone and Blue Dandy. And after a moment John watched them too.

"He's going to brush him a little this time," he said as Blue Dandy's lean head came under the wire. "Watch him take to the turn. I was afraid he'd keep rolling the way he did at home. But he don't. The world itself wouldn't be too big for his fancy."

It seemed to me as if my heart stirred in my insides and rose and went out after the sulky. The posts went past still faster and we saw the horse's back dropping lower as he sank into the perspective, until only his head and taut-whipped mane bored round the far turn.

"Pray God," said John, "we can bring him out tomorrow as good as that. With his heart in it."

Doone eased him round twice more and then gave him to John.

"Take him back, John. Cool him out slow. He's right."

I didn't move even when John took the bridle. The track was like a print in my eye round which the grey horse was still traveling.

Doone came over beside me and pulled out his pipe.

"They'll be bringing out the other two in a minute," he said. "Do you want to wait with me?"

I nodded.

Glancing back after Blue Dandy, I had seen activity at another stall.

"That'll be the mare," said Doone.

He lifted himself up on the rails and smoked thoughtfully. We were silent for a time, but when he spoke he surprised me.

"I wish it was over," he said.

"Doone!" I cried. "Don't you want to race?"

He turned to me with a smile. And in that instant it occurred to me that, whatever John Callant might say about George Beirne, Doone was as fine a gentleman.

"Don't worry," he said. "I'll race all right tomorrow, Teddy."

115

He turned his gaze back to the track. "But it doesn't seem worth it. All the money, all the worry. Whether he wins or loses, Blue Dandy isn't going to be a better horse or a worse one."

"Don't you want to know he's better?"

"Not very much," he said. "Not now. I used to when dad was running him down. But now dad admits it—that he's better than Greybriar. We beat Greybriar's time four days ago," he went on. "After that I didn't seem to care so much for the race. I get lonesome for Kathy. I wish she could come down here," he said.

"So does she."

He smiled at me again.

Then we heard a sulky come onto the track and I first saw Amber Girl.

A groom was leading her. Behind her shining, new sulky walked two men. One—a little, lean-faced fellow—was watching Doone and me.

"That's Joe Mason," Doone said. "And that's Mr. Crocker with him."

I had never seen anything like the picture she made in the hot clear light, with her small, bright, chestnut head and soft eyes, her sharp, pointed ears. She had an air of expense about her, not only from her new yellow sulky and shining tan harness, nor even from her polished round hoofs. It came from the way she walked, from the delicate arrogance of her head and the mild disdain of her glance at us. She seemed built to fly, with her sloping quarters and raked shoulders and cannons flat as knives. Her hocks were well let down—a sign, even I had learned, of real speed; but she looked short to me, and even allowing for her sex she wasn't ribbed out the way Blue Dandy was.

Mr. Crocker came up and leaned on the fence beside us. And Doone introduced me.

"Well, Armond," said Mr. Crocker, shaking hands, "what do you think of my filly? Can't she beat that long grey Boyd animal now?"

I remembered George Beirne's opinion, given a month ago, in the office at Boyd House. "I'll give her the first heat," I said, and heard Doone chuckling. But Mr. Crocker boomed with laughter.

"Hear that, Mason?" he called to his driver as the man let the mare step down to the rails. The driver shrugged and picked up the mare's head. She went off at a mincing jog. It was good as an answer. Mr. Crocker laughed louder. "Make a bet on it?" he asked.

I glanced at Doone, but he was looking away. My family, I knew, would have disapproved, but I had made a statement and Mr. Crocker was challenging it, and I had a dollar in my pocket over and above my fare home.

"I'll bet a dollar," I said.

"Do you want odds?" Mr. Crocker asked, smiling.

I flushed as I remembered that Mr. Crocker had already put up four thousand on the race. But I said, "No, do you?"

He became very serious as he entered the bet in his notebook. He shook hands with me soberly and rejoined his men. And I, also, felt sober. For to me it seemed the most serious transaction I had ever been party to; and as I looked at the mare once more, I felt that she had to be beat, and that Blue Dandy was as much my horse now as the Boyds'.

There was a strange smile on Doone's face, but I didn't pay any attention to it. In my own importance I asked how much he had on the race.

"Not a cent," he said.

The mare took it very easy, and when she went in Doone said, "I'm not afraid of her. George Beirne is dead right."

I flushed.

But, as if for our especial benefit, there was a commotion at the paddock gate, and McGinnis' Pascha appeared. I caught my breath and stared, and Doone's hand touched my knee.

"He's all stud," he said.

He brought a cloud with him. He was as big as Blue Dandy, but he was ribbed out fuller. He wasn't beautiful to my eye. He had the long head that came from his Dexter blood and that traced back to Messenger, and the enormous stifles and long sloping hips. They had him checked high, but the check was slack, and he stared out over the fleece buffer on his nose as if it wasn't there at all. He seemed built entirely on lines of savage strength, but when you looked closer you saw by the fine fall of the legs from the shoulder to the long pasterns that there was speed in the coal-black body.

A brawny fellow was hanging onto his head with both hands while another slipped a cord round his upper lip, and a little man with a stiff black beard and cold grey eyes climbed onto the black, battered sulky.

"That's McGinnis," said Doone. "And the pair of them is what Blue Dandy and I have to beat."

I caught the doubt in his voice, and I understood. The three men elaborately ignored us, and the horse's being was all for the track—though he kept turning his head right and left as he jogged, and rolling his eyes till the white gleamed, as if he were looking for horses.

But even so he didn't impress me as McGinnis, of Goshen, did, for the little man sat as calm and collected as a man on the box of a road roller. Only this roller had the speed of a wind let loose.

I saw that, when he wheeled beyond the wire and the horse fought the bit before he could be brought down. And I remembered Uncle Ledyard's tales.

"Now you've seen them. Come along."

4

From where I sat before Blue Dandy's stall, I could hear John Callant and Benjamin Daniel fussing over him—the slap of their hands down his back as they worked in the liniment. To my right, the two grooms were holding the black stallion's head while the small man, McGinnis, examined the set of one of his shoes. Beyond them, the mare was receiving a bath. Leonidas lay before me, chin on paws, watching them sleepily.

A group of ancient hangers-on paused before me to look in at our horse, speaking covertly to one another, and then shambling on to stand before Pascha, but at respectful distance; and then again moving slowly toward the mare.

Benjamin Daniel came out to start a fire in a small, cylindrical stove that stood out in the open. He looked at the sky and put on some water to heat, and then he went in.

An hour drew itself slowly out before I saw Uncle Ledyard coming with Doone past the grandstand. Uncle Ledyard didn't notice me, but shouted for John.

John put a rumpled head through the stall door.

"Yis?"

"Come out here," ordered Uncle Ledyard; and when John obeyed, "I heard this noon that the odds in town have jumped against Blue Dandy. Do you know anything about it?"

His voice rumbled in his chest, and looking at his face I was surprised at the passion in it. I had never seen Uncle Ledyard angry and quiet together.

John rubbed the back of his neck and shifted his feet.

"Well," he said, "I heard something a couple of days back."

"What did you hear?"

"That our horse couldn't win."

Uncle Ledyard's nod was grim.

"That's what's going about. But the harness maker told me something else too. There's a rumor he ain't going to start."

"No," said John.

The blood swelled Uncle Ledyard's cheeks.

"John," he said, "two people have got to be with the horse all the time. Understand? I want you to take him out tonight and walk him down the lane in the country. But both of you go with him. Doone and I have got to go to a dinner Crocker's giving. But we'll come right back. I'll bring you a revolver for tonight."

I looked at Doone.

He didn't seem to be listening at all. He was staring north over the grandstand roof. The beginning of sunset there was setting the edge of a cloud on fire.

There was an unexpected chilliness in the air and, feeling it, I shivered.

I didn't understand why John Callant was so surly with Uncle

Ledyard. I suppose his nerves were edgy. He merely grunted when Uncle Ledyard thundered at him to remember. And he turned his back on both of them as they went off.

His voice shook.

"Roaring and blathering," he said. "Yelling at me as if I was a beast in his stall. Does he think I'm going to kill me own horse?"

"John!" I cried.

"You're just the same. I've a mind to pack me bag this minute, I have. And leave the ugly beast."

"You don't mean that, John."

He turned his face upon me and I saw that his eyes were blood-shot. His long lip quivered. And at sight of it the world seemed insane to me, with Uncle Ledyard mad as a March rabbit, and Doone seeming apathetic, and John Callant threatening to walk out on Blue Dandy. I glanced at Leonidas for help. But he merely lay still as marble with the sunset on him, and his eyes were closed.

"If Kathy was here!" I said to myself. "Oh, God, if Kathy was here!"

I was lonesome. John had taken the horse to walk with Benjamin and Leonidas for escort—"down the lane to the duck pond, where he can look at the stars in the water. It's cool to his feet there, and he can be thinking of the honor of the Boyds." The shadows, stretching themselves through the grass, carried intimations of black darkness. As I watched them growing and joining together and slowly blotting the light from the grass that sloped up to the curve of the track, I found my hearing whetting itself for sounds. I wanted suddenly to go into the stall where John Callant had his cot, to find the lantern, but I did not dare to turn my back on the growing darkness. I looked for stars to see whether Blue Dandy could be seeing them in the water of the duck pond, as John had said he might, and I wondered whether they were still there or whether they were coming back.

A lantern bloomed suddenly down on the right, and I saw Mc-Ginnis pause for a minute, staring my way, before the stall of Pascha drank up the light through its open door.

And then I heard it. At first, not feet but a whispering in the grass. It wasn't Blue Dandy coming back, nor was it Leonidas coming ahead of him. It was coming down from the shadow under the grandstand. Then I did hear feet, but I could not have moved for my life. And at last I heard an outraged voice:

"You'll kill yourself coming over here. It's bad enough coming down for the race. But to come out here at night, tonight, walking like this. Good God! Ledyard and Doone won't speak to me after this! You might at least think of my gout in this chill."

I heard a low laugh.

And my heart rose.

"Kathy," I said softly.

"Teddy!"

She was all about me—her perfume, the faint scent of silk from her skirt, and her arms feeling for me in the darkness.

"I couldn't stay up there any longer. I couldn't stand it a minute more."

She was half laughing, half crying.

The admiral grunted and reached round her waist to shake hands and then stood off. I could hear him blowing through his mustache.

"Where are they all? Where's Doone, and Uncle, and John and Blue Dandy?" She surrounded me with questions and sat down on the box. Her breath came rapidly. "I had to come down," she said again.

I told her that Doone and Uncle Ledyard were at dinner, and that John and Leonidas were down the lane with Blue Dandy.

"They ought to be back any minute."

The admiral grumbled as he eased his feet, and I forgot about the darkness while I stood between them.

"What's that down there?"

The lantern had come out of Pascha's stall. It was too dark to see the face of the man who carried it, but his active walk was unmistakable.

"That's McGinnis," I said.

He lifted the lantern then to padlock the stall door, and Kathy laughed.

"The way Uncle talks about him, I've imagined McGinnis was an enormous man."

"Wait till you see the stallion," I said.

McGinnis stopped for a moment, looking our way, then he went into the next stall and the door shut off the light. The darkness seemed to inclose all life but our own and the deep vibrance of the crickets in the grass.

Kathy's voice caught the hushed depth:

"Will they bring Blue Dandy back soon?"

"Yes," I said.

I thought for a little while that she wasn't going to say anything more. But suddenly her voice went on:

"Teddy, it's all a strange business. I don't want you to think too hard of Peter. He's known for a long time that someone was going to try to cripple Blue Dandy, but he's had nothing to do with it himself."

The admiral snorted loudly.

"I know, Jim," she said. "He used the knowledge to cover the Boyd money. He had to borrow. But he's only a child, really, like the others. He had no business going to a college without enough money to keep up with the type of friends his uncle encouraged him to make. He signed the name of one of his friends to a check, Teddy. His friend didn't do anything about it, but he gave Peter two months to get the money back, and when Peter heard about this business I suppose he thought it was a providential chance."

The admiral muttered something.

"I know," Kathy said again. She hesitated, as if her urgency stifled her. "It's so easy to blame him. At first he laughed at us all for poor fools. And then, the last week here, because he had laughed at the Boyds for being such poor people, when he saw how their hearts were in the horse, he felt sorry for them. It wasn't that anyone ever would have found it out. He couldn't bear it. Last night he came back and told me."

"Why didn't he let us know?" I asked.

"No one must know but you and me and Jim, Teddy. Jim's promised not to tell. You must promise me. I wouldn't have told you at all, except that you know so much already."

"It's bound to come out sometime," said the admiral. "By God, it ought to!"

"I'm thinking of George Beirne," said Kathy.

"Do you know what she's done?" demanded the admiral. "She's given him the money to cover the dud, and she's going to cover the bets he borrowed to make, if the horse wins. And all she's got is his promise. Promise!" the admiral snorted. "You'll never see a penny of it, girl."

"I expect not," said Kathy quietly. "It doesn't matter. All that matters is that Blue Dandy has a fair chance to win. It isn't the money. Uncle and all the Boyds have the first real horse they've had in fifteen years, Jim. It's their lost youth."

I wasn't listening to her now. My ears were stretched through the throbbing of the crickets for the sound of the gate hinge in the lane. The admiral must have understood. His naval voice beat off the board walls and echoed as he swore.

"Do you realize we've been here half an hour ourselves?" he said. "Where's the horse?"

The chill was all over me now. There were no stars for John to have shown Blue Dandy in the duck pond. It was black night. The barns were invisible. Only the roof of the grandstand showed like the back of a sleeping monster against the arched effulgence of the city lights beyond it.

And suddenly, though I could not see him in the darkness, I was aware that a change had taken place among us. The admiral was no longer the old, gouty gentleman led here against his will by Kathy. His voice had become a terse, galvanic bark.

"Teddy!" My neck stiffened as I faced him. "Has John got a lantern?"

"No."

"Who's he got with him?"

"Benjamin Daniel."

"Who's Benjamin Daniel?"

"The groom."

"Is he able-bodied? Would he fight?"

"I don't know. But there's Leonidas."

"By God, that's so!"

The way the admiral said that made my heart swell. There was Leonidas.

123

"Teddy, can you get a lantern?"

"Yes."

"Get it quick. . . . Kathy, you stay here. Don't move, girl. I'll go after McGinnis."

I felt my way into the dark square of the stall John Callant used. As my hands went over the boards, I felt the blood pounding in my finger tips. It was a strange thing that I wasn't afraid. It was as if the admiral's voice had blown the very consideration of fear out of me. As my hands hit the table and slid up against the matches, I heard him pounding down the way.

"McGinnis!"

"Who is it?"

"James Porter."

The door must have opened.

"McGinnis, I think someone's making a play at Ledyard's horse. There's no time to lose. Come along."

The match fizzed and the flame crawled back onto the stick. With a sense of wonder, I saw that my hand was not shaking.

"He's down the lane somewhere, Teddy says. He ought to have been back here fifteen minutes ago."

I stepped outside. The admiral was coming back. With him was McGinnis, his eyes showing white over the black beard as the lantern light swung against it.

He made no questions. He obeyed the admiral as I had.

Kathy said, "Won't you need something? A pistol?"

The admiral's oath was a marvelous thing.

"I've got my cane."

He wasn't even limping.

"Leave Kathy the lantern," he said to me. "We'll use McGinnis'."

The three of us circled the stable together, with the admiral marching in front, his spats moving briskly through the grass. His hat was tilted back on his white hair and he held his cane like a sword.

"This way for the gate," said McGinnis, and he tossed me an aside: "Ledyard's a fool for sending his horse out to walk in the evening. But I suppose they didn't expect anything till late."

I didn't answer.

The admiral wheeled and made for the gate. As he opened it, the hinge squeaked familiarly. Before us, the lane bored down through small willow trees, and the admiral paused for a breath as though he surveyed his line of battle.

In that pause we heard Leonidas' deep growl.

"They're down there!" cried the admiral, and he started running. McGinnis went with him like a fox, and I doubled my elbows and followed the light. I thought I heard feet behind me, but I didn't look back.

The dog was enraged. Over the stamp of our feet in the cool sod I heard his rumble, so deep I knew he was crouching.

The thud of our feet must have acted like a fuse to dynamite. A man shouted; there was a piercing shriek that sounded to me like Benjamin Daniel, and that made my blood turn icy; and there was a crashing of brush and a queer muffled noise, like sobbing.

McGinnis' lantern cut the willow branches out of silver against the black sky and showed us the turn. We took it at full run; McGinnis in the lead, the admiral laboring heavily in his wake, and myself. And then we saw them.

Just for an instant. The grey horse with his blanket dragging under his legs from the surcingle, his head raised to the limit of the lead rope that seemed anchored in the grass. Before him Leonidas was a flashing tangle of white, moving so fast I could not see his shape, perfectly silent as he deviled something on the ground. And just ahead of him three men, swinging stupid faces to our lantern, dropped the sticks with which they had been aiming at the dog in darkness.

They saw only two men and a boy, and they stood their ground. McGinnis gave a short dry shout, but the admiral roared sulphurously. There was a queer fusion of bodies and the lantern broke with a clear, bright tinkle of glass and went out. The admiral grunted. I heard his stick strike hard. Leonidas roared. A man crashed into me and went over me, and I was lying in the grass. The man who had hit me yelped, and a wind passed over me as Leonidas cleared my face. I heard Blue Dandy snorting.

And then the turn of the lane grew bright and I let out a yell as Uncle Ledyard came round.

"Jim!" he roared.

"Come on, Leddy!"

The admiral's voice shook me.

I saw Doone silent and dark and passionate as he sprang past Uncle Ledyard. I heard a fist landing hard, and another cry. The knot of men broke apart. Three black shapes burst out of it and crashed into the willows. The light steadied and formed us. The admiral was standing in the midst, his hat askew, and looking down at his cane. Uncle Ledyard was rushing over to Blue Dandy with his voice almost motherly, "Easy, boy, easy."

Leonidas was facing down the lane and Doone was bending at the end of the halter rope, but McGinnis stood aloof, looking at Uncle Ledyard and Blue Dandy.

I got to my feet.

"John's all right," Doone was saying. "He's been cracked hard on the head, but he's coming round."

"How's the horse?" asked McGinnis.

"I don't see a mark on him." Uncle Ledyard was feeling the hocks and hamstrings. "You got here in time."

The admiral breathed loudly on his knuckles.

"I overreached," he said disgustedly. "I had my aim, but the light went out. They ought never to have got off."

"One of them didn't," said McGinnis dryly.

A man was lying still on the ground with his arms up over his neck.

His shirt was torn back from the shoulders and there were red gashes in his skin.

"The dog got him," said McGinnis.

He pointed.

There was a gurgling sound and John Callant sat up and looked at us, his long lip preternaturally sober.

Consciousness returned with pain. His stubby hand went to his thatch of hair.

"You're all right," Doone said to him. "Just take it easy."

John stared at us comically.

"What's happened?" he asked.

Doone laughed.

"They've gone. Leonidas is still chasing them."

His laughter was easy, quieting.

Uncle Ledyard came away from Blue Dandy.

"Do you know who he is?" he asked McGinnis, pointing to the stranger.

McGinnis shook his head. "He ain't dead, luckily. Do you want to take him in?"

Uncle Ledyard stooped over him. His big hand rolled the body over. I felt sick, in spite of McGinnis' words. The man was limp.

But Uncle Ledyard suddenly slapped the seat of his trousers. "Playing possum. . . . Get up and beat it. All I want is my horse."

But the man didn't stir.

John Callant groaned.

"Call the dog," he said. "He'll go fast enough then."

I whistled. We all stood still, listening. I whistled again.

Then we heard Leonidas coming back. He broke out of the willows at an easy lope, waved his tail as he saw me, and stiffened suddenly at the man he had downed. The hair lifted on his shoulders and his head dropped. As I caught his collar I felt him rumbling; the man came to life. He cast one wild look at the dog, scrambled round and bolted like a rabbit.

The admiral roared with laughter.

"They've cured my gout!" he said.

He stamped his foot on the ground to prove it, and went pale.

"For the love of God," he said. "Can you understand that?"

"Come along, Jim," said Uncle Ledyard. "We'll take you back. Maybe McGinnis will help you."

"I don't need any help," said the admiral.

So we started. McGinnis holding the lantern, Doone steadying John Callant, Uncle Ledyard leading Blue Dandy, myself holding Leonidas by the collar, and the admiral, a limping figure of defiance, acting as rear-guard.

We had just got to the turn when a voice cried behind us.

"Fo' de Lawd's sake, gen'lemen, don't abandon a po'r frightened soul!"

A black face crawled out of the bushes.

"Benjamin Daniel!" roared Uncle Ledyard. "Where the devil have you been?"

Benjamin Daniel's face gleamed with sweat.

"De whole passel on 'em burs' onto us," he explained. "Dey come dis way an' dat way, and dey come onto me from behine. I seen I couldn't argumen' no resistance, Mistuh Boyd; so when John Callant drap down, I drapped down too."

"I'll bet you did," said Uncle Ledyard.

"But I didn't jes' do nuffing," said Benjamin Daniel. "De whole time I was studyin' how we goin' get away from dere."

He rolled his eyes at us all.

"Dat horse," he said, coming up to Blue Dandy, "he ain't got a scratch on him!" His voice was proud.

We went up to the gate together and through the gate and round the barn.

Kathy met us there, her eyes searching for Doone's.

"All right?" she asked.

I saw Doone's teeth flash at her as he smiled. His eyes seemed at peace. And I knew his heart was in it again.

McGinnis studied us all for a moment.

"We'll have a real race tomorrow," he said.

"You're damned right we will," said Uncle Ledyard.

McGinnis grinned a little and said good night. He wouldn't wait for thanks, not even for Kathy's.

But as I watched her and Doone, and as we got John Callant to his cot and heard, on the far side of the wall, Benjamin Daniel fussing over Blue Dandy with a soft, bossing voice, I knew it wasn't the race that counted for us. We were all together again, even to the admiral's gout.

5

We stood in front of Blue Dandy's stall: John Callant with the headstall and collar hanging on his arms and a great blue lump on his forehead; Uncle Ledyard smoking his after-breakfast cigar, his bold eyes still as he gazed at the grey horse; and Benjamin Daniel, his black face totally absorbed as he folded the warm wrap. Doone had the sulky out on the grass and was testing the air in the tires. Leonidas pressed close to my knees, his yellow eyes moving from face to face, though he followed my heels with a restlessness as persistent as my own.

"Benjamin," said Uncle Ledyard, "quit messing with that wrap and hang it up."

"Yassuh," said Benjamin Daniel, and I wanted to laugh at the way his eyes showed the whites. "Yassuh, I'm direc'ly goin' do jes' dat."

He shuffled into the next stall and I heard his endless movements as he arranged the blanket just so on the shelf.

"You don't want 'em too hard, Doone," said Uncle Ledyard. "You don't want those wheels skittering on the stretch bend, not if McGinnis is up to you."

Doone turned his lean face and grinned.

His lips looked tight to me, as if they stretched unwillingly. "They'll do, Dad."

"If you don't give him every decent inch," said Uncle Ledyard, "the old rip will smash you. That black devil he's driving would eat up a sulky like hay."

"By God, yes," hissed John Callant. "The ugly bison."

Doone said, "We won't give him the chance, will we, old boy?"

We all looked at Blue Dandy.

Alone of us, he was at ease. He was standing at the threshold, leaning his breast lightly against the closed half of the stall door; and his ears were pricked and his eyes staring over our heads, up the slope of grass to the banked curve of the track. The floor of the stall was raised above the level of the ground, so that he seemed to stand upon our shadows.

Uncle Ledyard drew in his breath.

"He don't seem any the worse for last night, Doone."

Doone grinned again, and John Callant said, as he fingered the lump on his forehead, "Not him, your Honor, Misther Boyd"—as if he were inducting Uncle Ledyard into a strange business. "Sure he trains as peaceable as a hog. He's that clever and easy, you could have him in your parlor, and he'd set down and drink tay with you like a lady."

Uncle Ledyard blew out a blast through his nostrils and turned his back on John. His face looked swollen.

Doone said quietly, "As long as he races for me—"

"He won't have to," John said grandiloquently. "He'll just imagine he's trotting a mile for you, Misther Doone. And if you'll just imagine the same, the both of you'll come home in front."

"Oh, for the love of God, John!" snorted Uncle Ledyard.

"Yes, your Honor," said John, still in his noble voice, "for the love of God and Boyd House."

"M'm'm—m'm'm'm!" murmured Benjamin Daniel approvingly from the fastness of the other stall.

"Will you stop jabbering, you old baboon!" roared Uncle Ledyard.

6

It seems to me, looking back on that morning, that Uncle Ledyard was the most worried of all of us. For I had to take but one look at the grey horse to feel sure of his winning, and John Callant talked to everyone like the prophet of the Lord of hosts. Benjamin Daniel had only one thought—to do nothing that would bring down Uncle Ledyard's wrath upon him, and so far he had been almost supernaturally unsuccessful. Doone kept to himself. He answered Uncle Ledyard's questions quietly, but I noticed that he kept his eyes toward the grandstand. And it was easy, even for me, to see that his mind was not all on the race.

And Uncle Ledyard must have been aware of that.

We all knew what Blue Dandy had done in his training, but Uncle Ledyard knew that it takes the lust for winning to make a great race horse. "Greybriar," he was saying, "wanted to run everything that moved, dead into the ground. But Blue Dandy has never been up against a great horse, and McGinnis hasn't let anyone see the best the Pascha can do."

"Sure, the best he'll do is get a smell of Blue Dandy's wind," said John Callant.

"I wish we hadn't gelded him," said Uncle Ledyard. "I'd like to see him more savage."

Doone stared at the grandstand. Early as it was, the tiers were beginning to fill.

"Has anyone heard from Kathy?" he said to me.

"No," I said.

"What's the matter with her?" asked Uncle Ledyard.

"She was asleep when I left the hotel," Doone said. "I didn't want to disturb her."

"Listen," said Uncle Ledyard, "stop worrying about her. She can look out for herself. You've got a race on your hands."

"Damn the race!" said Doone quietly, and the expression on Uncle Ledyard's face as he turned back to the horse was startling. He was almost pale.

George Beirne was coming along the outside rails of the track. He walked down to us and said "Good morning," coolly, as if he were dropping in for a trial heat, and Uncle Ledyard's eyes relaxed at the mere sound of his voice.

"How's the horse?" he asked. And then he laughed easily. "Needn't tell me. I can see for myself." He put his hand on Uncle Ledyard's arm and went on, "The whole Boyd family is turning up, Ledyard. I thought they were all here yesterday, but they've been coming into the stands this morning—faces I've forgotten all about."

Uncle Ledyard cursed.

"I hope we'll win for them, George."

"You've got a good chance."

Uncle Ledyard said, "When I made this match with Crocker and McGinnis, I thought it was just between the three of us. Who would have thought that all the rest of the family would buy into the thing the way they have?"

George Beirne laughed again.

"They can't help it. They'd take the pacifier from a baby to put their money on a real Boyd horse. And they haven't had the chance for a good many years, Ledyard. If it hadn't been for Doone and John working on Blue Dandy, they might never have had it."

"It beats the devil," said Uncle Ledyard, "why I never caught onto him till last year."

"It took Kathy," said George Beirne. "She's waked up the lot of us. Where is she, by the way? I heard about her coming down— a regular Boyd—but I haven't seen her this morning."

Doone turned.

"She said she was coming," I said.

Uncle Ledyard said savagely, "She'll turn up, Doone. Quit worrying. She's got Jim looking out for her, hasn't she? What do you suppose she did before she got married?"

A thin sort of grin came over Doone's lips.

"That's just it, dad."

George Beirne whistled.

"I'd forgotten that. Good Lord, Doone, she's all right!" His cool eyes swung over us all in turn. He smiled at me and Leonidas. I remember thinking how strange it was that a man so wise in horses and dogs and people had had no inkling about Peter Beirne and what had really brought Kathy down to us.

"Look there," he said, almost casually, "Crocker's got his mare harnessed. You'd better get into your silks, Doone."

"Thank God," said Uncle Ledyard.

Doone turned his eyes from the grandstand and went into the empty stall. Uncle Ledyard, John Callant and Benjamin went in to Blue Dandy, and George Beirne and Leonidas and I were left alone. He moved a little to one side.

I watched the stripping of the grey horse. In the dimness of the stall it seemed to me that there was a gleam upon him, like a light shining. He gave me a feeling of coolness, fitness and great strength, and also a quiet that came not so much from his own being as from the old blood lines that traveled his veins. I felt a shiver come over me as John Callant buckled the bellyband and Benjamin knelt down like a black heathen worshiper to fasten the boots. The horse lowered his muzzle to sniff the woolly head, and then raised it again. His eyes did not seem to see the things my eyes were seeing, but his ears pricked sharp, and his nostrils fluttered suddenly.

The men were quiet, all of them. The purpose of the race was upon them and they knew what they did.

Doone stepped into the sun with his silk blouse and cap, and for the first time I saw Uncle Ledyard's colors—crimson and green. Doone went past me into the stall. He stood for a moment looking over my head. I saw Uncle Ledyard covertly studying him, and Uncle Ledyard's face was still and pale.

Then I heard George Beirne chuckle.

"McGinnis is having a wrestle with that horse of his," he said. I turned.

Mr. Crocker's chestnut mare, Amber Girl, was mincing up the slope to the track gate, with Mr. Crocker in his bright, checked suit, and Mason, the driver, in yellow silks, walking behind the sulky while the groom led the mare. My heart turned in me to see the shine of her, the bright, new, yellow sulky, the gleaming tan harness, the glitter of varnish on her hoofs. There was a costliness about her outfit that found an echo in her own slim neatness. The sunlight moved in gleams back and forth against her withers as she walked, and the polish of her brown boots reflected a green light from the grass. She went up and over the rise and through the gate and sank down into the curve of the track. I saw her head rise as she was checked by the groom, and heard Crocker's voice as Mason climbed over the seat.

Then her ears danced and she moved slowly out of sight.

"Look, Teddy," said George Beirne. He was laughing.

Before the McGinnis stall, two men and McGinnis were trying to get the black stallion into the shafts. Their figures looked small beside his great bulk; they were like ants swarming against his sides. He reared and shook off one man and squealed triumphantly.

McGinnis remained calm. He had on his silks, coal black, relieved only by the number band on his right arm. His eyes, even at that distance, shone coldly blue as he held the shafts and eyed the horse. Suddenly—so quickly that I nearly missed his action—he brought the shafts down over the quarters, and the stallion came to earth and raised his head and bugled.

The sound split the still sunlight like a wind.

I felt George Beirne's hand on my shoulder.

He said quickly and urgently, "Run round to the grandstand, Teddy. The admiral's waiting there. Run like the devil!"

"What is it?" I asked.

"Run," he said.

"Is it Kathy?"

"Don't worry."

His face was as composed as ever, and he smiled. I gulped and doubled up my arms and ran, with Leonidas, a white shape, bounding easily beside me. The Pascha turned his black, thick head to see us go by, and the sun made small scarlet firepots of his nostrils.

At the back of the grandstand the shadow retained the coolness of the night and the dew still lay on the grass. It had wet the edges of the admiral's spats. He left a dark trail in it where he was walking up and down. As I doubled round the corner, he turned and saw me.

"Hello," he said gruffly. "Here it is."

His red face was portentously solemn and the side of his white mustache, which he was accustomed to pull in moments of stress, had lost its curl. But with that lopsided effect, he made a fine figure marching up and down in his quarter-deck stride. His blue coat looked freshly pressed, the dew beaded on the glossed toes of his shoes, and his hat was jauntily cocked.

The admiral's voice, however, was troubled and his nattiness was like a shell he had automatically assumed.

"Good morning," I said. "How's Kathy?"

His bulging eyes stared at me.

"She's fine!" he said, and he swore.

I saw that his thoughts were tangled, and I said, "Yes, sir. How's Kathy?"

"Didn't I tell you she was fine?" he roared. Then he looked at me again, and his voice thickened: "You make me sick. The whole lot of you. Ledyard's just a roaring ape and don't know any better,

I suppose. Coming in this morning after Kathy'd gone to the hospital and wondering what the devil he was going to do to keep Doone from knowing. He made me sick, I tell you. And you make me sick, too," he added.

"Hospital," I asked.

"Yes, hospital—hospital—hospital," said the admiral, trying a few variations. "Would you expect her to have it in a hotel? She went there last night sometime. She's having a baby, in case you don't know."

"Today?" I was struck with a kind of wonder, I remember, that Kathy should have selected this day of all days.

"Today," the admiral echoed me. "Today. Didn't I come out of her room and tell Doone she was asleep, when he came round to see her this morning? The ninny didn't even think of going in to see for himself, and old Ledyard at the foot of the stairs sweating blood. She's supposed to be in the stands now, watching, and here's a letter she's written for Doone, and you're to take it, so he won't be worrying about her. She wrote it herself. Ledyard went round and told her all about Doone—some kind of rot about his not liking the race, or being worried, or something—and they cooked this up between them."

"I'm sorry," I said, staring at him. I couldn't think of anything else to say.

"Sorry!" said the admiral. "What are you sorry for?"

"You'll miss the race."

"I'm damned if I'll miss this heat, anyhow," he snapped at me. "I've hired a couple of messengers to bring me news from the hospital. Bulletins. On bicycles!" he added, and he stamped off for the steps, striking his cane against the wall of the grandstand as he went.

I lingered a moment with the letter in my hand. There was a stirring of voices over me, a low-pitched muttering, in which I seemed able to trace some kind of rhythm, as if at last the great, monstrous bulk of empty stands had come to life and breathed. Then I saw Blue Dandy in his sulky, with John Callant at his head and Doone picking up his whip from against the wall, and

Uncle Ledyard talking to George Beirne. I had been wasting time.

I ran with all my might, and Leonidas went ahead like a white spear and bounded tremendously under the horse's nose. Except for the silks on Doone, it seemed strangely and peacefully like a morning at Boyd House.

But I rushed up to Doone and panted out that I had a note for him from Kathy. His dark face looked drawn to me. I wondered if he were afraid of racing, now that it was actually upon him. I wondered if he thought, as I did, of that savage black brute in the unscrupulous hands of McGinnis. But he read the note and handed it back to me. "Keep it safe for me, Teddy," he said.

I said, "Yes," with the sturdiest intentions, but my voice shook. For I couldn't get the idea of Kathy in the hospital out of my head, and I thought Doone ought to be told, but I didn't dare step over the heads of Uncle Ledyard and George Beirne, and even the unwilling one of the admiral. I suppose I looked white and miserable, for Doone suddenly grinned widely and held out his hand.

"Wish me luck, Teddy." His hand squeezed mine hard and he looked straight into my eyes. His eyes seemed sad to me, and, in a way, frightened, but at the same time they reminded me of Kathy's—why, I don't know, unless they were laughing too.

"Good lad," said George Beirne; and Uncle Ledyard said, "Come along."

And John Callant said, " 'Tis time," and he led the horse up the slope against the hot slant of the morning sun.

I think, as long as I live, I shall remember the grey horse standing among us at the track gate on the little crest made by the banked curve. His head was poised so high that even when John had latched the check, the rein hung slack. He stood with his forefeet placed close and his hind feet drawn deep under him, so that his quarters were raised against the slope, showing his full power. There was none of the flashing dancing of Crocker's expensive mare, nor the half-harnessed savagery of McGinnis' stallion. But in that instant before Doone swung his legs over

136

the seat, I saw the fine breeding in him. He was cool, but not a muscle quivered, his nerves were as much iron as the color of his hide. His head was lifted to face the world which was to see him for the first time, and he did not look afraid.

I think Doone drew some of his courage through the reins, for his lips set close, but without muscular force, and his shoulders relaxed as his feet pushed home in the brackets.

"God love you," said John Callant; and Doone did not smile, but said, "All right, old boy," and Blue Dandy went gently into motion. He seemed to glide off from us, smoothly and effortlessly, and as he went away down the track, his mane and tail lifted a little, and the posts came back through the wheels like clockwork.

George Beirne tapped his hat.

"There's nothing more we can do, Ledyard," he said. "Nothing but watch."

I could not hear what Uncle Ledyard said; his voice was choky, and the blood had all of a sudden rushed into his face.

But the gate steward said, "Clear the track, gentlemen," and together we moved back and the gate rolled shut in front of us.

"Nothing," said Uncle Ledyard loudly.

He moved toward the grandstand with George Beirne.

John Callant stayed at the gate. He had hooked his fingers in the wire mesh under the top rail and he leaned with his face against it.

"John," I said, "where's the best place for me to be?"

But he didn't answer, and I realized bitterly that none of them wanted me now. With Kathy in the hospital and Doone on the track with Blue Dandy, I was shut out. I was shut out of the race entirely. Uncle Ledyard and John didn't even want me watching with them.

Leonidas poked his cold nose in my hand and I looked up from the grass to find the gate steward examining me kindly.

"Do you know what I would do if I was a spry lad like you?" he said. "I'd run up to the top of the stands. Right at the top in the middle. If you've got eyes good enough, you'll see every small thing in the race from there." He grinned, and pointed to John

137

Callant. "This poor chap has to stay here, and he won't see hardly a thing."

"Thanks, mister," I said.

7

I was panting as I climbed the last tier into the shadows of the great roof. At the top, behind the highest row of benches, there was a long and narrow kind of promenade, and all along it, let into the back wall, were windows that put bars of the morning sunlight slantwise down the long slopes of seats.

My heart raced with the relief of sudden level going as I pounded along this promenade to get to the middle of the stands. I was afraid I would get there too late for the start. But when I took my seat, all alone on the top tier, the horses were down at the right-hand curve, the mare swinging wide as she turned back, Blue Dandy making a short, sharp, easy loop. Leading them back to the wire was the Pascha, his hard stroke breaking suddenly into buck jumps. I stared, as it seemed, straight down upon his broad back and saw McGinnis' face from above, for he wore his cap back on his head. And he was grinning with what seemed to me a devil's grin, as if he relished pulling a horse out of his break.

"Look at that son of a gun," said a voice right beside me. "He's a cute hand with that brute."

I turned round sharply. But there was no one there but Leonidas, who was lying in a sunny patch and licking the dew from his paws.

"It ain't hardly going to be a race, with that stud in it," said another voice, and I whirled back. A little shiver possessed me. And I looked down. A third voice said, "That's right. The mare won't last and that grey of Boyd's goes like a cab horse. He ain't got no lust."

I saw an old man in the last occupied row, far below me, shaking his head, and I understood that the voices were carried up and back to me by the long incline of the roof.

The stands were not more than half full, but to me it seemed a great crowd. Right and left under the roof the steady mutter of their voices was a sibilant roar, like deep breathing; but now and then, of the people directly below me, I could hear every word.

I looked at Blue Dandy to see whether he actually went like a cab horse, but I didn't see that he did. He was doing his trot back to the wire as easily as he would at home. His head was up and he was looking over the mare and the stallion, and I saw that Doone was, too. He was driving with a light rein, with the horse gathered easily.

"The old fools," I said to Leonidas. His tail tapped on the floor. I wanted to shout down to the old men, "Wait till they start."

But one of them said, "They're scoring this time. Moulian's telling them."

In the judge's stand, a man leaned far out over the rail and swung a green megaphone after the sulkies. His words bellowed hollowly past me.

"Mr. Mason, you're outside. Mr. McGinnis has the rail. Mr. Boyd is next him."

Though they were now down the track beyond him and his megaphone was pointing away from me, I could still hear him as he talked to the three drivers.

"Now, gentlemen," he was saying. "There are only three of you and you're all experienced drivers. You've got all the room in the world and there's no excuse for not getting off the first time. I want you to take one short score past the turn and then come back to me."

The mare had wheeled first, moving neatly in the track and then abruptly coming up on her toe calks at what seemed to me a full trot. She was fairly skimming as she shot out under the wire and her neat hoofs clipped off the track with a light, almost brittle, tattoo. I watched her spin out into the turn with the ribbon of dust swinging wide behind her, and then in the tail of my eye, I saw Blue Dandy coming down past the stand.

He was moving fast, but it seemed to me that he didn't show

half the pace of the mare. Doone, however, wasn't urging him at all. As they went out for the turn, Moulian pointed the megaphone after them and I heard his voice saying in an almost conversational tone, "Pick up your reins, Mr. Boyd, when you have an opportunity."

Doone raised the tip of his whip in acknowledgement, and as they entered the turn, he reached back with his left hand and tucked the trailing end of his reins under his seat.

At that instant McGinnis brought the black horse through the stretch on his score. He was all dynamite: he didn't trot smoothly but looked to me to be on the edge of breaking at every other stride. It was almost as if he was not only fighting the icy wrists of the little man driving him but himself as well. But then, as he hit into the turn, for an instant he really trotted, and the way he hauled up on Blue Dandy and Doone shot my heart suddenly down into my shoes.

The mare was now coming back to us with her neat, quick gait. Doone was turning Blue Dandy. But the Pascha's rush had carried him almost to the backstretch, and McGinnis was fighting him there. He half reared as the little man brought him around and as he returned to us he was still fighting the bit, with his eye showing white and a bib of froth under his throat.

The three horses went down past the stand close after each other, and Moulian was calling after them, "I want you to turn together, gentlemen, and come back to me even. There's no reason why we can't get away the first time out."

As he finished speaking, the murmur of voices in the stand died away with something resembling a sigh. In the sudden stillness I became aware of pigeons humming on the roof. Then all my senses were caught in the turning of the sulkies.

They came round at a short walk, Doone and McGinnis turning in towards the rail, Crocker's mare swinging to the outside in front of them. They wheeled like hawks crossing in flight, and in the next instant they shot toward us down the straight.

My eye became all-embracing. I saw Moulian leaning even farther out from the slant. His face was purple as he shouted, "Pull back your mare, Mr. Mason!" with his hand reaching toward the bell. "Pull her back, I say!"

Mason leaned back on the reins and the chestnut's pointed face lifted and her ears set back hard. It brought the stallion up like a thundercloud. Mason's face was set tight and his eyes were all on McGinnis. McGinnis was calm, his eyes like blue glass—bits of sky, midsummer blue. They held me.

I saw him cast one glance at Blue Dandy, a length back, between them.

"Go!" roared Moulian.

Then I heard the stroke of hoofs against the dirt, heard, as the horses shot past, the deep hard breathing round my face, heard one clear, sharp word from Doone, and it was swallowed in the roar of voices, as if all the crowd had held their breaths from the beginning of the score. One of the old men yelled, "Did you ever see a start to beat it?"

I was enraged at the start's holding, with Blue Dandy a length back. It seemed to me a gross unfairness. But my eyes were irresistibly drawn after the sulkies. The dust spun from their wheels, sudden and live, six ribbons almost breast for breast. I saw Mason touch the mare with his whip, and the billowing yellow silk back of his shirt dipped like a bird, and, as the horse rifled clear of the dust on the curve, the yellow was leading and the mare was going prettily, with a length of open air between her and the Pascha. She went like a swallow. She was all gold and amber, like her name, beyond the shining green grass of the inclosure. The rails swam past her. Just her head showed, her slim, pointed head like the point of an arrow, and Mason's face running along the rails as if it were flanged to it.

I had never seen a horse go like her. She drew out and out from the black and Blue Dandy until she had two lengths, and I felt my heart swelling unbearably. The Pascha was beginning to reach out. As I watched, his withers sank into the white rail and dropped slowly level with them and the dust obscured Doone entirely. Only the grey head of Blue Dandy showed in it, a length and a half behind the black shirt of McGinnis.

They streamed past the half-mile post, one, two, three, as they had come up to it, and the mare began to sink into the curve. Suddenly McGinnis swung his whip and the black horse shot up and hung to the wheel of the yellow sulky.

There was a shout from the crowd that raised me to my feet. I had lost all sense with that shout. I was on my feet, but there was no sensation in me. As I looked down, I seemed to be floating, and the white oval of the rails, the green grass and the streaming dust headed by the trotting horses made me the pattern of a dream.

And then the blood was in me and every nerve was whipping. I let out a shout that brought Leonidas in one bound to the bench at my side, and we pressed close, staring down.

They were in the cup of the bend now, with the bank rising to the horses' breast collars. Blue Dandy hung three lengths back, and the crowd was beginning to lift its incoherent shouting into names: "Amber Girl! Amber Girl! . . . The Pascha! . . . McGinnis! . . . Look at him!"

There was a hush as sudden as the break in a storm.

A shrill voice was crying, "Blue Dandy! Oh, Doone, Doone, Doone! Come on, Doone!"

It was my own. I became suddenly abashed, but the crowd took me up. "Boyd!" yelled somebody. It was like an old familiar shout. "Boyd! Boyd!"

For Blue Dandy had risen over the dust. He was coming into the straight on the outside. He was leaning into the turn, and for the first time the world saw what Doone and John and I had seen at Boyd House training track more than a year ago. The lift of the grey horse before he opened, the thrust of his tremendous stride, with his head out and the cups of living flame in his nostrils. One saw then why he was short in the saddle place and long underneath. He came up, making half as much ground again as the other two, who were locked against the rail, and McGinnis and Mason turned, not to look at each other but to see the green-and-crimson Boyd silks. They went to their whips together. The mare's ears dropped and the stallion squealed suddenly, and they flashed under the wire, and I saw then why the gate steward said to get high up.

I felt ill and weak. The crowd was tossing names, but I could tell that Amber Girl had held her place, and Pascha had nosed out Blue Dandy. He had come too wide and too late. I watched them slowly down the track, taking the bend wide to leave good going for the next heats, and I hardly noticed that the mare was dropping her ears, and that Pascha was blowing hard as he wheeled his sulky round for the gate, and that Blue Dandy was springing on his pasterns with his head up and a nicker for John Callant.

A voice boomed, "Well, Buddy Armond, how about our dollar bet?"

I looked down into the face of Mr. Crocker, and I hated him.

He was clambering down to the track.

Behind him, glum and red-faced, went Uncle Ledyard, but George Beirne stopped and came up toward me. He put his hand on my shoulder.

He said, "The Boyds feel sick too. But, boy, Blue Dandy didn't rightly know what it was all about. He waked too late. Doone waited for him. We expected the first heat to go like this. Remember, it's only the first heat. He damned near broke them both as it was. The mare has had a bellyful."

His fingers squeezed.

"Don't show it, boy, if you do lose. But we're not beaten yet. They're scared to death—McGinnis and Mason both."

I got up, trembling.

"Come along," he said.

As we went down, I saw the admiral in a front seat. He was reading a message.

He saw me as I went by, and he swore.

"A horse!" he said. "A horse. Give me a bicycle!"

But I saw his hand was shaking. . . .

I didn't look for the other horses. George Beirne said it wasn't good form for one stable to look in on another between heats. "They've got things to hide. But we know what they are anyway. Look, McGinnis is walking the Pascha before he takes him in."

Blue Dandy stood still under the ministering hands of John Cal-

143

lant and Benjamin Daniel. His head was dropped, but he pricked his ear at me and Leonidas.

"Don't bother him," John said tartly. And then, "Oh, Misther Teddy, did you mark him as he waked? Oh, glory saints!"

"M'm'm'm—m'm'm'm" said Benjamin, as his black hands slapped a tattoo down over the loins and the stinging scent of liniment filled the stall.

"He scraped out as easy as the twelve apostles," said John. And his hands joined Benjamin's. I turned away to Doone.

"Doone," I said, "will you win the next?"

Doone was breathing deep. He looked at me as if he didn't see me.

"He went," he said. "He went to win. I didn't dare to touch him."

George Beirne came down from the track again.

"2:03 for the heat!" he cried.

Uncle Ledyard stuck his stick into the ground.

"He'll go from the beginning, Doone. Let him go. Maybe you'll distance the mare."

Doone grinned.

He turned away from them and said to me, "Have you got Kathy's letter?"

I gave it to him.

He read it again.

"Look here, Teddy," he said, and showed me the note.

> Doing fine. I wish I were there.
> But beat them for me anyway.

I gulped.

"You knew, Doone?"

"I took her over myself. But she didn't want dad to know. She said he was so worried. His heart's not too good. So she let him cook up this business to occupy his mind."

"Oh, Kathy," I said. He grinned a close little grin.

"Run ask the admiral, Teddy. And show him this."

I ran. I found the admiral swearing at another messenger boy.

"Go like hell and bedamned," he finished, "and tell the doctor I'll hang him dead as mackerel if she isn't all right."

He stopped as he saw me.

"Doone wants to know—"

"Oh, he does!" roared the admiral, and he drew a breath to launch himself.

"Doone said for you to read this," I said, handing him the note. He swallowed and took it. Then he did let loose himself. He forgot all about Kathy. And when he at length remembered her, he included even her in his swearing, and then he met my eye and something like a smile lifted his white mustache.

"Teddy, my lad," he said, "those two young pigeons have made donkey ears grow on us. Every last one of us. You too. I don't doubt even that dog of yours has 'em. Ledyard!" he roared aloud. "He'll never get over it."

"Is she all right?" I asked.

"The doctor says he'll have news in half an hour at most. But Lord, why worry? She can look out for herself."

I went back to Doone, and I told him. He looked at his watch. There was still sweat on his face, but he said very calmly, "We'll hear when the heat starts, maybe." And he got up and went in to Blue Dandy. And I went after him, completely puzzled.

8

Uncle Ledyard was right. This time Blue Dandy was first on the track, and he went away from the gate swinging his head to watch for the other horses. Doone was keeping a tight rein on him.

The stallion came out without any rearing, but he fought the bit as he went after Blue Dandy. They came all the way round to the grandstand before the mare was ready, and when she came on, anyone could tell with half an eye that she would do well to keep her distance. The mutter of the crowd swelled up under the roof as Blue Dandy trotted through the straight, still swinging his head in an effort to watch the Pascha.

Doone swung him round at the end of the stand, where the admiral was sitting, and I ran back to catch their voices.

"Nothing yet, you young hellion," said the admiral and Doone's teeth flashed as he grinned and swung his whip and went back.

He gave Blue Dandy a trial score and slid past us for the curve, going light and free to the beginning of the back stretch, swinging wide of McGinnis and cutting in under Pascha's nose. I saw McGinnis shake his whip after him and the Pascha dug his hoofs into the track and tried to take after him. Doone looked over his shoulder and laughed. Besides the others, both he and the grey horse went gayly.

They scored twice; the Pascha carrying McGinnis right away both times and being put back. But on the third, Blue Dandy and Amber Girl came down on the wire like a harnessed pair, and Moulian's "Go!" fairly lifted the roof.

It was a beautiful start. The mare was flying. Her stroke was so rapid that she seemed to be leaving Blue Dandy standing still. It was obvious that Mason was out to build a lead and hold it— putting everything into the second heat. And yet she couldn't leave Blue Dandy before the curve. He was trotting with pricked ears, and a breath rose out of the crowd as Doone pulled him in behind the mare's wheels. He was so close that Mason must have felt the breath against his collar.

The pulling let McGinnis bring up the stallion as close again to Doone, and the three horses fled the curve like a train of cars. I felt my knees knocking as they went into the backstretch. "Doone!" I was praying. "Now, Doone, now!"

And the crowd let out a roar as Doone pulled wide coming out of the curve. For the grey horse was trotting hard at last. His ears had come back. For an instant he teamed the mare, leaving the Pascha a length back, and then, though his stride gave no increase of speed, it lengthened, and he pulled out so fast that the mare lifted and broke.

Mason sawed her savagely to the outside, so roughly that she

146

broke again as she came down, and McGinnis, who had been waiting, shoved the Pascha through on the inside and swung his whip and set out on Blue Dandy's trail.

But my blood seemed to be singing. The heat was over there. I knew it in my heart. I sat down again in a kind of prickling calmness. Blue Dandy did not come back. His stroke was longer than even I remembered, and I realized that the difference lay in the mile track with its wide curves.

Doone had him on a close rein as they struck the bend, and horse and man leaned together. They came with a kind of joy. I seemed to see it even that far on Doone's face, as I saw the joy of trotting in the great stride of Blue Dandy. The thrust of his forefeet was tremendous, as if he snatched with each stroke an extra foot of ground, and his hind hoofs came through like pistons, barely clearing the track.

The crowd were roaring, they seemed to make a wind that tightened his mane and tail beyond bearing. He whipped out of the curve with the Pascha two lengths back and he gained half a length again coming down the stretch. The mare was so far back that no one looked for the flag of the judge in the distance stand.

And then, as Blue Dandy slid under the wire and whipped out for the curve as if he had the taste of another mile on his bit, I saw the Boyds in the crowd. I couldn't mistake them. Nobody could have mistaken them. They were standing on their benches. They were flinging paper and waving reticules, and their voices were like wild Indians. I saw Aunt Phoebe far down to the left, yelling with all her might and opening and shutting her parasol, until suddenly she overpushed it, and then she whooped and flung it backward over her shoulder with a full sweep of her arms, squashing the hat of the gentleman behind her.

I jumped up and tore down the promenade to the end stairs, with Leonidas barking hysterically, and clattered down to the admiral's seat. The old gentleman was laughing and cursing.

"Damn it, Teddy!" he roared, hooking my neck with the crook of his cane. "I left my brandy at the hotel! Ask Ledyard if he's got any!"

"Yes!" I yelled.

147

"Lord, boy!" he said. "Did you ever see anything to beat it? There's the time!" he bellowed. "Be still, can't you?" he roared at the people round him.

Moulian was swinging his megaphone at us. His voice came hollow and thunderous, and quelled the shouting:

"Time for the second heat—time for the second heat: Two minutes flat! Two minutes flat!"

"Hey-hey!" shouted the admiral.

"He didn't even bother to name the winner! Just the time! Teddy, if Ledyard ain't got it, snitch me that bottle of John Callant's."

"Admiral Porter," said a voice in our ears.

A messenger boy was standing there. He held out a message. The admiral took it and tore it open.

"Tell Doone," he shouted, "that the doctor says he should have news in twenty minutes."

I nodded wordlessly.

As I ran down the slope to the stables, I met Mr. Crocker. He looked very crestfallen, but he smiled wryly and called after me, "You were right, boy! I hope you take McGinnis!"

I just waved.

Before Blue Dandy's stall, in some manner that no one was able ever to explain, I found Uncle Ledyard looking completely purple and standing solemnly on his hat. And for once, John Callant was speechless. Benjamin Daniel was saying, "M'm'm'm— m'm'm'm!" over and over till everyone's ears buzzed, but nobody noticed him. And Doone was sitting on the box against the wall and just staring.

"Oh, Doone!" I cried.

"Didn't he go, Teddy?" Doone said.

Uncle Ledyard drew a shuddering breath.

"Greybriar—" he began, but he broke off. "Greybriar never ran a heat like that," he finished.

Doone smiled.

I said, "The admiral's heard that the doctor should have news for us in twenty minutes."

"God bless her!" cried Uncle Ledyard, but he couldn't move

148

his eyes from the horse. . . . "He's cooling out beautifully, John."

"And the admiral says he needs a drink," I said.

"Buy him a barrel," said Uncle Ledyard.

"He wants it right away," I said, but Uncle Ledyard said, "I've only got the sherry, and he can't have that."

Doone said, "Tell him to let me know as soon as he hears," and he got up stiffly and went in to Blue Dandy. So I snitched the bottle John Callant had hidden under his shoes, and went back to the admiral. I couldn't walk, I had to run.

The admiral drew the cork and smelled it.

He said, "I never smelled liquor like that, my boy," and tilted his head back. "I never tasted that kind of whiskey," he said, after a long pull, as he wiped his mustache. "Have you?" and he passed me the bottle.

So I took my first taste of straight corn whiskey.

"No," I said, handing it back.

But instead of returning to the stall, I felt my giddiness increase, and I sat down suddenly beside the admiral. He sat down, too, remarking that it was a good idea, and had another pull of the bottle. We perched like two owls for twenty minutes, and until the admiral put his hand on my shoulder, the voices swayed round me and blurred indistinguishably with my swimming sight of the green inclosure.

But little by little my equilibrium returned to me; and when the admiral said, "Here they are." I saw Blue Dandy following the Pascha onto the track.

Somebody said beside me, "That boy of Boyd's better look out this time," and turning my head I saw them down beyond the wire, swinging hard and coming into the straight. I left the admiral suddenly and scrambled up to the top of the stands. There was a roaring in my ears, "There they go!" and I stopped to see them come past the starter nose for nose, with Doone and McGinnis staring like dogs from the corners of their eyes.

I sat down hard, and felt my breath go out of me as the Pascha suddenly let all out. He gained a bare length, barely enough to justify McGinnis' taking the pole on the curve; but even so, Doone had to pull up, and the crowd yelled incoherently.

The dust spun wide to the outside of the curve as they came into the backstretch, and this time there was no mistaking the ability of the stallion to trot. It seemed to me that Blue Dandy was just hanging on. The little black beard of McGinnis was pointing the way for his face, low down on the rails, and the great beast went like a locomotive, a black incarnation of power. He caught the eye, now that he was in front, and Blue Dandy, at his heels, traveled like the ghost of a horse. As they passed the half, it was a wonder at all to find him still there.

I tried to see what Doone was doing, but it was too far off. All I could tell was that he was not using his whip.

Just before the stretch bend, Blue Dandy seemed to move up a little, or else the Pascha had faltered, for the gray muzzle disappeared on the far side of McGinnis' black shirt.

Someone cried, "The fool! McGinnis will carry him wide!"

And McGinnis had taken the whip again, and the black stallion hit the curve like thunder. And still Doone kept Blue Dandy just to the outside.

I looked for Uncle Ledyard, and I saw him under me, standing up, and still as a wooden image, with his hat squeezed to a muss in his hands. I couldn't see George Beirne at all. And my eyes swung back to the turn.

They were into the last quarter now, and McGinnis was edging out. He came wider and wider, and he had the black going full blast.

The crowd stilled and the shadow under the roof became cold for me.

I heard the hard, wonderful, steady striking of their hoofs in the dirt. I saw them come out of the curve, and now Blue Dandy seemed behind McGinnis' back.

And an unholy yell lifted me. For Blue Dandy's ears pricked and I saw his nose on the inside of McGinnis. And McGinnis must have caught the change of stride, for he tried to pull in. But he had overdriven his horse on the turn, and in the breath Doone's hands eased and Blue Dandy caught his flight again and drew up to the black's quarters, and they drove now straight for the wire.

I heard McGinnis' voice, unbelievably deep, as he shouted. But Blue Dandy had the rail and was coming. His stroke was longer than the stallion's. He got his nose up to the throat latch and hung there for two posts, and then the black squealed and broke, and Blue Dandy pricked his ears and bored through, and the race was over.

The stands rocked and rocked to the shouting of the Boyds. They did not care about the time. Their horse had won.

He had beaten the two best on the Grand Circuit in his first race. That was what they cared about. The Boyds had a horse again.

I think I was their only supporter who heard Moulian's stentorian bellow:

"Time of the third heat: Two minutes, one and a half seconds!"

But even I did not much care about it. I could not get up. I could not move, even when Doone brought Blue Dandy back, black and lathered, his legs cased in dust, but his ears up. He came back along the stands lightly and easily.

All I remember of it is the sight of the admiral leaning far over Doone's head, and his naval voice uplifted above all that pandemonium:

"It's a girl!"

IV

1

Just why Uncle Ledyard had gone in for sheep, I doubt if he could have explained himself at the time; but he had. He had come across an advertisement in a February farm journal of a flock for sale in Chittenango, and he had ordered the lot by mail without consulting a soul. They had arrived, according to Doone, in the middle of a March snowstorm, so it had taken the whole force at Boyd House and four of the neighbors with their teams and sleighs to get them over from the station. The next night the first ewes had started lambing, and since then they had entirely disrupted the life of the farm.

Boyd House was geared exclusively to the needs of the horses and always had been. Of course a certain amount of time and thought had to be put in on keeping up the dairy herd; but they after all were mere adjuncts, whose purpose was to provide money for the stables and manure for the fields. But the sheep were another matter. John Callant complained that their baaing at the end of the barn disturbed the horses and resented each bale of straw that went out of the stable loft for use in their pens. Adam Fuess fell so far behind with the spring plowing that he was in a constant sweat for fear he would not get the oats into the ground in time; and when he did have the twenty acre piece ready for seeding, Uncle Ledyard sent him out with all the hands on the place to build a new page wire fence round the big back pasture. As no man among them had ever tried stretching this sort of fence in rough territory, they had a bad time with it.

What with one thing and another, even Doone was obliged to break off training the horses some days; but when he finally turned on his father and asked why in God's name he wanted to have sheep at Boyd House, the only answer Uncle Ledyard could give was that he thought the lambs would be nice for little Fanny to play with.

That was probably as near the truth as anyone was likely to get, Uncle Ledyard included. He had lost his heart to his grand-daughter, and nothing in his opinion was good enough for her. It made no difference that she was not yet quite two, or that a couple of lambs in a small pen near the house would have been a good deal more suitable. His mind did not work that way. If there ought to be lambs at Boyd House for her to look at, he felt that they should be of his own raising, and that meant a whole flock, complete with a ram. He called them "Fanny's sheep" and went out with her every morning, while they remained in the barn, to inspect them. He would allow no complaints to be made of them in her presence and perhaps because of this and perhaps also because of the pleasure the little girl took in these visits to the barn, the men became reconciled to their presence on the farm.

No one foresaw then the trouble they would bring to Boyd House. I don't mean the lambing and fencing, which were only a nuisance and were over and done with in any case by the time I arrived from the city at the end of May. I mean the killing which came to the valley. It was like a nightmare for a while; even the horses were forgotten. Nor was it only the Boyd flock that suffered. Other flocks down the river had their share of it, too; and if it had not been for Leonidas, who finally put an end to it, I think the sheep would have been given up altogether, for men seemed to be powerless against the sheep killers.

Kathy brought Leonidas to meet me at the station. The lilacs were blooming in the back yards when the train pulled into the village; and when I saw her on the seat of the gig, as lovely and

153

fresh as she was the first time I saw her at Boyd House, with the white bull terrier cocking his ears beside her, my heart turned over in me. I cannot describe how I felt, coming home that spring, though it was the same every year for me. Ours is in no way an impressive landscape; but there are more woods than farmland in it, and besides the river, it is full of springs and running brooks; and perhaps if you are born in it, as I had been, it gains meaning. My own family were going abroad that year, and I was to spend the summer at Boyd House; but Uncle Ledyard and Kathy and Doone had always made me feel that the place was as much my home as theirs; and it was like Kathy to have thought of going round by our house to pick up Leonidas and bring him to greet me.

Leonidas was in his sixth year now, and right in the full of his prime. He was a good bit heavier than when he had fought the drummer's dog that night in Bender's barn, but he hadn't begun to slow up, and his body under his smooth white hide felt hard as whalebone under my arm. He wasn't demonstrative with me; he just licked my hand once; but that touch assured me that nothing had changed between us.

I could hardly speak, and I kept my arm round him and just sat still as we drove out of town. The blue sky was warm over us; the meadows were sprouting the year's best green; and where the road led through the woods, I could see ferns like silver springs uncoiling from the brown leaf bed.

Kathy gave me the news of the place as we drove. Mostly she talked about the sheep and made a funny story of the trouble they'd made in the lives of Adam Fuess and John Callant; and she also described the way Fanny had got Uncle Ledyard under her tiny thumb.

"It's almost scandalous, really," Kathy told me. "I honestly think she must be the first Boyd woman that's ever had the run of the office. She thinks it's her play room and uses it so."

Uncle Ledyard had not paid a great deal of attention to her to begin with, while she was still in what he referred to as her babyish stage and spending most of her time in her bassinet. He had been too absorbed during those early months by Blue

Dandy's campaign on the Grand Circuit. But once she had started to walk, she had made a dead set for him, and his capitulation had been complete and immediate. And therefore the sheep.

It was strange at first, but it became a familiar sight to see the sheep drift over the bald top of the hill to the west of the house. They came in that way from the back pasture which had been fenced with page wire, and after them came old Francis Hughes, whom Uncle Ledyard had appointed shepherd in addition to his duties with the poultry, because Francis had once worked with sheep, but so long ago that even he could not remember when it was. He was an old Welshman who claimed to have been bully of the Chenango Canal in his day, and he still had heavy fists, though the flesh had thinned out with time, and a misused nose. The first thing he had done was to acquire a sheep dog in the town of Steuben. It was an odd pup, which he called a "pure-bred English shepherd," and it had cost him seven dollars. It was a gray-brown, woolly animal, with a beagle's way of using its long tail, and about half as big as Leonidas. He had named it Femus, for some unknown reason, and the first time I saw him, Francis told me how masterful Femus was with a laggard ewe. And Francis also credited the pup with potent tastes and tried to teach him to chew tobacco.

I think that Femus was as puzzled as Francis by this new career of theirs, but he was an honest little dog and did the best he could, and because we had had a beautiful, dry, warm spring, the sheep prospered, every one.

The lambs became frisky, and in spite of Francis' most patient attentions, they grew wild as fawns. There was an old dry ewe who had got into the flock by some mistake, I suppose; for she was an obvious cross with a Rambouillet, leggy, and with a startled leap like a doe rabbit's. According to Francis, she wasn't good for either mutton or manure any more. She found every flaw in the fence, and for the first three weeks she had had every hand on the place busy pegging the wire down. Francis finally had a bell put on her—an old sleigh bell with a high-pitched note. And he named her the Widow Pierce, after a woman he had disliked in his young manhood.

155

At first, of course, I didn't take much interest in the sheep. I went off fishing all day. The water was clearing, but it was still too high in the river to wade, so I fished the beaver-meadow brook that ran along the western line of the Boyd place. There weren't any good trout till you came out in the beaver meadow at the back of the sheep pasture, but through that the brook followed a meandering course which was prodigal in deep holes on the bends, holes in which trout lived that were more than a pound. They hid under the banks, with their bellies on cold springs, and they had plenty of room to fight in, and you were lucky if you brought one home.

But when I was all through fishing in the late afternoon, I would leave the stream and cut home across the sheep pasture, and generally I would pick up the flock, or hear Francis calling, "Nanny, nanny, nanny," embarrassedly through his nose, and then I would see the Widow Pierce coming along at full gallop to the back fence and Francis clumping along a good hundred yards behind, and in between would be the rest of the flock, with Femus looking worried and running all the way round them and back again, and no more able to turn them than he would have been able to turn an avalanche. He just didn't know how. If he tried to nip one, Francis would curse him like forty canal boatmen, and ask him whether he called that being a sheep dog. And if he just let the sheep run over him, Francis would weep at him for his lack of gimp. But as soon as the sheep got tired and made up their own minds to go home, Francis and Femus would trot along side by side, looking confident and proud. He said they were reading a book about sheep-dog trials, and by the end of the summer he would take Femus to England maybe, and then he would bet the universe against a glass of beer, himself and Femus would take the grand prize. And Femus would look up at him with his tongue hanging out a yard, and wag his tired tail.

Kathy and Uncle Ledyard generally brought small Fanny with them to see the sheep come in, so we four would walk back to the house together for Fanny to get her supper. It was very peaceful in the dining room, with Uncle Ledyard grinning at Fanny and looking at my trout, and Fanny switching her black curls

156

and talking about the "more sheep," and Kathy quietly watching us. Doone would come in from the paddock with the faint sweat and leather smell from driving and sit down too. And generally after supper we would move into the office, where Fanny played with her dolls in front of the warm stove while Doone and Uncle Ledyard discussed the day's workouts and maybe check back on the blood lines of this or that colt, for none of the young ones showed the same sort of promise Blue Dandy had at their age.

The names of the horses being passed back and forth seemed to have a fascination for Fanny; she would leave off her playing and sit raptly listening. There was nothing she loved more than to hear her grandfather read off a pedigree, which, if the colt came of Greybriar's lineage, could be a ringing performance.

Nothing was missing but the admiral, and Kathy said he was coming the last week of June; and it was such a quiet, peaceful time that it seemed impossible that anything could break it. And yet in one short week the peace was broken and a kind of red horror lay at our doors. We felt then a little, I suppose, the way the first settlers felt when they thought of the Indians. We didn't know when the trouble would find us, but we felt sure it would come.

2

As it happened, I saw the first sign of it; but at the time I didn't know what it meant.

I saw it when I was fishing. I was lying on my belly at the edge of a deep hole in the beaver meadow, and Leonidas was lying just behind me with his chin on my ankle, and for ten minutes neither of us had moved nor made a sound. An old willow stub leaned out over the water, its roots undercut by the eating curve of the brook, and right under it was a wary old trout. I knew him from previous unsuccessful encounters, so I had taken great pains in crawling up on the bend, and now I was there with my worm trailing slowly towards the spot he ought to be lying in.

It was a good day for brook fishing. A cool, gray, misty rain seemed almost to rest on the deep grass. So fine and thick was the rain that I could just barely make out the old spruce stubs here and there and the line of the fence of the sheep pasture on the far side of the brook, and the thorn apple trees just beyond it, like parasols in the rain. The tall beaver grass hid me, bending over me with the weight of the rain on it, and dripping wet on my neck. It was chilly, lying still, but the admiral had come up the day before and was keen for a taste of trout. Even as I lay there, the rain seemed bending the grass lower and lower, and gradually it came on a hard pouring that made a sound on the earth.

In the midst of it Leonidas stirred suddenly and got up on his haunches. I looked round angrily, but his ears were pointed over my head and his yellow eyes had a queer kind of uneasy blaze in them; so I forgot the trout and looked up. I got cautiously to my knees. And then I dropped my rod and took hold of his collar, for as I watched with him, I felt an uneasy stirring in myself, as one feels waking through a bad dream.

They had drifted into sight through the rain with no sound at all. There were five of them. But they ran close together behind a little half collie that had a head like a fox and was almost the same color. At first I thought it must be four dogs following a bitch, but then I saw that the red one wasn't a bitch. There wasn't a bitch in the pack. I whispered that to Leonidas, and when I did I felt a queer chill at the back of my neck. One doesn't expect to see dogs in a pack. And this was a pack, and it was hunting something.

I had better describe them here, as I was the only person ever known to have seen them running in daylight. The red dog was obviously the leader. There were two ordinary-looking shepherd dogs—which means any dog that will herd cows and has a strain of collie—and they looked to me as if they came from the same litter, for both had black masks on their muzzles. They were heavily set up, with thick, curling tails, and they galloped

158

strongly. The fourth dog was a black-and-white shepherd with a real collie's head. It was the fifth that made me wonder. He was a big black-and-tan foxhound, the kind the old trappers used to breed for running deer. Such dogs were rare even then; we called them Adirondack hounds; and this one was a beauty, big, deep-chested, with the bloodhound head, the lovely, long ears and a coat that was like silk, even in the rain.

They slipped out of the grass with the red dog a little ahead and went all along the back fence. They seemed to be sniffing the foot of the wire, and they did not stop till they came to the north corner; and then they halted and looked for a long time through the wire into the pasture. They had the look of talking things over, and they also had the look of dogs who had come a long way, but who knew exactly what they wanted to find.

They seemed not to have found it, for they stood only a minute about the little red dog, who was sitting down on his tail and looking more like a fox than ever. They seemed to be talking over their next move; and then, as suddenly as he had brought them, he rose and led them down into the deep grass again.

I got to my feet softly. I couldn't see them any more. But I could trace their passage through the meadow by the wave they made in the deep grass. And in only a minute more they were completely gone. That was the queer thing about them—the swift-ness of their coming and their going—that and their muteness.

I found I was shivering, and so was Leonidas. He had made no sound either. I had made no sound. There was just the rain. Then I saw that a trout was on my line and I, luckily, kept him and went home with what I had.

Uncle Ledyard and the admiral were on the back verandah having their afternoon bourbon, and it seemed very comfortable and dry behind the eaves' drip, so I stopped to show them the fish and to tell them about the dogs. Uncle Ledyard asked for a description.

"I don't know any of those dogs," he said, when I gave it to him.

I said they looked as if they had come a long way.

"Running deer, probably," said Uncle Ledyard.

159

The admiral sipped thoughtfully and wiped his mustache dry. "They don't sound to me like dogs running deer, Ledyard."

"What are you talking about?" said Uncle Ledyard.

"I don't know," said the admiral. "I just said it. I'm not a damned farmer."

I left them chaffing each other and went up to change.

It was cool enough that evening for us to have a fire in the living room, and we were gathered there before dinner when old Francis came to the office door.

He looked wet, and so did Femus. He had his chewing tobacco in his hand, out of deference to Kathy's tastes, and he looked worried.

"Mr. Boyd," he said, "it ain't as if me and Femus had been minding animals like them stiddy for the past forty years, so I don't rightly recollect. But it seems kind of cold and what you might call damp out for them there lambs. I was wondering hadn't I better drive them into the shed tonight."

"I don't know," said Uncle Ledyard. "What would you do with sheep on a night like this on Long Island, Jim?"

The admiral said, "I'd give them all a finger of whiskey. Only I'd put it in the milk for the youngest ones."

Uncle Ledyard swore at him and told Francis to put the sheep inside.

"They won't be bothered by dogs there anyway," said the admiral.

"What the devil?" said Uncle Ledyard.

And Doone said, "Dogs?"

I told him what I had seen. I think it was the first time any of us stopped to think about those dogs. But Uncle Ledyard laughed.

"Those dogs were out on a spree, that's all," he said. "They don't know any more about sheep than I do."

Francis shuffled his feet.

"Femus," he said apologetically, "he's a real active sheep dog."

"You get out and tend to them," suggested Uncle Ledyard. "It'll be dark pretty soon."

Francis looked thankful and went.

But I kept thinking about those dogs and the sheep. . . .

About four o'clock the next afternoon, Doone and I were out at the training track with Blue Dandy and one of the young ones when we saw a rig drive up to the house, and by the time we had finished the heat, Benjamin Daniel had come out to take the second horse and to tell us that Uncle Ledyard wanted to see us.

He was on the back porch, and with him were the admiral, looking purple and blowing at his mustache, and Kathy, with a white look of pity on her face. Seated in front of them was a heavy-set farmer who held his glass of bourbon as if he would crush it any minute.

Uncle Ledyard said shortly, "Doone, you know George Peasely. . . . This is Teddy Armond, George."

The big man acknowledged us by getting heavily to his feet. But his frozen eyes scarcely saw us.

Uncle Ledyard spoke for him:

"George came this way because he knows I have sheep. He wanted to know if we had any trouble last night and he wanted to warn us. I think it was damned decent of him. Last night dogs got into his flock and killed more than twenty of them—lambs, ewes, and his Shropshire ram."

The farmer listened attentively to what Uncle Ledyard said. Then he downed the rest of his glass and sat down again.

The admiral's blue eyes swelled with sympathy.

"What you need, Mr. Peasely, is a little more whiskey."

"Maybe I do," said the farmer, in a thick voice. "I don't know."

"The dogs got into his back pasture about nine last night. Maybe earlier. George didn't hear a thing until he heard a dog barking at his neighbor's. George hadn't a sheep dog."

"I never needed none," the farmer said, apologetically, looking at all of us. "They minded me real handy. They done well for me this spring. I only lost one lamb." He looked down at the glass the admiral gave him. "We ain't never been troubled this way afore now," he added.

Kathy looked as if she were going to burst out crying.

George Peasely went on like a man talking in his sleep:

"I just woke up and I heerd that dog a-barking like he was crazy. I didn't think nothing of it. He's a crazy dog anyway. But after a while my woman said, 'I think I hear something running,' she said. It was real still, and after a while I thought I heerd something myself. So I went out with a lantern, and I seen some of what I had in the corner of the pasture, and the rest was just laying around."

"Teddy," said Uncle Ledyard, "I think you saw those dogs. I think Jim was right."

"You saw them?" asked the farmer. "What was they like?"

His eyes were bloodshot. For the third time I described the dogs I had seen. "I didn't know what they were up to," I said.

The farmer looked at me pityingly.

"The devil wouldn't have guessed half of it," he said. "I don't know any such parcel of dogs. But that hound must have come from a great ways. There ain't but a dozen or so of them left in the woods." He stared into his glass again.

"What can we do?" asked Uncle Ledyard. "I've never had any experience in this business."

"I know what I'm going to do," said the farmer slowly. "Any dog I see on my place that looks like any one of them dogs, I'm going to shoot him, no matter what he's doing."

He got up heavily and thanked Kathy for the whiskey.

"I got to go home," he said. "I got to get back to chores. Milking. Cows. I'll be up all night, I guess. I guess you'd better be, too."

He went away. Kathy went into the house. Uncle Ledyard sat still, his mouth looking like stone through his beard.

"Go get Francis, Teddy," he said.

3

When Francis came, Uncle Ledyard gave him the news. Francis swore incredulously.

"That wouldn't happen here," he said. "Not with me having a dog like Femus."

But we locked the sheep in again, and I think all of that night and the next and the next we lay waking. But nothing happened. It seemed as if, with their big night at Peasely's, the dogs were surfeited, and little by little we began to lay by our worry. Francis began to mutter things about George Peasely's not being much of a sheep hand to let his sheep get killed that way. He got sick of gathering clover for them every day. And the sheep, which had been strangely docile for several days, began to get restive and to object to being locked up on warm nights. It took three or four of us to get them in, and little Femus began to look like skin and bone.

Then, without any warning, Mr. Roper's flock was got into. He had a man and a couple of thoroughbred collies, and one of the collies was killed and the other was cut half dead, and eighteen sheep were counted next morning with their throats torn out. The man had gone home early that night. He guessed there wasn't anything going to happen and he was bothered quite a lot with his teeth, he said, from being out in the night air. But that didn't do the sheep any good.

And two days later the dogs broke into the pen George Peasely had built. He heard them breaking in and they only got two ewes. And then we had peace again.

But this time we knew that it wasn't real peace, only a truce, and that the dogs would run as soon as they were rested.

Uncle Ledyard and Mr. Roper and Henry Martin began scouring the backwoods. Uncle Ledyard had an advertisement in the Herald for a black-and-tan Adirondack hound. He offered seventy-five dollars for a good one, and I had to go round with him looking at the dogs whose owners answered. But none of them were the real thing. As the heat of mid-July came onto us we had to let the sheep out at night, and Francis and Doone and John Callant took turns watching them with shotguns. The three other sheep owners did the same thing. We knew it wouldn't do any good just to keep our sheep out of the way. Those dogs had to be found and exterminated.

It didn't make any difference to us that they had not attacked

163

our flock. We knew that it was only luck and time. All except Francis, who laid the whole thing to Femus.

"That there's an intelligent pup," he said to me. "He's put out Injun signs and that's the only thing those dogs know. They're scared of us, that's what."

Femus was exchanging important civilities with Leonidas, but when he heard his name he trotted over to us with his comical head cocked on one side and his earnest, ineffective, brown eyes fixed on Francis. Leonidas walked slowly after him and sat down and looked at him also.

Francis swelled like a turkey with pride.

"Look at him," he said, "and you'll see that it's the fact. Look at him alongside that white animal. My dog's all full of brains and intelligence and knowing how to be a useful article. That white un's only good for fighting—but when it comes to farming, where is he? Downright farming like tending sheep, I mean?"

I didn't argue with Francis. Femus had become the better part of his existence. And there was no gainsaying that he was a nice dog. So I patted him and sniffed covertly of my fingers. He had a strong smell. He was a little like Francis that way.

4

That night was a full moon and a clear, warm night with a slow wind from the south, and that night the dogs came to Boyd House.

It was so quiet at bedtime that none of us thought about the possibility of the dogs' coming to us; and when I got into bed I lay awake for only a short time listening to the high, clear notes of the sleigh bell on the Widow Pierce. Just before I dropped asleep, I remember thinking that she must be leading the flock over the hill.

I woke with the sweat starting out all over me. I got out of bed with one jump and ran to the window. What I heard was the high, frantic barking of a dog.

I recognized it at once. It was Femus. It had a beagle note in it. But now it was choked with sheer, stark terror and also with a pathetic kind of bravery that made me feel my heart coming up toward my throat.

At the instant I heard Doone at his window and Kathy's low voice, and I heard Doone say, "Hell's loose," and he was tearing down the stairs. I rushed after him. Our feet filled the house with thunder on the stairs. Leonidas was at the front door, clawing the screen. Doone rushed for his shotgun, and I after him, and we put out across the field. Then we heard a distant boom of Francis' shotgun, and Doone said shortly, "He must have been asleep."

At the report, lights sprang up in the farmhouse. Adam leaned from his window.

"Wake John and Benjamin," Doone shouted, "and come along!"

They were far behind when Doone and I got to the top of the hill. Leonidas had passed us. He was fading down toward the beaver meadow. As we paused to get bearings, we heard a patter of hoofs and the flock came up directly at us, running like sin, their eyes lambent in their dark faces. They came right against us, and saw us only at the last minute, for they parted like water against stone and swept past on each side, so close packed that they rubbed both my legs.

Far down the hill we saw Francis running clumsily, a dark, bent shape. He stopped and stooped down and got up and ran, and stopped and stooped again, and Doone cursed softly, and said, "They got some of them."

Francis ran for the north corner of the pasture, but I noticed that Leonidas had veered and was heading south. He ran in long bounds, low to the ground. I whistled to him and shouted, but he kept on.

Doone said, "We'll follow him. He's got twice the sense Francis ever had."

We began to run again. In the south corner we found Leonidas nosing along the fence. I collared him. He felt sickish under my hand and was trembling.

"They crossed the fence here," Doone said. "This is where they did the last kill."

He moved on ahead of me, and then I saw, in a hollow of the ground, three shapes lying. There was a hot smell in the air when I came into the wind. It made me feel sick and I understood why Leonidas was trembling. Then, just ahead, a pathetic note clinked once, and in the corner of the fence we found the Widow Pierce standing with a dark stain covering her right shoulder. She was rocking unsteadily on her feet, her eyes closed, and the blood had soaked her sheared fleece into a solid mat.

"They've got away," Doone said. "Where's Francis?"

A lantern was moving fast down the hill toward the north corner, bobbing and swinging in Adam's red hand. In its light the legs of John Callant and Benjamin Daniel, one pair white and skinny, the other black, followed in order. I remember being startled by the pinkish look of Benjamin's foot soles.

As the light traveled into the corner we saw Francis huddled down by the fence.

Doone took a last look at the Widow Pierce.

"Come along," he said, turning. "We can't do anything more here. They've gone this time."

We walked slowly over along the back fence until we came to the men. The three standing were silent, but Francis was making a queer, hysterical, sobbing sound. He was doing something with his hands on the ground, and the men just stood and looked at him helplessly.

Then he turned up his face against the lantern light. His seamed cheeks were streaming and his mouth trembled under his dank mustache, so that he had trouble with his quid.

"They got him," he said.

He backed away, still squatting.

Adam moved the lantern.

Femus lay there. His throat was literally torn out and there was a great wound on his loins that gave his hind legs a meaningless appearance, and they sprawled whichway behind him. That bite broke his back. As I looked at it I had a picture of the two big dogs with their black muzzles.

166

Francis' voice was oddly dry for his wet face:

"I guess he must have heard them digging under. I guess he went down there. I was getting over to where I heard that damn dry ewe a-ringing her bell. I guess maybe I was resting. I heard him barking. The whole business was quite a ways from where I was, I guess. I guess maybe I was having me some sleep. I come over the hill just after he quit barking. And then the sheep was spattering all around and I seen them dark devils wherever I looked. I loosed my gun off at one of them. I guess maybe I didn't hit him. He had hold of that damn dry ewe." He looked down again with sick eyes. "I guess that Femus heard them digging. It's mostly the only place they could of got through, I guess. I guess he tried to hold them off. I guess he done the best he could."

Francis was silent. Adam hawked, and said, "I guess he did."

"I guess that's right," said Benjamin awkwardly.

John said nothing, and Doone stooped suddenly, his dark face coming keenly into the lantern light. He touched Francis' shoulder.

"You pick him up, Francis, and take him home."

Francis looked stupidly at Doone. "I guess," he said, "maybe I will." He picked up the broken, small shape and stood in front of us. "How many of them's dead?" he asked.

"We'll have to see," said Doone.

Francis looked at him.

Then he said, "Most anybody could buy a sheep," and he took the dog off.

The stamp of feet came down the hill and we saw the admiral and Uncle Ledyard. Uncle Ledyard yelled to Francis, "Where are you going to?" But Doone called, "Dad," sharply, and Uncle Ledyard let Francis go. The admiral stopped to look at Femus, and then looked off and began swearing heavily. He was still swearing when the two old gentlemen came up to us.

"They've gone," said Doone. "They killed Femus. Francis is half crazy."

Uncle Ledyard didn't say anything, but we spread out and began counting the dead sheep. The night distorted us, the seven of us walking back and forth in line, with the lantern on the outside edge, and counting the dead sheep. The admiral was next to me and all the time I heard him swearing to himself. There were nine dead, five of them lambs. The admiral was fond of lambs.

When we came into the south corner we found the Widow Pierce still rocking dizzily on her feet. Adam gave the lantern to Benjamin and picked her up in his huge arms.

"I'll take her home," he said. "You'd better round up the other ones and put them in the shed."

Some of the dead sheep were hardly touched except for the tears in their throats. They suggested licentiousness in a strange way, like victims of a kind of pagan raid. When we had dragged them together they made a kind of monument, but all we could say about them was that they were dead.

We left them there and went back to the farm. We went to the shed and saw the other sheep. One or two of them were cut.

There was a light in the farmhouse kitchen and we went to it. Francis was with Adam, watching him dress the shoulder of the Widow Pierce. She was lying down and making sounds like two pieces of sandpaper rubbed together. Her shoulder had been laid open to the bone, but Adam was putting in some salve and stitching down the flaps.

"She's a tough old thing," said the admiral admiringly.

Francis said, "She ain't got blood enough in her to bleed to death."

I wondered where he had left Femus or what he had done with him, but nobody ever asked him. He was ten years at Boyd House, he died there, and he was buried in the lot on the Hawkinsville road, with a proper prayer and service, but none of us ever learned what he had done with Femus.

That ended the night. I don't know why, but we felt completely tired out. And everyone, even Kathy, had a queer, nervous look next day. It was no use thinking that the dogs had had their fill. Now that they had tasted blood at Boyd House, they would come again and again. There would be no quiet while the sheep were there.

"Why don't you give them up?" the admiral said that evening. "They just cost you money anyway."

168

Uncle Ledyard didn't answer for a minute, but his mouth set heavily under his short, grizzled beard. And then suddenly his cheeks darkened and he said quietly, "I'll be damned if I'll give them up to a parcel of dogs."

"I feel that way too," Kathy said quietly.

Doone squeezed her hand. He had forgotten all about the horses.

"We've just got to watch," said Uncle Ledyard. "We'll watch every night till those dogs show up, and we'll get them, if we have to get them one at a time."

Next day he went down to Hawkinsville and interviewed Pete Freelands, who was one of the old-timer trappers, and Pete agreed to camp out at the back of the sheep pasture and patrol the woods. Uncle Ledyard had agreed to pay him a hundred dollars for each of the dogs he shot. And after that it became as familiar a sight as the sheep to see old Pete nosing along the woods trails.

But Francis had no use for Pete Freelands. "There ain't no man going to fix those dogs," he said. "No man alive can touch them." He hardly ever said anything to anyone any more. He seemed to be brooding over Femus, and Benjamin Daniel declared he was going crazy and wouldn't go out of the house at night for fear of him. But since the killing, the sheep had been won over to Francis. He could do what he wanted with them now. Even with the Widow Pierce.

That was queerer than the undeniable fact that Francis was trying to make up to Leonidas. And Leonidas was nervous of Francis. He seemed to feel shame in the old man's sight. I came on them one day, Francis feeling Leonidas all over slowly, and talking to him, and the bull terrier with his eyes shut and trembling slightly at each touch.

"You're a fine, big dog," Francis was mumbling. "You got power; you got heft. You ain't just a little dog, half sized like Femus was. You ain't going to be wrasseled over by the weight of them. You ain't."

Then he saw me and moved off, but I saw his lips still muttering under his lank mustache.

169

Uncle Ledyard said to me that evening, "You know, Teddy, I'd keep Leonidas locked up at night. Make sure the doors are hooked." He must have read my questioning before I spoke. "Somebody might let him out," he went on. "There are five dogs. I know Leonidas is strong, but those dogs run together."

"Yes," I said.

"You see," Uncle Ledyard said, "I think Benjamin Daniel's right in a way and Francis is just a little out of his head."

The time was when we used to sit with the shades drawn; but now the shades were always up, so Uncle Ledyard could make sure that Adam or John or Benjamin, as the case might be, went out to take a stand in the pasture. Francis, of course, was always there.

He was there that night, ten days later. He was herding the sheep into the lower end of the pasture and he had sat down on one of the hurdles facing the house. Uncle Ledyard and Doone and I watched him take his place. It was cool enough that evening for a fire, and the admiral had fallen into a doze while Kathy played fragmentary pieces to us from the rose room.

"It was three days ago they killed those two strays at poor George's, wasn't it?"

Doone nodded.

Uncle Ledyard let out his breath.

"They're hardly likely to run again for a few days then."

5

The coolness made me sleep quickly. All of us must have gone to sleep, I guess. Nobody heard the door open downstairs, but Francis admitted later that he opened it half an hour after the lights went out in the house. He took Leonidas with him back to the sheep pasture. They waited together in the dark. Then Francis went to sleep himself. But he wouldn't say how he opened the door. That has always been one of our mysteries.

All I remember is that when I went to sleep, it was beginning to rain very lightly. I woke up again about one o'clock. The rain had then stopped; there was only a spent drop or two falling off the eaves. The house seemed very quiet. And then I heard the sound that we always heard at night. The tinkle of the bell on the Widow Pierce. I barely heard it. But it wasn't the usual, slow, grazing note. It was a spray of notes, and then silence. It brought me out of bed, and I went to the window. The stars showed clear and large, and they gave enough light for me to see the mist filling the river valley. Tails of mist reached up through the barnyard and out toward the bald hill. I couldn't see the fence posts of the pasture, but as I stared for them I thought I heard a sound out there.

It wasn't the bell. It sounded to me like running, a lot of running, but so faint I couldn't be sure. It was like a gust of rain against dry brakes.

I heard my name called softly, and looking along the house wall, I saw, dimly, Kathy and Doone leaning out of their window together.

"What is it, Teddy?" Kathy asked.

"It sounds like something running."

"Francis hasn't made any sound. And Adam must be out on the north fence."

"I don't know," I said.

Doone said, "I'm going out."

He drew back, and I did also. I put on pants and shoes over my pajamas and a sweater. When I slipped out on the landing, Doone was already going downstairs.

He went down and then stopped.

"Hell's up," he said suddenly.

"What?"

"Leonidas has gone."

I looked over the back of the red-leather sofa, but he wasn't there. Then Doone showed me the unbolted door.

"Hurry," he said.

He had his gun in an instant and we were running out over the wet lawn and making for the pasture. But still there wasn't a sound. There wasn't any sign of anything except the mist. But the sheep had moved.

"Francis must have gone to sleep," Doone said. We ran up the hill and we found Francis at the top of the hill, rubbing his eyes and looking round for the sheep.

For an instant the world was yet still under the mist. It lay like a thick down puff, softly in the hollows of the ground, putting the world to sleep. It veiled the beaver-meadow grass and all the pasture beyond the hilltop. And we could hear nothing and see nothing except the dim, dark, floating shapes of trees upon the mist.

"Where's Adam?" asked Doone.

"I ain't seen him," said Francis. "But the sheep are all right. That white dog's out here somewheres. He'll let us know."

"You fool," said Doone. "He never speaks."

"For God's sake," said Francis, and I saw a shadow under his mustache as his mouth opened.

"We've got to find them," said Doone.

He stepped down into the mist and I followed him. For an instant our eyes seemed to be looking level along the top of it, then we were in another world. And then, too, we knew that hell was up.

A couple of ewes came by us at a dead run. Their ears were flat, their breaths beat against the mist, we heard their dry panting, and then they were gone. Doone swore and ran ahead. We were running blind, and I was suddenly scared to death for fear I would lose sight of him. For the mist had surrounded me with the instinct of the sheep and I knew that the killers were among us.

We ran blind, and then we stopped. Now we heard signs in the mist, not definite sounds. Just life, or death, if you want. And before we moved again and my eyes cleared from the labor of running, I saw Doone raise his gun and heard him curse again. But I had managed to see it—the frantic ewe running with her head up, and the low, scudding, dark shape. Just as they faded, I saw the dog bound high and far, but I could not tell whether he had got her. Doone sounded as if he was crying with rage. He cursed the mist. But he broke with long strides for the spot to which the dog had last leaped. He ran hard and I almost lost him.

I got a little to one side, and then I saw the ewe. She was down and torn, but there was no dog.

"She's here!" I called, and Doone came feeling back to me.

He stopped a moment, listening.

"They've scattered," he said. "They're taking them anywhere."

And at last we heard a dog's voice. It was a long, high snarling, and all at once it choked, and Doone shouted aloud:

"Oh, good dog! He's got one, Teddy! He's got one surely!"

We dove blindly for the sound. Now and then, sheep passed us. Then we heard a thumping on the ground, but it died suddenly, and as we turned for it, I had just one glimpse of Leonidas, like a whiteness in the dim white, so close I could have touched him. I shouted, but he was gone. And Doone, ahead, shouted, "What's that?"

"Leonidas!" I said.

"He's got him!" yelled Doone. "Come and look at him!"

I saw the match like a yellow flower in the mist and made for it. When I got to him, Doone had struck a fresh match.

"Is that one of them, Teddy?"

"Yes," I said. "There were two just like that."

It was one of the brothers. He was dead.

A little beyond him was the shape of a dead ewe.

6

I don't know why, but as I looked at the dead shepherd dog and the dead ewe, I had a picture of Femus in my mind's eye, and I lost my uneasy feeling of the mist. It seemed as if my feelings got completely tangled, as if everything in the world got tangled, with the dogs all wild after the sheep, killing blindly, and Leonidas hunting them one by one. He must have had a stroke of luck with the dead shepherd, getting his first hold in the right spot; and as I took my last look at the dog I realized the power there must be in the white neck and the muscle-filled jaws. Seeing Leonidas, quiet, self-effacing, round the house, day after day, allowed one to forget what he could do when circumstances turned him loose.

He was loose now, a white dog in the white mist; but where he had gone to there was no way of telling. Doone and I stood together as if we were upon an island. There was the shape of a thorn tree a little way off and three or four of the sheep crowded together under its low-reaching branches.

"Listen," said Doone.

We heard the rapid running of feet sweep down the hill past us, another ewe in full flight, and then she doubled and turned right for us and fell dead in front of us. She pitched straight forward all along her neck, with her nose out flat. And when her momentum was used up, her hind quarters teetered over with a ghastly kind of slowness and she did not even twitch.

I heard Doone muttering, "Ran herself to death," and then I heard the rapid sound of the following dog, and for some reason we saw him quite clear in the rift of the mist, a dark shape, with his bloody tongue hanging out on one side and his eyes rolling at us and a hot fog from his throat. Doone's gun sprang to his shoulder, and at the last knick I hit it with my fist. It went off like thunder and the explosion seemed to close the well in the mist which had allowed us to see the dog. And Doone swung on me.

"It's Leonidas!" I cried.

"It's that black-and-white collie," he said.

"Listen."

Just to our right the collie snarled. There wasn't a sound out of Leonidas. Just the voice of the other dog, but from the way the voice sprang back and forth in the mist, I knew Leonidas had him cornered. We broke for the sound, and then it was shut off as the first had been, all but a short worrying, choking imitation of the voice, and then that died. And Doone blundered into the fence.

At that instant another couple of sheep broke in and out of view, and like a parody of hell the black hound followed them. This time Doone had no chance even to raise his gun. The hound was gone. But at the same time we heard a flurry along the fence and the hound yelped.

Over on our right, Adam Fuess' voice broke out. He had answered Doone's shot, and we had not heard him and he had come on the first dead sheep. He was running now. We heard his heavy feet pounding above us. He said later that that shot was the first he knew anything was happening.

That was the horrible queerness of it, the silent dogs, with Leonidas hunting them down without a sound, and the sheep running—running blind crazy till they dropped, like the ewe we had seen, or till the dogs got to them; and even when the dogs got to them, the sheep made no sound. They just suffered it. And not a thing to see unless you were down in the heart of it, in the mist, and then little, but enough.

Doone shouted to Adam, and he came panting up to us, his great legs breaking eddies out of the mist, and he had a lantern. It made just a faint, wet, yellow spot to show our shoes and the beads on the shotgun barrels. A couple of the sheep saw it and started for it, and the little red dog flanked one of them.

We didn't see him till he turned tail. He saw the light and went. But he seemed running straight and Doone let off a shot after him. The dog headed for the fence.

Adam breathed hard.

"That Leonidas," he said, "he got one of them right under a thorn apple."

"Which one?"

"A shepherd with a black muzzle," said Adam.

"That's not the one we saw, Teddy," Doone said. "That makes three."

"Three," said Adam.

"He's chasing the hound now," I said.

"I wish to God I'd got that red one," Doone said.

Then we heard in the woods the crack of Pete Freelands' rifle, and Adam said, "Maybe Pete's got the red one." And then, out in the beaver meadow, we heard the hound yell. We climbed the fence and started breasting the deep grass. Adam's lantern showed us the brook and the beaten place where the dogs had crossed. We waded over. Beyond the brook the grass was beaten down erratically, but there wasn't a sound.

But we followed the trail, which made plain reading, over a log and round a tussock, and our light bored into a kind of nest in the grass and we saw the hound. He was dead, on his side, with his chin stretched out tight, and fast to his throat was Leonidas, his eyes closed and ears hanging loose. His white coat was dark and slashed, and blood oozed slowly from his flanks, but his lips curled against the silky tan markings on the hound's throat with a kind of voluptuousness.

We dropped down beside him and Doone felt of him.

"He's not dead. Teddy, take the gun."

I picked it up and Doone tried to pick up Leonidas, but he wouldn't break his hold. We had to slosh him with a hatful of water before he would. He got up himself then. He could just stand. But he was all right.

Doone carried him over the brook and a shape raised up on us, and I saw that it was Pete Freelands.

"The red one must have got away," I said.

"To hell with the red one," Doone said.

"You needn't worry about him," said Pete. "No hunderd dollars ever got away from me, once I laid eyes onto it."

He held up a tail like a fox's brush.

"Where's the others?" he asked.

Adam said, "They're dead. He got 'em."

"Crimus," said Pete, "that's some dog! He could have four hunderd dollars if he could write his name."

And he came along behind us, muttering "four hunderd dollars" all the way to Boyd House. Probably he wished he was a white bull terrier himself.

The family were all awake, and we told them the dogs wouldn't run any more, and Adam went out to the kitchen to deliver the news there. We put Leonidas on the hearthrug and Kathy helped me in tending him all night. The admiral wanted to give him whiskey and poured him a good peg, and then had to drink it himself. About three o'clock, Francis came in, and he started to cry, so Uncle Ledyard sent him out.

Leonidas was all right after a week or so; he was stiff, and his coat was spoiled with welts from his scars. The people who came to look at him bored him, but he treated them politely.

There has been no more sheep killing in the valley since then though.

V

1

There were just three weeks in the year, according to the admiral, in which Boyd House lost its resemblance to a chapter out of Gulliver's Travels, and a man could draw a full breath in the house without smelling horse. They came after John Callant let the air down in the tires of the sulkies and cleaned and oiled and stored the racing harness for the winter. Now and then of course there would be a year when this didn't happen, like the one of Blue Dandy's great campaign round the Grand Circuit, when the whole place was kept in a ferment of excitement right on through Thanksgiving. But ordinarily, with the first white frosts and the falling of the leaves, you could count on a recess, and though you might meet John Callant or Benjamin Daniel at almost any hour jogging a horse along the highway, the training track was deserted. It was then that the admiral came into his own, for on every good day, he and Uncle Ledyard, and often Kathy and Doone, would be out gunning for birds.

There were good partridge covers all up and down the valley, from the night pastures of the big, riverside farms to the little, brush-grown and abandoned backwoods clearings, and I believe they hunted every one of them; but for the admiral the high point of each season came when they traveled over to Mrs. Roger Bourbon Castle's place in Steuben and hunted the alder draws for woodcock. He declared that they were the finest woodcock covers in New York State. All the hunting he did up to then was in his mind really no more than training for the work he put in there; and John Callant had often described to me with awe in his voice "the grand way the admiral will go in after them long-nosed birds, loosing off the barrels in his gun, and swearing, and trampling down the underbrush, and making more noise and exertion than a boar looking for nuts in a brickyard." I had always hoped to go along on one of these expeditions, so it was a great event for me when they asked me to make up one of the party.

It was the season after Leonidas' fight with the sheep-killing dogs; the opening of school had been delayed that year, and I was filling out my time at Boyd House on Kathy's suggestion. I had gone out after partridges on several occasions with Uncle Ledyard and the admiral, but more often I had chosen to hunt by myself, hoping, as a boy will, to come home with a bag to beat theirs, but feeling lucky indeed and more than satisfied if I had a single bird in my pocket. But now for several evenings the admiral had steered all the talk to their prospects at Mrs. Castle's, and I was wild to go with them.

We traveled over in the new Brewster wagonette, stuffed in with the duffel like sardines, while Artemis, the Gordon setter, flowed round our feet like a kind of nervous oil. It was the great time of the year for her as well as the admiral; and the preparations of the evening before, the packing of bags and food hampers, the laying out of guns and ammunition, the trip to the cellar for the wine to be taken along and its careful bestowal in baskets—all recognizable omens—had wildly excited her. She thrust her head far out the rear window, barking hysterical farewells at Kathy who stood on the porch with small Fanny and Leonidas to see us off, and as the wheels started to roll, Uncle Ledyard was only just in time with his grab at the scruff of her neck.

"Get down, you fool dog," he growled, dumping her between our knees. "You'll break your own neck, if you lean out much farther, Jim," he admonished the admiral, who was flourishing his hat and kissing his hand from the side window.

I had been waving my own good-bye to Leonidas who seemed

to understand that this was not a bull terrier's junket. Doone was the only completely calm one among us. He merely grinned at Kathy from inside the window, and when he caught her eye she burst out laughing at all of us.

"Well," said the admiral, hauling himself back through the window and lighting his after breakfast cigar. "We're on our way. I only hope George got your letter."

George Beirne was to join us at the farmhouse.

"Of course he's got it," Uncle Ledyard said. "There's no reason why he shouldn't have."

"Just the same," retorted the admiral, "I'd feel better if he was along."

"Then there wouldn't be room for Teddy," Uncle Ledyard pointed out.

"That's so, there wouldn't," agreed the admiral, turning to smile at me and relaxing all of a sudden behind a cloud of cigar smoke. "I'm delighted you're going to have a chance at Mrs. Castle's shooting. Does she ever come up there now, herself, Leddy?"

"Not that I've heard of, and Lord only knows why she bought the farm in the first place," Uncle Ledyard said. "Roger used to talk at one time about their living in the country and raising horses. He got a very good pair of mares to start off with. But Marian wouldn't budge out of Utica. I don't believe she's seen the place more than twice in her life, and since Roger died, not at all."

"Well, we needn't worry about it," said the admiral, "as long as she lets you have the shooting."

"All we have to do is send her a few birds," said Uncle Ledyard. "The old girl likes her food as well as you do, Jim. She sits all day over the finest cellar in the state, and you can't tell me she don't nip down to it once in a while. I've always thought Marian might have turned out a good Boyd if she hadn't married a lot of money like Castle."

"What was the matter with him?" asked the admiral.

"Nothing at all," said Uncle Ledyard. "That was the trouble. When she made him lay off his liquor, he just went to pieces. He hadn't a vice left."

The admiral nodded solemnly, and said he'd seen the same thing happen himself. But Uncle Ledyard went on:

"Old Man Castle, that made the money, was a man. He had seven children and he named them all after his favorite drinks. I remember Julep. She was a handy little piece of baggage and I might have married her myself if she hadn't run off first with a naval man."

"What was the matter with that?" demanded the admiral.

"Nothing at all," said Uncle Ledyard, "except her daughter did the same with another sailor, and they had a daughter, and now she's been sent back and Marian's adopted her, and I feel damned sorry for that poor girl."

The admiral swore. "What's the matter with that?" he demanded belligerently.

Uncle Ledyard chuckled.

"Marian blames the whole thing on me," he said. "She swears if it hadn't been for me bedeviling the girl's grandmother to marry me and my horses, she wouldn't have run off with the sailor."

2

It was good woodcock weather. When John Callant turned off the highway, the northwest wind had slackened and a fine rain was slanting over the alders. We all climbed out and stood on the porch, and the admiral stamped his feet to get the stiffness out of his knees. He looked very handsome, with his cheeks red and shining and the drops of rain on his white mustache and beard, and his blue eyes staring out at the gray sweep of the alder bottom as if it were the sea. The lust of shooting was on his face, and his feet made a thunder on the boards.

"John," said Uncle Ledyard, "drive round to the barn and see where Ira is and ask him why the devil he keeps us standing out here."

"Yes, your Honor," said John.

"And bring in that bottle of brandy!" roared the admiral. "I need it!"

Ira was the caretaker. Under his guidance, Castle Marian, as Mr. Castle had poetically named it, had run to seed. The house needed repainting; the shingles of the barn roof looked like the hair of a shedding buffalo; the barnyard was weedy; and four half-Guernsey cows stood miserably out in the wet.

"She's let the man do what he likes," growled Uncle Ledyard. "Good cattle run out, and Lord knows what's happened to the horses. I think they run wild."

"What do you care?" said the admiral. "You have the shooting."

That was the big point with him. He stamped his feet again and the house shook.

"Why doesn't that baggage open the door?"

I saw the door opening behind us, and then an amused, cool voice said, "I don't know if I qualify."

The admiral wheeled, eyes popping, an oath on his lips that he seemed to catch in his mustache, for he swallowed it with some effort. Uncle Ledyard turned, too, in utter astonishment.

She had dark eyes that were very bright, and reddish-brown hair that, in its lack of order, was like an impertinence. Her face was small and narrow, but her mouth was large, the lips full, and as she met their angry stare, I saw the corners twitching at the two old gentlemen.

"Don't you recognize me?"

"I don't," said the admiral. "Who are you?"

Uncle Ledyard laughed, and she smiled at him and gave him her hand.

"Jim," he said, "this is the product of those two naval elopements. It's Sally Dean. She's by way of being a cousin of mine . . . This is Admiral Porter, Sally. And this young shaver is Teddy Armond, a neighbor of ours."

The admiral bowed.

"Delighted," he said politely; then he added, "Is Mrs. Castle here?"

She read his apprehension as easily as I, and she laughed, putting back her head a little.

"Don't worry," she said. "You couldn't stir Great-aunt Marian out of Utica with the whole American Navy. No, I'm up here in exile. We've had a disagreement, you see, and I got tired of listening to what happened to my mother and grandmother."

"Oh," said Uncle Ledyard. "So that's how it is."

She nodded and stood aside.

"Come in," she invited. "There's room for you all. Mrs. Potts has been wiping around your rooms with a wet rag and Ira's gone for potatoes."

"Potatoes!" exclaimed Uncle Ledyard. "Didn't he plant any?"

"I believe so," she said. "But he couldn't be bothered to dig them."

The farmhouse was a small square building, of small square rooms, with stoves in them instead of fireplaces. The one in the parlor was burning.

"There are plenty of birds," said Sally Dean.

The admiral nodded. "Good weather," he said, and started putting up his gun.

John Callant came in with the brandy and a tray of tumblers and a siphon, and Uncle Ledyard measured out the drinks. The girl watched him and nodded. She called him Cousin Boyd.

"I'm glad you came," she said. "I was getting lonely, after all, and thought I'd have to go back. Jack and I can't marry till spring, and I'll have to stay somewhere."

"You ought to have come to us," said Uncle Ledyard. "I gather Marian's set against him." She nodded again. "Then he's one of two things," went on Uncle Ledyard. "He's a sailor or he's a horse breeder."

Sally Dean accepted her glass. She seemed to be bubbling at Uncle Ledyard. She gave me the feeling of liking us all immensely.

"Which is it?" said the admiral. "No, don't tell us yet. . . . She's a handsome intelligent girl, Leddy, and I'll bet you ten dollars it's a Navy man."

"I take you," said Uncle Ledyard. "Who is your young man, Sally?"

She became surprisingly demure.

"His name's Jack Prentice, Cousin Boyd. He lives near Bath."

"Prentice!" cried the admiral. "No relation to Commodore Prentice?"

"A nephew, I think, Admiral Porter." She was bubbling again. "But he belongs to the horsy side of the family. He's trying to make a go of his father's place, and he says he's got just enough to feed his horses this winter and can't take me on."

She was still laughing, but I thought with a kind of rebellion.

"Prentice," said Uncle Ledyard. "I used to know Ralph. He had some good stock in the 8o's, but he let them run out."

"That's what Jack says. He hasn't a first-class colt in the stable. He says if I could bring him just one as a dowry, he'd take a chance on being able to feed me this winter."

"But what does Marian object to about the young man?" asked Uncle Ledyard.

Her mouth became hugely sober.

"Great-aunt Marian says he reminds her too much of you, Cousin Boyd. She doesn't like horses or the men who raise them. And she says before she'll see me throw myself away, the way Mother and Granny did, she'll cut me out of her will."

Uncle Ledyard roared with laughter.

"My dear girl," he said, "no wonder she's disturbed. You've doubled the offense, you see, for he's both horseman and sailor by breeding and inheritance. Why don't you just say bedamned to the old girl?"

"I would if I could," she said seriously. "I don't give a curse for the money, but I haven't a thing to take Jack, and he hasn't a thing to take care of me with. Or at least, so he thinks, poor boy."

"We'll have to find you that colt, then," said Uncle Ledyard.

3

It cleared gradually through the morning, and by noon, when we came back to the farmhouse, we had nearly a dozen birds. The admiral was in high good humor. He passed out into the kitchen to consult Mrs. Potts about luncheon and to give Ira a couple of dollars for protecting the birds. Artemis had come in with us and dropped herself like a wet mop in front of the stove to drain, and as she drained, the heat made steam of the water and coated the windows.

We sat round the stove, all four of us, as wet as the dog, and watched her lolling tongue. It is one of the pleasantest sights there is, after a long session in the brush, to come into a warm place and watch a tired dog's tongue and know that good work has been done by all hands. For I had shot my first woodcock, and the admiral made as much of it as if I had, single-handed, sunk the Spanish Navy.

Even Sally had got a bird, though she had done almost no shooting, but Uncle Ledyard said she showed a natural aptitude. For the most part, however, she had walked behind one or the other of us, swinging lithely through the tangles, with the alders poking into her hair, her head bare to the wet. She had put on a pair of man's overalls, which was a daring thing to do in those days, but both the admiral and Uncle Ledyard seemed to approve of them.

As she sat now in the hard leather rocking-chair with her legs out and her hands in her wet pockets, she was oddly boyish. Uncle Ledyard's brows drew shaggily together. He took a long pull at his pipe. It was the look he had when he was thinking of Greybriar, or one of the good mares, or the old days of his young manhood.

Sally gave a little shake of her shoulders.

"Do I look so very awful?" she asked. "I'll go put a skirt on for luncheon, if you'd rather."

"You'd better put on something dry," said the admiral over Uncle Ledyard's shoulder, "but I must say, those things are becoming."

She gave him a long look, and I noticed then that her eyes had a pleasant trick of narrowing when you said something she liked.

"Jim's right, my dear—about the dry things, at any rate," Uncle Ledyard said. "And he's right about the pants too. I was thinking about your grandmother, Sally. She was very much like yourself."

"In what way?" Sally asked eagerly.

"She had all the instincts of a hoyden," said Uncle Ledyard seriously, "but she had a pretty way of making them acceptable. She led me round by the nose for two years, I remember."

Sally got up, still with her hands in her pockets, her eyes bright.

"You're being very nice to me," she said, and she included me in her smile.

I thought the admiral and Uncle Ledyard looked rather silly staring after her and keeping such complete silence until she had gone upstairs. I couldn't see why two elderly gentlemen should look so fascinated by a young girl. For she seemed very young to me, the way she had put on overalls and all, though I had to admit to myself that she was a courageous walker.

But as soon as she had vanished, and her bedroom door had closed, the admiral swung on Uncle Ledyard. "She's a piece of the right stuff. A devilish nice little piece of it. I was right about the pants, wasn't I?" he said.

"I expect you were," said Uncle Ledyard. "She's got a pretty good leg to carry it off with."

"Good leg!" The admiral blew his nose like a trumpet. "Why, she's got the finest leg I've seen in New York in twenty years!"

Uncle Ledyard loaded his pipe complacently. He stole a sly glance at me, but at the same time I saw he was more than half serious about it.

"You may be right, Jim," he said. "I suppose we Boyds get used to them. It's a characteristic of our women. Even Marian has them, the old pickerel. And this girl is built like a Boyd woman and no quarter-deck inherited from her sires that I can see. Why, my lad, we marry them instinctively. That's what horse breeding does to you. There's a lot of similarity between the lines of a good horse and the lines of a handsome woman."

The admiral used an unrefined word.

"There's something in what you say," said Uncle Ledyard. "You see them and get excited, but we take them in instinctively."

The admiral coughed and looked at me.

185

Uncle Ledyard grunted. "It's time Teddy was learning some of the philosophies of life," he said.

"Well, there's some truth in it, Teddy," admitted the admiral. "You keep your eyes open when you're thinking of getting married and make sure the girl has a good leg. Women can fool you any time with their faces, but they have to use the legs they were born with. A good leg is something that doesn't spoil. You don't get tired of a good leg, my boy."

Uncle Ledyard said, "I guess you've got the point. And I'm glad this girl isn't going for a sailor. It would be a waste."

The admiral let the remark pass in favor of the brandy. And we sat very comfortably, sniffing the fried potatoes and coffee doing in the kitchen, until John Callant poked his head in the door.

"Misther Ledyard, your Honor," he said.

"What do you want?" demanded Uncle Ledyard.

John's watering blue eyes had a conspirator's gleam.

"I wish you'd just step out with me behind the barn, like," he said in a hoarse whisper.

"What for?" said Uncle Ledyard testily.

"I wish you would, your Honor." John glanced back over his shoulder cautiously.

"Can't you tell me what it is and stop mummering like a blind ape?" roared Uncle Ledyard.

"It's a colt!" hissed John, and seeing Uncle Ledyard gather himself for another curse, he added, "With a trot to him like a railroad train."

"I suppose I've got to go out, or he won't stop pestering," said Uncle Ledyard. "Is it still raining?"

"A drop in the sky, maybe," said John. "One or two. But the sun's just ready to have a look at the colt himself."

I rose with Uncle Ledyard. The drop or two turned out to be a hard shower, driving across the valley on a fresh gust of wind. Uncle Ledyard rumbled and yanked on his hat.

"If you've got me out for a two-dollar mule I'll skin the hide off you and put it on the beast to keep him dry."

The dignity of the back of John's scrawny neck was more eloquent than a dozen replies, as he led us round the corner of the barn and then walked openly into the teeth of the wind. The muck in the yard was ankle deep and Uncle Ledyard swore again. But John marched up to the far fence and pointed dramatically.

"Look there," he said, and then in his teeth: "Ape is it? Indeed!"

"Where?" said Uncle Ledyard, with automatic sarcasm, but I saw his shoulders stiffen and he leaned his wrists on the top rail as he would at a training track. I climbed up beside him.

"The white-nosed one," said John softly. "He's standing just behind the mare. He's got the four white feet on him and the white nose. The black one."

"I see him, you fool. He's marked like a circus horse."

"Your Honor knows better than me," said John impudently, "but you stand where you are and I'll just take a handful of earth and move him out." He clambered over the fence and ran into the pasture. "Go wan! Get up with ye!" And he heaved a great clod at the rump of the colt. The colt lifted his hind legs like lightning and then broke out of the shabby group of horses and went down the field at a ringing trot.

I heard Uncle Ledyard grunt gently.

The colt had distinction. Even I could see that through the rubbish of brakes and dirt that stuck in his ungroomed coat and made witches' brooms of his full mane and tail. He was higher over the rump than the withers as he traveled, oblique shoulders dropping his forelegs straight—the line of all lines to find—withers broad and low, muscled deep in his quarters, with a long barrel, that seemed too long for his clearance. But when he reached the boundary fence and followed it across our sight, I saw the smoothness of the gait, as if he went on rails. Even his comical white muzzle couldn't take your eye from that.

"I'll be damned," said Uncle Ledyard.

"Yes, your Honor, surely," panted John Callant, running back to us on his bowed legs. "Isn't he the sight in seven counties to be finding among all these long-nose birds?"

"I admit he's a good-looking youngster," said Uncle Ledyard, "but I don't understand it. He's got all the Hambletonian earmarks. I'd bet five hundred on it. But none of that blood is in

Marian's mares, and she hasn't kept them up. Or maybe she has."

"That old bay mare he keeps pestering was a good-looking horse in her day," said John. "Will I give him another clout, your Honor, just so he'll stretch himself? You'll notice he didn't run when I belted him. He trotted as easy as natural."

"I noticed that," said Uncle Ledyard. "It's a funny business, John, but I'll tell you one thing—that colt's too good to be left here."

4

"Looking at the nag, Mr. Boyd?" asked a drawling voice, and we turned to see Ira Potts standing behind us and sucking air distastefully through an abused-looking straw.

Ira Potts had one of those disarmingly unhappy faces, as if he knew he was a rogue, and as if he knew you knew he was, and as if he were trying to get up his courage to ask you what on earth could be done about it.

"Where'd that colt come from?" asked Uncle Ledyard.

"That black one?" Ira looked. "Oh, I guess that's the old mare's colt. She dropped him a year ago last spring. He looks to me as if he was going to be a horse."

"He does to me," said Uncle Ledyard shortly. "Out with it, Ira. Where was she bred?"

Ira folded his hands and looked down at them, and I noticed with sudden fascination that he was looking through the straw.

"Why, I don't mind telling you how it was," he said. "Since I persuaded Mrs. Castle we'd ought to give up dairying and there wasn't no milk to draw, I got kind of tired seeing that mare just stand around doing nothing all the while, so I drove her down to Syracuse last year for the fair, and they had a likely horse standing there, and the man in charge was my brother and he said he'd do me the favor of a service if I liked, so I thought she might as well do something besides just eat grass, and it wasn't every day you'd get that good a service for nothing, so I done it."

"You mean you served her. What's her name?"

"Chancery," said Ira.

"You mean you got her served for nothing?"

"Uh-huh," said Ira. "My brother, you see. He wouldn't do it for a stranger."

"Wasn't that Hambletonian Graustark?"

"Some three-dollar name or other. I thought I might as well, and maybe I could pick up something for the colt. I ain't broke him. Him and me don't get on too good. He's one of these here joking horses. Seems I can hardly bend over cleaning out the barn but he takes a pass at me. You ain't thinking of buying him?"

"I'm just thinking," said Uncle Ledyard, "that if you sell him without permission you'll find yourself in a pretty unpleasant mess."

"It was just an idea," said Ira, smiling sadly.

"I warn you," said Uncle Ledyard.

"I was afraid you'd see him. Last year I had him hid in the silo," Ira explained naïvely, "but this year he didn't want to go in."

At that moment the sound of the admiral exploding on the back stoop came to us convulsively against the wind.

Uncle Ledyard took a last look at the colt, and then he turned and walked thoughtfully back.

"Where the devil have you been?" asked the admiral. "We rang Mrs. Potts' dinner bell, and Sally's been blowing a tin horn, and when the dinner came on the table I went out and called."

Sally came to the door. She had changed to a skirt and a striped green-and-white blouse with a high white stock, and done up her hair on the top of her head. The change in her was amazing. In a way she was prettier, but in a way I did not like her so well until she moved again and I saw that even clothes could not hamper her free style of going. She was flushing prettily too, at the approval in Uncle Ledyard's face.

He took her hand and put it on his arm.

"Sally," he said, suddenly and loudly, "I've found your dowry!"

"What do you mean?" she cried. "Oh, I know! The colt, the one with the funny white face." She bubbled. "I thought he was awfully nice, but is he really any good?"

"All I can say," said Uncle Ledyard, "is that I'd give a round sum to have him in my own paddock."

"Oh, Cousin Boyd. Then take him." She had read his face; the acquisitiveness wasn't out of it yet. "I wouldn't for the world. It isn't as if I'd found him myself."

"Sally," said Uncle Ledyard, "I said I'd find you a colt for a dowry. It's my opinion if I looked for three years I wouldn't find a better prospect. . . . Don't you think so?" he said to John Callant.

"Yes, your Honor," said John. "That's what I told you myself, but you wouldn't believe me."

"Of course she ought to have the colt," said the admiral stoutly, "but if you don't start on these eggs and potatoes, they'll be cold. Marriage will keep, but an omelet won't, and I made it myself."

The admiral looked down his nose as he parted the omelet.

"It was one thing I never could teach the Navy," he said, "so I had to learn the art myself."

Sally and I admired the omelet to his heart's content, but Uncle Ledyard ate mechanically. I knew his mind was working round the matter of the colt, and at last he said, "Maybe I can manage Ira. He's a damned rascal, but I might be able to put enough of the fear of God into him so he won't give us away. I'll offer him the price of the service, and we can say that your great-aunt gave you the rest of the colt as a dowry. Nothing would please me better than to put it over on the old girl," he added, "but she'll raise the devil with me if she ever finds out."

He paused to look solemnly at Sally.

"And then," he said, "you can go down to Bath leading him behind you, and if your Jack doesn't take you both in, he isn't a Prentice at all."

"Is the colt really so good?" asked Sally breathlessly.

Uncle Ledyard continued his solemn tone.

"Just walk up to his barn," he advised, "and tell him he can have the colt if he'll take you in too. Stand close to the barn, mind you, so he can see you against the doors, and the idea'll be too strong for him to resist."

Sally rose solemnly and walked over to him and put her arms round his neck and kissed him. I could see Uncle Ledyard enjoyed that, for he got quite red and didn't quite meet the admiral's eye.

"Of course," he said, "I'll have to see Perkins and get a pedigree, but he's a good sort and won't mind the joke."

"You'll have to have a name for him," I said.

"That's right," said Uncle Ledyard. "Let's name him and drink to his career, which will mean yours, my dear, and your Jack's."

The admiral leaned back.

"I understand the mare's name is Chancery," he said. "In that case, considering all the circumstances involved, I think there's only one suitable name for the horse."

"What is it?" cried Sally.

The admiral did not answer until he had poured out the brandy. He raised his glass.

"Ward," he said. "Ward, out of Chancery!"

We shouted together, and the admiral looked very pleased. He wiped a hole in the mist on the windowpane and looked out.

"The wind's died," he said. "Looks perfect. I've got my eye, and with half a pint of luck we'll get more birds than we have in three years."

As it turned out, the admiral was right. It was the last great woodcock day in the history of Boyd House, and the memory of it still persists. Uncle Ledyard stayed with John to help capture the colt, but George Beirne turned up, meeting us in the lower swamp, and between him and the admiral and two lucky shots of mine we got fourteen brace.

George Beirne, naturally, was made a partner in the conspiracy; and Uncle Ledyard said he would have been anyway, because Great-aunt Marian had always fancied him for his good looks, and he might be useful, and besides, said Uncle Ledyard, he had a greater instinct for the pure points of skulduggery than the rest of us put together. Watching his thin, cool face, that never seemed to age, I saw that the whole business delighted him. But he shook his head.

"I wish you all the luck in the world, Sally," he said, "but don't put too much faith in the colt. Marian's an amazingly sharp woman; she's the worst rascal of all the Boyds, and she'd rather make trouble than eat." He lifted his handsome head and we all heard John Callant at the back porch.

"It's stopped raining, your Honor," he called. "And I thought Miss Sally might want to look at her colt."

We went out. The colt was nervous of the lantern light, but after a minute he fell to monkeying with the top of John Callant's cap. And we saw that John had spent a busy afternoon on him. He was curried and polished till his coat glistened. His mane had been plucked and John had braided his tail with a couple of brown shoestrings.

"It's the best I could do, miss," he apologized. "But when I get him home I'll trim up his fetlocks and he'll look better. He's a fine gentle beast, but a terrible joker. . . . Leave that hat be!" he roared suddenly. "Haven't you any decent respect before the mistress?"

"He's beautiful, John," said Sally. And I heard a sad voice at my elbow echoing her.

"I thought he had quite a bit of horse in him," said Ira Potts. And he sighed. "Easy come, easy go. That's the way life is with me."

Uncle Ledyard had given him fifty dollars to split with his brother, and had promised to see the brother was fired by Mr. Perkins if Mrs. Castle ever got wind of it.

5

All Boyd House turned out to see us come in. I looked closely at Doone, for, to my mind, he knew more about horses than either Uncle Ledyard or John Callant. And I saw that the colt filled his eye.

Kathy was cordial to Sally Dean, and very much amused by the illegality of Uncle Ledyard's procedure.

"If it wasn't for your sake," she said to Sally, "I wish the whole thing might come out. Imagine a pillar of the county and a retired admiral robbing an eighty-four-year-old lady of her one decent horse. It would make a twenty-year scandal."

Sally bubbled over, but neither Uncle Ledyard nor the admiral was amused.

Uncle Ledyard said seriously, "It's not stealing. She never did anything but neglect old Chancery. It was no effort of hers that got this colt dropped, and if I didn't do something about it, the boy would have got out of the family for keeps."

"Quite right," said the admiral, "and besides, as gentlemen, we have to consider Sally's interests."

At home, Kathy took command. She decided that Jack Prentice should be invited for a visit, that an engagement should be announced from Boyd House, if Mrs. Castle was still hostile, and that things should move fast enough to sweep the old lady off her feet, even if she caught on to the show.

Uncle Ledyard seconded her. I have a suspicion that he wanted to make up his mind whether Prentice was worth the colt as well as of Sally. But the way he put it was that Prentice should have a chance to say whether the colt suited him or not.

Prentice came. He was a nice, quiet fellow, somewhat shy, and rather impressed by Boyd House and the family and the stable, and he went quite white with excitement when he found Sally. But the colt filled his eye and he spent a good part of each day in the paddock with Doone and John Callant, working the animal. And even after tea time, he would sometimes get up abruptly and walk out to the barn for a final look at the horse in his stall.

"I think," Sally said one evening, watching him go, "that he thinks more of that horse than he does of me."

"Not really," Kathy said, smiling. "Though it's something one has to get used to."

"Was Doone ever like that?"

"Oh, yes. He still is, for that matter. I sometimes think the Boyds have a way of translating us into horses in their minds, and back again," Kathy said. "Though I'm sometimes not sure of the last." It was a great week in the house. Mrs. Callant told Sally that Mister Prentice had a way with him that put her in mind of the days Mister Doone was courtin' Miss Kathy. Mrs. Toidy, finding the admiral in bed when she went in to make it one morning, stopped behind the screen to tell him about the birth of her first boy; and Minna strode about taking long and audible breaths through her mouth and dropping dishes, "the way she thinks she's love's dumb dreams itself," said John Callant, who was forever trying to wheedle Prentice out to the stable.

We all liked him, except the admiral. The admiral couldn't understand him. He would sit watching Sally go into the rose room with Prentice or waiting for him on the piazza with the snow blowing through her hair; and her eyes, said the admiral, melting for him like a good dog's.

"Why the devil doesn't he just take off and be damned?" he exploded.

"Uncle thinks there ought to be a regular announcement," Kathy said. "I think he's right. Especially after both her mother and grandmother eloped."

"She ought to herself!" roared the admiral. "She would if she could move him too. More power to her. Why don't you send out the announcements?" he added.

"Because her great-aunt ought to have the chance to do that, Jim dear. After all, she raised the child."

The admiral merely swore.

"Why don't you write the old——" But Kathy had put her hand over his mouth, and, as Prentice came in, said, "Uncle wrote two days agu"

The admiral grumbled and scowled under his hand at Prentice.

I have always wondered how Uncle Ledyard couched the announcement. I remember that Kathy had been rather upset because he had not first showed his letter to her. But he maintained that if he had done that he would have had to recopy the letter half the day.

"I just told her plain and simple they wanted to get married and that I was for it, and that if she didn't want to come up to the wire like a decent member of the family, we would. What's the matter with that?"

"It's the way you may have said it," said Kathy.

"I didn't swear at her," said Uncle Ledyard. "I'd have liked to, though. But I did make it short, so I'd get an answer out of her. It'll do her good to be roused."

Mrs. Castle's answer came by return mail. John brought it over in the evening. We were sitting before the living-room fire and the admiral was dreaming over his woodcock in the wing chair with Artemis at his feet. Uncle Ledyard made his usual futile attempt to read Mrs. Castle's infinitesimal spidery writing and passed it over to Kathy.

My dear Ledyard: I am very much surprised and shocked at your letter. I am also very much surprised that Sally should have continued in this mulish obstinacy. What you say about Prentice's father being nearly as good a judge of horses as yourself may be true; it may also be true that he is a damned sight better than Roger, but the fact remains that young Prentice hasn't a sou, and that you are a very poor judge of people, as you always have been, or you wouldn't have let a sixteen-year-old girl like Sally's grandmother make an ass of you. I am considering Sally's future, which you are not. She is not yet of age. She cannot be expected to see that this Prentice will probably turn out as poor as all the horses in the Boyd family. I have told her that if she marries this boy she will not get a cent from me. If she marries a proper man she will get a hundred thousand. I said so to her, I say so to him. If he wants to make a beggar of her, that's his lookout.

As for you, Ledyard, I've never had any use for you, as you very well know. I regard you now as a senile old fool.

Faithfully yours,
MARIAN CASTLE

Uncle Ledyard drew a rasping breath and laughed harshly. I

looked at Sally and Prentice. Her lips were set and she was looking at him, with battle in her eyes, but he would not meet them. He was staring at the fire with a peculiar, fixed expression on his face. I wondered why Kathy had not stopped reading. I saw that she was covertly watching the pair. But it seemed rather cruel.

"Well," said Uncle Ledyard, "that lets her out. Kathy, we'll get out the announcements ourselves."

Prentice looked up then. He seemed oddly hesitant and very much embarrassed.

"Mr. Boyd," he asked, "what is the legal age for marriage? I—I never looked into it."

"Eighteen!" roared the admiral.

He did not look at the admiral.

"Just the same . . ." he began, turning to Kathy.

Sally got to her feet. She looked very slender and very young in the swaying light of fire and candles. Her hair caught a reddish glow from them and her cheeks were bright.

"Jack doesn't want you to send out the announcements just yet, Cousin Kathy. And I don't either. . . . Jack, come with me. I want to talk to you. . . . You'll excuse us, won't you?"

She took his hand and led him toward the rose room. I thought she looked tragic, and I was grateful to Uncle Ledyard's deep voice shouting after them, "Remember, Sally, I'm giving you that colt!"

She stopped then behind Prentice's shoulder and blew Uncle Ledyard a kiss. Her face flashed with her wide smile, and then she shut the door.

The admiral cursed like a twelve-inch gun.

"Now," said Uncle Ledyard, getting up and moving for the office, "I'm going to send Marian a letter."

"Be gentle, Uncle," Kathy admonished him.

He grinned at her.

6

What he wrote in that letter to Mrs. Castle, I do not know, but by the way he was chuckling I think he must have worked off some old scores. Whatever it was, it never got to her. She got to Uncle Ledyard first. A telegram arrived in the morning.

IF YOU HAVE GOT RID OF THAT COLT I WILL BRING ACTION

CASTLE

"Ira must have given us away!" said Uncle Ledyard.

The admiral's eyes swelled. He stood a moment on the porch, and the next I knew, without saying a word, he had started for the barn. Sally and Prentice were out at the time, which was just as well, according to Uncle Ledyard, for we would have to think up some scheme for hiding or disguising the colt. And Prentice was sinfully honest.

"Disguising won't help, for the first thing any man looking for him would do would be to wash the face of every horse in the place. We'll have to think fast, Doone. Likely as not she'll be sending the sheriff up after him." He summoned John Callant. "John," he ordered, "hitch Blue Dandy into the runabout and get George Beirne. Bring him with you. Tell him I want him in a hurry." He turned on Doone. "Yes, Doone. I'll bet you a ten-dollar bill she'll have somebody up here inside two days."

Uncle Ledyard was not quite right, for, about half an hour later, before John had had time to get back with George Beirne, Mrs. Callant came bursting into the office with a face like a beet and her eyes staring like telegraph poles, to gasp: "Glory be to God, your Honor! 'Tis the sheriff calling for you and him with a warrant for the white-nosed horse!"

"That's done it," said Uncle Ledyard grimly. His jaw set under his beard and he put his hat on slowly. He went out on the porch with me at his heels.

"Hello, Blake," he said.

The sheriff was rather sheepish.

"Good morning, Mr. Boyd. I'm real sorry, but I've got a warrant sworn out by Mrs. Castle for the recovery of her two-year-old stallion. Do you want me to show you the warrant?"

"No, I don't," said Uncle Ledyard. "But how are you going to pick him out?"

"Oh, I've got Ira Potts along," he said.

"Do you know if he told Mrs. Castle anything?" said Uncle Ledyard with a wry grin.

"No. But I made out from him on the way up that you give him something for the colt, and he went down with half of it for Mrs. Castle and confessed the deal, and she told him to keep the money and gave him as much again for the chance of getting after you. He was regretting all the way from Stittville he hadn't been honest with her and taken the whole amount down."

"Thanks," said Uncle Ledyard. "I appreciate your telling."

The sheriff said with a sober face: "Of course he told it in confidence, and you'll treat it that way, sir, won't you?"

"Of course," said Uncle Ledyard, equally sober. He glanced up at the barn. "Your deputy's got the right one. Treat him easy."

"We will, Mr. Boyd. I don't see Ira anywhere though."

At that instant some agonized yells broke out from the rear of the stable. They rose in pitch, frequency, and anguish.

"I guess I hear him," said Uncle Ledyard.

The sheriff grinned again.

"Well," he said, "if Iry wants to stay, it ain't my business. I was told to fetch the colt to Utica."

"So long, Blake," said Uncle Ledyard.

We watched him off along the Boonville road, with his deputy and the colt. A stiff wind was blowing and the colt was skittish. From the barn, the sounds of wailing reached a crescendo, then ceased. Uncle Ledyard sat down with a grim face.

Then he began to chuckle. I looked up, and behind me I heard Doone break into laughter.

The admiral had issued from the barn. He had lost his hat and his white hair was mussed; his face looked purple; and his eyes, even at that distance, showed very blue. He was walking with his quarter-deck stride, but he was looking down at the fragments of a farm whip which he carried in both hands.

He kept that attitude all the way to the edge of the piazza.

He glanced up, there, to see us. He looked a little confused.

He said, "I remembered that whip when the telegram came, and I was lucky to find it when they came in after the colt. I didn't believe it would break though."

At that moment we saw Blue Dandy coming out of the woods road at his full stretch, with John Callant hunched along the lines and George Beirne holding his hat and the cape of his coaching coat fluttering.

"You're too late, George," said Uncle Ledyard. "The sheriff's been here and gone with him. He had a warrant."

George Beirne whistled.

"I thought she'd get on to it. How?"

"Ira gave it away," said Uncle Ledyard, "and she gave him a present for doing so."

"Well, I did too," said the admiral, staring round. "John, for God's sake bring me some whiskey to the office. I'm tired."

He led us inside and sat down slowly and comfortably and sipped at his glass. Gradually his face cleared. He wiped his mustache dry and straightened his beard. He looked up at us and beamed and said to Kathy, who was bending over him in a solicitous way, "I want to sit down and think about the first time Ira tries to sit down, too, Kathy, that's all."

Doone broke the news to Sally and Prentice, for Uncle Ledyard couldn't bear to tell them. And Doone said they took it perfectly calmly. A little later Sally came into the office to see Uncle Ledyard.

She kissed him. Her cheeks were very pink and her eyes had sunlight in them.

"Uncle Ledyard," she said, "I'm so glad! Jack says that if I'm willing to starve, he'll take me without the colt. He says that now

I can't have it, the last barrier has been removed, as far as he's concerned, and the rest is up to me."

Uncle Ledyard gave her one of his gentle smiles.

"Good for you, Sally. When do you want it to happen?"

"I'm not giving him the chance to change his mind," she said. "We're going to elope. I want to carry on the tradition, but I'm altering it in favor of the horses."

She went out like a bird.

They left that afternoon.

"They'll do," said the admiral with a sigh. He returned to his bourbon. "It's all over."

But Uncle Ledyard was glum.

"It's too bad about that damned old woman," he said. "She oughtn't to cut them off that way. And losing that colt's still worse. What in God's name will she do with him?"

"Oh, she's going to make a buggy horse out of him, according to Ira," said the admiral. "I found out about that while I was talking to him."

"Buggy horse!" roared Uncle Ledyard, with the vein standing out on his temples.

George Beirne broke in quietly.

"I wouldn't give up hope," he said. "I believe it might be worth paying her a visit, and I suggest we go down tomorrow."

"You, maybe," said Uncle Ledyard. "She wouldn't let me in her door."

"Yes, she would, Ledyard. She wouldn't miss the chance of crowing over you, for one thing."

Uncle Ledyard agreed glumly.

"But I don't see what good it would do."

"Well," said George Beirne. "I shouldn't wonder if the colt is taking charge of his end of this affair. She's not equipped to handle a stud horse there. Her coachman's been with her over thirty years—and he was timid when he started." George Beirne let this sink in. "You see? It's a small barn, too."

Uncle Ledyard's eyes became speculative.

"She won't be able to keep him," George Beirne continued. "And I think, salty old crone that she is, there's enough Boyd blood under Marian's crust to keep her from letting a good horse go back to Ira's attentions."

7

That was how we found ourselves on Mrs. Castle's doorstep, the following afternoon, with our backs to Genesee Street, and our faces very grave. The admiral had supplied the transportation with his car and had insisted that I ought to come, too, as a party to the original conspiracy.

It was a high gray house of great dignity, with long French windows all around, and a narrow piazza. The lawn looked combed, the shrubs were expertly trimmed: even her sidewalk wore an air of refinement.

The door was opened by a maid with a fortified face. I have never seen so grim a woman, and Uncle Ledyard seeing the admiral stare after her, whispered, "She's an heirloom."

We went into the afternoon parlor. Like the morning parlor, it fronted on Genesee Street. The afternoon sun was streaming through the French lace curtains over the tall windows. It found reflections in the gilt French mirror on the opposite wall. It fell on the mauve velours carpet and white damask chairs. There was an impeccable respectability about the room that put me into a dazed state of awe.

I stole behind the admiral and instead of looking into the room, I looked into the mirror. For that reason I was the first to see Mrs. Castle. She was sitting in the shadowed corner by the rear wall of the room, and she was grinning—I did not think of it as smiling at all—grinning from ear to ear.

I had often heard of her, Lord knows; how she kept track of every last one of her relations, how she sent a napkin ring at every birth and a wreath at every death, and how in her time she had sent both to more than one of the family, how she never mistook their names and how she hardly ever said a good word for any of them.

Uncle Ledyard and the admiral and George Beirne were standing as men do in a strange house when they are not quite sure of themselves, and she was enjoying the spectacle. And then she caught my eye in the mirror and shook her finger at me. I saw myself flushing to my ears, and as I watched the two of us in the glass, her image rose from the chair. I turned to face her.

She was not at all the crooked, bent witch I had expected to see. She stood straight as a ramrod in her black silk dress, that, in contrast to the furniture, was distinctly shabby. And I saw the white stocking where she had slit one of her shoes. Her face was long and angular, more even than Uncle Ledyard's, and she had the same piercing dark eyes and the curved nose, and round her throat she wore a black velvet choker with diamonds stitched to it. Her sparse white hair was drawn back to the knot so tight it gave, from in front, the impression that she had a man's haircut. But her voice was quite feminine, though rather harsh.

"It's nice of you all to call, Ledyard. I haven't seen you in ten years. Ah, so this is Admiral Porter. Admiral Porter was probably responsible for the tactics you have employed, though I should think he had learned them in Yale rather than at Annapolis. I have heard of Teddy Armond also," she continued. "The name used to have a good reputation." And her eye chilled me.

"Emmeline," she said to the maid, "draw up chairs to the windows. I have found that country visitors always enjoy looking out at the street."

We took the chairs appointed by Emmeline, while Mrs. Castle sat in the room facing us. She was quite at her ease, and her dark eyes watched us sardonically. I could see Uncle Ledyard flushing up under their stare and the admiral gnawing his mustache and muttering inaudible comments behind it.

"To what," asked Mrs. Castle, "am I indebted for this unexpected call?"

"Aunt Marian," said George Beirne, backing out in a way that Uncle Ledyard said afterwards was absolutely poltroonish. "Ledyard, here, would like to speak to you about the colt."

"To apologize?" she said calmly. "That's much nicer of you, Ledyard, than I should have expected."

"No, damn it!" Uncle Ledyard burst out. "I've come down to beg that colt off you, Marian. And that's all of it. I'm ashamed of myself for doing it, but I can't bear to think of a horse of his breeding out of training. It's a sinful thing to let a colt with his possibilities go to waste, Marian."

"That may be," said Mrs. Castle. "But I have no intention of turning him back to thieves."

"Thieves!" exclaimed Uncle Ledyard. "What's Perkins going to say when I tell him you've stolen a service from his prize stud?"

"Whatever Mr. Perkins may say, or his stallion either, is a matter of indifference to me. It's not been proved that I stole the service in any case."

"If you didn't yourself," Uncle Ledyard interrupted her, "your mare did, anyway."

"Don't be coarse, Ledyard."

"Don't be a fool, Marian."

Their resemblance increased as their tempers rose. Bright spots appeared in Mrs. Castle's cheeks. The assiduous Emmeline entered behind her long face and extended a smelling bottle.

"You've got to look out for your heart, Miss Marian," she whispered loudly, throwing a dirty look in our direction.

Mrs. Castle struck the smelling bottle from her hand. Her voice acquired a sudden richness of tone.

"I can look out for my heart. Get out of here, Emmeline, and go upstairs and lock yourself into your room and throw the key out the window. I won't have you snooping."

She never glanced at the maid. Her eye was fixed on Uncle Ledyard's.

"If it wasn't for the family name, for which you seem to have no regard, Ledyard, I'd bring action against you."

"Go ahead!" roared Uncle Ledyard.

"I will!"

"I have proof that I bought the colt from your man for fifty dollars."

"I don't believe it."

"It's the truth, Mrs. Castle," said the admiral.

"When I want your testimony, Admiral Porter, I shall ask for it."

"Ask anybody here," suggested Uncle Ledyard.

"Damn that rascal," she said. "He told me you'd paid him twenty-five. Which was a ridiculous price for any colt, let alone one of Hambletonian stock."

"You admit, then, you knew of the stolen service."

"It makes no difference what I knew," said Mrs. Castle. "I am keeping this colt. I am going to have him broken and use him in the cutter this winter."

George Beirne said, "But, Marian, it's criminal. That horse ought to be on the track. He'll do as much as Blue Dandy did to make the Boyds famous again. Haven't you any family pride?"

"Plenty," she said grimly. "I can look out for him. Robert is quite capable of breaking him. He's in the stable, and he's much more contented than he would be in any of your rural barns."

"Rural barns!" Uncle Ledyard guffawed. "Have you looked at your own lately, Marian?"

"I have no intention of doing so."

There was a lull and I became conscious of the breathing of Uncle Ledyard and Mrs. Castle and the admiral.

The admiral got up.

He said, "Madame, it is obvious that we are getting nowhere, but before I go I feel compelled to say that apart from this colt, I consider your behavior unnatural, cruel, and tyrannical. I mean in respect to Miss Sally. Prentice is a thorough gentleman. He is honest, modest and simple."

"Fiddledeedee," said Mrs. Castle shrilly. She swung on Uncle Ledyard. "That's another thing I have to say to you." She drew a deep breath. "What's become of them?"

"They've eloped," said Uncle Ledyard with a wolfish grin. "As soon as you took the colt, young Prentice saw that there was nothing standing between him and an honorable marriage with Sally. He's poor, but you've made her a beggar. The county will see it's a step up for the girl."

Spots of white appeared beside Mrs. Castle's autocratic nostrils.

"The ungrateful little hussy!" she said stridently. "The image of her mother and grandmother."

"Thank God she isn't of her great-aunt," said Uncle Ledyard. He happened to glance out of the window and said with sincere astonishment, "What's the crowd about?"

All of us rose and looked out at the street. I think there must have been fifty people pressed against the fence. They weren't looking at the house; they were looking into the drive. It was then, with the last echoes of Mrs. Castle's voice humming in our ears, that we heard the frantic voice of Robert, her stout and aged coachman.

As one man we rushed to the side windows.

8

The colt was in the yard, his halter dangling a broken rope.

"That rope was punk rotten," said Uncle Ledyard disgustedly.

The colt was standing quite still with his forefeet together and his head erect and ears pointed. His white nose was turned to Robert, who was approaching him with a measure of oats and saying, "Nice boy, nice boy. So, so, so. Steady." But somehow Robert's voice lacked conviction. I noticed that his head was bare and, looking down at the colt's forefeet, I saw his hat.

It was the hat, not the colt, Robert wanted. He made a dive for it, but the colt was too quick. He snatched it and pranced sidewise.

"My maidenhair," shrieked Mrs. Castle.

Ward, out of Chancery, had cut across the bed of ferns, which was the pride of her garden. But he wasn't through yet. He obviously decided that the hat and Robert were pretty slow, so he tossed off the hat and looked around for better game. A bed of ornamental cannas caught his attention and he broke them off at the head, flung up his heels, and pranced onto the lawn. He stopped there with great demureness under a ten-foot potted palm.

The palm must have awakened an echo of the itchy life at Steuben. He leaned against it to rub himself, and the tree went over; and due to the slope of the lawn, he went with it. There was a momentary tangle, an explosion, as a helpful bystander thought of closing the gate with a bang and the colt flung himself to his feet and charged straight for the house. He landed on the piazza before he saw it and braced himself to whirl. He skidded on the clean hardwood and stopped opposite one of the French windows. He may have seen himself reflected, he may have recognized Uncle Ledyard, or it may have been due to his rustic lack of knowledge. At any rate, with a determined gesture he put his head through the window with a shower of glass just as Mrs. Castle reached it.

In spite of Uncle Ledyard's laughter, Mrs. Castle's imperious dignity was not shaken.

"Get out," she said to the colt. "Go home and behave yourself."

The colt was so surprised at the voice that he pricked his ears.

"Of all the dithering, helpless old women," snorted Mrs. Castle. "Why doesn't one of you catch him and take him in?"

"I wouldn't interfere for worlds, Marian," rumbled Uncle Ledyard. "I've had my lesson."

The colt appeared to listen with intelligence. Perhaps the pressure of the sash frame behind his ears made him think he was captured.

Mrs. Castle snorted and said, "Very well, I'll take him in myself. . . . Emmeline! My hat."

Emmeline fetched it.

Mrs. Castle's hats were famous. They stood high on her head with ribbons and vegetation or plumage, and they were very vividly colored.

This specimen was one of the largest and highest. And it attracted the colt's notice. Stretching his upper lip delicately and dexterously, he made a pass at it. He caught it just as Emmeline held it out. Emmeline gave a piercing scream; Mrs. Castle swore; and the colt reared.

The French window ripped like tight breeches. The sash gave way from its hinges and, as he broke down the porch with the hat in his mouth, it balanced for a moment round his neck—what was left of it—like a preposterous collar. The crowd yelled.

He charged them. "Oh, Lord," said Uncle Ledyard, "he'll hang himself up on those palings."

But the colt cleared them with a magnificent leap. The crowd broke like a swarm of minnows and the horse stood in Genesee Street, between two trolley cars that had stopped out of curiosity, with Mrs. Castle's French window round his neck and Mrs. Castle's unmistakable hat in his teeth. He appeared to grin, and very slowly he dismembered the hat.

It was at that point that Uncle Ledyard went out and caught him.

He led him back through the gate and gave Mrs. Castle the remains of her hat with gravity. "What shall I do with him, Marian?"

She seemed utterly speechless, but she waved toward the barn. Escorting him together, we stabled the colt. Then we went back to the house. Emmeline met us at the door, her face as sour as an unbelievable gooseberry.

"Madame says for you please to come to the morning parlor."

We obeyed.

I had expected to find Mrs. Castle on the verge of apoplexy. I think she was very near it. There was a strained look on her handsome old face, and she had her back turned to us, and she was shaking.

"Ledyard," she said in a queer voice, "you were quite right. He won't make a buggy horse. He needs to be trained. He needs more work than I can give him. What shall I do with him?"

Uncle Ledyard cleared his throat. He spoke in a calm voice:

"I could train him myself, of course, but I wanted to give him to Sally and Prentice."

Mrs. Castle turned slowly on us. Her face was working.

"Understand," she said sharply, "I won't give him to anybody. Here's fifty dollars, which puts you out of the deal altogether, Ledyard. But I wish you'd see Perkins and get his pedigree—the colt's, I mean."

"You'll want that."

"Yes. And I want him trained." She paused. Her fine old face seemed to mellow. "How about this Prentice fellow? Is he capable?"

"I should judge so," said Uncle Ledyard.

"Then he and Sally shall have the colt to train and I'll pay them for his keep. Half the winnings—and how much ought I to pay them a month?"

"Say three hundred dollars," said Uncle Ledyard without batting an eye.

"Well——" Some of the old glitter was coming back to her eye. "I'll offer two hundred."

The admiral was nosing around the room. He stopped by a table in the corner. I saw him touch an ancient bottle set there with sherry glasses.

The sound Mrs. Castle emitted was almost a giggle. Certainly she snickered. "Admiral Porter," she said. "Do you remember a bottle of sherry I sent to Blue Dandy before his first race?"

"I do."

"Was it good?" she asked sharply.

The admiral's eyes seemed to grow slowly in her direction.

"Then if you'll pour five glasses we'll drink to my new colt." She drew up her aged figure to its full height and I saw the white stocking showing again through the cut in her shoe. But the glitter was back in her eye. "Nothing in the world would give me so much satisfaction, Ledyard, as to get a horse to beat you with. I've dreamed about it, but I never thought I'd have even the chance. Here's to him."

Uncle Ledyard drank with good will if not with George Beirne's grace. The admiral drank with his soul and an eye on me, as if to say such stuff was wasted on a boy. Mrs. Castle drank, and she smiled a Boydish grin.

"Wasn't he pretty," she asked, "with his head through the window and pricking his ears at us all?"

VI

1

It was on a Monday in November that we received word that Candida Brown was going to make Boyd House a visit. I recall this quite clearly because it was on that same evening that John Callant for the first time remembered to take off his boots when he came in from the barn. Uncle Ledyard had sent him over to Boonville late in the afternoon to pick up the mail at the post office, and we had finished dinner by the time he got back. The sound of his feet stamping off the snow on the kitchen steps made the living-room fire seem doubly comfortable, and a moment later he came in with his cheeks still stinging red from the northwest wind to put the New York newspapers down on the table and hand Kathy the only letter there was.

"It's got an elegant smell to it, Miss Kathy," he said. "Violets, it might be, or one of them French perfumes."

"Did you stop and see Morris, John?" asked Uncle Ledyard.

"I did," John answered him, "and he says he can't come up here till the end of next week because he's condemned to take a party of hunters from Brooklyn in to North Lake. But he said to tell you that him and Pete will show up the Saturday after next at sivin sharp to drive the south woods for you. And he told me that his young Joey had seen the old buck's tracks in that woods last week as big as a cow."

"What was Joey doing there?" demanded Uncle Ledyard.

"It's something I wouldn't be knowing," said John in a reasonable way, turning his eyes to watch Kathy.

She had lifted the envelope to her face to get the perfume for herself; but as she sniffed, she sniffed again, and her eyes swung accusingly on the little Irishman.

"John," she said, "how many more times must I tell you to change your boots before you come into this room from the barn?"

John drew in his breath, and his face seemed to swell with triumph.

"Sure, and haven't I just been after taking them off, Miss Kathy?" he cried. "And aren't they just as bad wherever they are? The things!" And he held them up at the ends of their laces for Kathy to see for herself.

Kathy got very pink, but Doone burst out laughing, and the admiral woke with a bellow, demanding his port, and discovered the glass in his hand. John cocked a comical eye at Uncle Ledyard, who was roaring at him to take himself and his smell away, and Uncle Ledyard grinned through his beard and looked quizzically at Kathy.

"You've tackled quite a job in John," he said. "It's even worse than being Doone's wife—or any Boyd's, for that matter."

Before she could answer, the admiral, who was now wide awake, became curious about the perfume.

"Who's it from, Kathy? It's not often we get a letter up here that smells of more than the mailman's horse."

Kathy opened the letter, and then she cried out and looked up at us, her eyes silvery with excitement against the firelight.

"It's from Candida Brown," she said. "She's coming up to make me a visit."

"That's fine," said Uncle Ledyard, beaming at her. "When will she get here?"

"She'll take the Empire on Wednesday. That's day after to-morrow."

"Good God!" ejaculated the admiral. "What will she find to amuse her up here?"

"She says she needs a rest before rehearsals start on her new play. She wants to see me." Kathy caught her breath. "You know, it's three years since I've seen her."

"It will be fine to have her," Uncle Ledyard said heartily; "but who is the lady?"

"Oh dear!" cried Kathy. "Everybody knows who Candida is! She's the making of any play she gets into."

"It's too bad she didn't come here in summer," said Doone, "when there'd be something to amuse her. But if she wants a rest . . ."

"Her idea of a rest," the admiral broke in, "will have you all running around with your tongues slapping against your knees. That girl's extraordinary."

"How?" asked Doone.

The admiral refilled his glass, sipped thoughtfully, and wiped his mustache with care.

"I've been told by four separate gentlemen of my acquaintance, who are all of them qualified to know, Doone, that Candida Brown has the best pair of legs in New York."

"I don't see what's so remarkable about that," Doone said.

The admiral spluttered.

"Don't be so god damned provincial!"

Kathy laughed at them both.

"Oh, Doone. She really is a celebrity. And you'll have to go meet her."

"Me?" Doone was startled. "Why, Kathy?"

"Because I'll be much too busy getting the house in order," Kathy explained. "And besides, she'll adore a drive alone with a good-looking man in a cutter."

Doone's grin was sheepish, but I thought he looked pleased. And then I noticed that the admiral's eyes were bulging at him with a rather dubious look in them.

2

Kathy was right about being kept busy. I doubt if Boyd House ever before underwent such a turning out. No corner was too dark to be overlooked, no moulding too high to escape being dusted. Kathy had infected Mrs. Callant, Mrs. Toidy, and Minna with a kind of competitive fervor of cleanliness and was herself right in the thick of all the activity, directing their efforts with a white dustcloth round her head and looking dishevelled and happily feminine. She moved in an aura of wax, excitement, and furniture polish, and she only regretted that there wouldn't be time to repaper the guest room. As Uncle Ledyard said, the only safe spots in the house for the rest of us were the office and the back kitchen pantry where John in a solitary and unremitting state of self-pity had been set to polish every last piece of silver and brass in the house.

In the evening, however, there was a brief respite when Kathy and the admiral, each in his separate way, tried to prepare us for Candida Brown; but Kathy had so many household details on her mind, and the admiral was so preoccupied in correcting his memory, that all we were able to gather was that she had soared into the public's favor in a single brief season, she had managed to stay there, and when we saw her, they both declared, we should understand why.

Yet I had a strange sense of disturbance when Doone hitched Blue Dandy to the cutter at three o'clock on Wednesday and went off to Boonville, with the seat piled high with fur robes for her knees and a pair of soapstones to comfort her feet. I felt it when the admiral went to put on his striped trousers and black coat. All at once the house seemed to have no place for me. Uncle Ledyard was smoking by himself in the office. Mrs. Callant was pressing out Minna's best uniform, and Kathy's feet made quick restless sounds through the house as she saw to a hundred last indispensable things, and no one knew where John Callant had vanished to. There was no one to keep me company unless I chose to visit the kitchen where Mrs. Toidy was getting Fanny's supper or went to the nursery, where the little girl was turning out her doll's house in a wild though unconscious parody. So I stayed with Leonidas on the living-room hearth, where I might hear the first notes of the sleighbells when they came out on the open flats by Kruscome's.

I heard them in an intermission of the wind, a far, silvery run that seemed to slide down out of the sky with the snowflakes. I yelled to Kathy, who came running down from her room in a golden dress that she had had made up in New York and that none of us had seen before. The admiral issued from his own room, twisting the ends of his mustache and patting down his white hair and smelling of eau de cologne. He looked up at Kathy with a curiously critical glance.

"Do you like it, Jim?" she asked with a light, almost breathless anxiety. "Is it all right?"

"It's very good," he said, after a moment.

"Very good!" Uncle Ledyard echoed him scornfully from the door of the office. "It's a perfectly, god damned lovely dress."

"Thank you."

Smilingly, she touched the edge of her skirts and swayed towards him. He planted a smacking kiss on her cheek and glared at the admiral. "Good!" he repeated, "My God, Jim, she's beautiful."

The admiral puffed through his mustache and muttered, "She better be," but he led us out briskly onto the porch.

From there we saw Blue Dandy flashing out of the twilight at us, with his mane tossing off the snowflakes; and the cutter pulled up with a cool humming of bells. We all looked at Candida Brown.

Doone had her tucked in tightly, so that all we could see was her pink face and the curling wings of blond hair on which her small black astrakhan cap sat jauntily. But when Doone sprang out and opened the robes, she rose to her feet, crying, "Kathy!

Oh, darling!" in a clear, light voice that was like an echo of the bells. And she and Kathy rushed together and kissed.

"Admiral Porter," she said, her voice warming, when Kathy released her, and the admiral stepped up to take her hand and bent over it in a courtly way in spite of his gout, and then Kathy introduced her to Uncle Ledyard, who looked rather bewildered by such beauty, and to me, whom she pounced upon with a laugh and kissed.

She had a faint feminine perfume, made thin and sharp with the drive through the cold, and I was uneasy when she kissed me and not at all sure that I liked her. For all the men stared at us as if they had never seen a woman kiss a boy.

John Callant came out for the bags and we accompanied her into the living room. But Kathy swept her on to her own room and we were forced to wait for more than half an hour, listening to their stirring, their voices, and their continual exclamations, before we got a real look at her.

She and Kathy held hands as they came through the door of her room together. For an instant before they moved towards us they hesitated, as if they were well aware of the effect of their entrance, and I think I never saw anything more lovely than the picture they made against the old yellow plaster.

They were both tall women, both beautiful, but there their resemblance ended. For Candida Brown had pale yellow hair; her skin was marvelously pink and white; and her eyes were a dark, exciting brown. She gave an extraordinary sense of perfection; but her beauty was not natural, as Kathy's was, but seemed engraved upon her, as if, with loving care, she had made a picture of herself. And as anyone could see, she had drawn it for the male eye. I know I thought of porcelain and fragile, perfect things, like the Dresden shepherdess on the mantel in the dining room.

I cannot really explain it. I don't think any of us tried to explain it then to ourselves. For the admiral bowed, and Uncle Ledyard beamed on both of them with a look of great satisfaction, and Doone stood still before the fire, looking very tall and dark, and rather shy. And both of them, when they came in, were looking only to him, and suddenly I got the impression that in spite of their light talk and laughter, they had been measuring themselves against his eyes.

I did not understand it, but it was there. And then, in a breath, as Uncle Ledyard said to them, "Come over to the fire and get warm," it was gone. They dropped hands and Candida laughed. She passed by Uncle Ledyard to stand beside Doone on the hearth, and she drew in her breath deeply.

"It's marvelous, Mr. Boyd. I've never been in such a place—so far off. The ride over was wonderful, the fast horse, the bells"— she seemed to be building up a part for herself—"and then this simple old house, with its warm hospitality, and the sight of Kathy again. I haven't seen her for years." She turned to Kathy and smiled with her beautifully etched lips. "You don't know how New York misses you, dear. When I said I was coming up here, they almost went down on their knees to me, begging me to bring you back." She paused again, and we all watched her. "But now I've got here I can understand why Kathy wants to stay." And she looked up at Doone and smiled at him.

"It's very rough, I'm afraid," said Uncle Ledyard. "Kathy, you know, was used to it. But we'll try to make you comfortable."

"Oh, I shall love it, Mr. Boyd. I've never had anything like it before. It's so quaint. The guns, the heads of deer, and then, so surprisingly, all your lovely old furniture. And the dog on the rug, even." And she put out her slim slipper to point at Leonidas. "It's simply ineffable. It's perfect."

I stared at her suspiciously.

"He's my dog," I said.

Doone burst out laughing at me. But Candida turned her dark eyes and said, not at all upset, "Is he?" And then she knelt down suddenly beside Leonidas and we all saw how slenderly she was made. "I don't wonder you claim him. He's perfectly beautiful, Teddy."

Leonidas examined her with his yellow eyes, and I saw his nose puzzling over her perfume.

She did not get up, but stayed on the rug with the firelight flowing over her bare shoulders that even there showed no flaw.

Perhaps she was aware of the striking contrast the dog's white coat made to her black dress.

"You who've lived here all your lives have no idea how exciting it all is. It has a tang. It makes me think—do you know?—exactly of the first time I tasted caviar."

The admiral had sat down. Now he touched her shoulder profanely with the tip of his cane.

"You won't find any caviar in this house, my girl," he told her dryly. "But Ledyard's got some whiskey that is damned good."

Candida gurgled and made a mouth at him, and he withdrew the cane, staring down at it as if from her skin it had conveyed some kind of message to him. For several seconds a rosy imprint of the cane tip remained on her shoulder, but she seemed unaware of it.

I glanced at Kathy. She was staring at Doone like a person trying to remember something. But he was not looking at her. Like the rest of us, he had been fascinated by the black-and-white figure on the rug. Kathy must have sensed my watching her, though, for she gave me a quick look, and I saw that something had excited and, I thought, also frightened her a little.

She stood at the end of the sofa, one hand dropping to the red leather arm of it; but when our eyes met, she lifted her head sharply and her body, which had been like the statue of a woman, suddenly charged the golden dress with life. At that instant Leonidas's tail started whipping on the hearth rug; there was a commotion at the head of the stairs, punctuated by deep whispers from Mrs. Toidy, and as we all turned, Kathy called in her warm, full voice, "Come down, darling."

In the silence that followed we heard the small, careful pumps start down the treads, and then Fanny herself came into view, wearing her best dress and plainly impressed by the formality of her entrance. For it was an entrance, and as I glanced back at Candida, I saw her body stiffen. She looked up at Doone, then quickly from face to face round the room; but though I was the only one watching her, she had no recognition for me. Instead, as Kathy led Fanny into the circle, she leaned forward from her hips with her hands outstretched in the prettiest gesture in the world and cried softly, "Oh, Kathy! Oh, Doone! She's so lovely!"

She put one arm round Fanny, drawing her close till her own blond head almost touched the child's curly dark hair, and looking from Kathy to Doone, she asked, "Aren't you proud?"

Doone grinned, and Kathy smiled without speaking. It was Uncle Ledyard who answered her.

"I'm the one who's proud. She's my girl."

At his voice, Fanny disengaged herself carefully and went over to him; and Minna, who had been standing open-mouthed and helpless with admiration in the dining room door, chose that moment to announce dinner.

The admiral rose promptly, for he never liked dinner to be delayed, and Uncle Ledyard, after patting Fanny's shoulder, followed suit.

Kathy said, "You'll have to go up now, darling."

"But I've just come down," Fanny protested.

"I know. It's too bad," Kathy said. "But we must go in to dinner."

"Can't she stay?" asked Candida, pleadingly; but I felt that she didn't mean it, and so, I think, did Fanny, for she turned to the stairs with no further protest and only the measured raps of her heels to show how offended she felt.

"Poor little thing," said Candida. "It doesn't seem fair," and she rose with smooth grace to stand beside Doone.

"Take Candida in, Doone," Kathy told him, still wearing her smile. "And Uncle, please take me."

I felt the admiral's stick rap my elbow.

"Well, Teddy," he growled, "since we can't have beauty, you and I must do the best we can with each other."

Doone led Candida through the door into the candle light, and the rest of us followed them; Uncle Ledyard looking at Kathy with his eyes so kind that she patted his arm as she put her hand through it, while the admiral, full of grumbling, and I brought up the rear. But I paid no heed to his muttering, for it had suddenly come to my mind that except for four little sentences, Kathy had not said a word for all the time she had been in the living room.

3

Next morning at breakfast time, a fine powdery snow was falling, without wind, without weight, it seemed to hang in the sunshiny air as if it had no hope of reaching the ground. There was a vivid frostiness on the country, and Uncle Ledyard's homespun coat had a stirring horse and tobacco scent as he entered the dining room.

He nodded to us and said to Kathy, who was sitting in a pool of silver glitter behind the coffee service, "Where's your friend?"

"I told her to stay in bed for breakfast. Candida doesn't know what it is to get up early."

Kathy always spread calm around the breakfast table, but more so this morning than ever before. It seemed as if after last night we were reunited again; Uncle Ledyard carrying his steaming cup to his place, the admiral stirring his chocolate with a moody spoon, Doone looking quietly across at Kathy's fresh morning face as if he were seeing her for the first time in his life. She always made us think of her as a brand-new person.

And then Uncle Ledyard crushed his eggshell and asked, "What will we do to entertain her today?"

"It depends on when she gets up."

Doone said, "I have to go over to Boonville this morning at nine and have ice shoes put on Blue Dandy."

"Is the canal frozen over?" Kathy asked.

"So John says. Kruscome hauled his milk in on it this morning. If your friend were up, I could take her for a real ride coming home."

The admiral grunted:

"Candida Brown? You won't see the end of her nose till lunchtime."

"That, Admiral Porter, is a gross and libelous statement."

We turned together to the door.

218

"Blister me!" said the admiral.

Candida stood there, poised, exquisite, and tailored in a dark mulberry dress above which her fair hair gleamed as golden as the sunlight. And she was wrinkling her powdered nose at the admiral as if to prove his lie.

"Good morning, all," she said, laughing at our faces. "I couldn't lie in bed a minute longer. I think the air—it's so incredibly clear—is making a country girl of me. And I'm ravenous. Mayn't I have some breakfast?"

The color waved in Kathy's cheeks.

"Candida! I never expected you so early. Of course you can have breakfast!"

She rang the bell and the notes made a little silvery sparkle all through the house.

"It's too heavenly," sighed Candida. "I can't stay in. The idea of all of you sitting here and thinking up lies about me! I should love to go with you, Doone. Just think. I've never seen a horse shod." She turned to Kathy. "And you'll be busy anyway, dear, won't you? All your household things and doings?"

Kathy said "Yes," quietly, and glanced at Doone.

Doone smiled rather vaguely at her and said to Candida, "I want to start promptly."

Candida opened her eyes at him. She seemed to be able to make them darker at will.

"I'll be ready when you are, mister."

Doone grinned.

They would have to take the road to get to Boonville, but coming home they could follow the canal. I knew what that meant, going smooth as silk, the dry, brittle squeak of the runners on the ice, the thunder of Blue Dandy's hoofs as if he ran upon a drum, himself at full stroke and the ice particles cast up by his points coming back at you like birdshot; and if you heard the sleigh bells at all, they seemed to be behind you.

The snow was falling on them when they left, the air was winy and sharp. Candida was nestled down under the robe until the cocky astrakhan cap came barely to the shoulder of Doone's coat.

"Kathy, my dear," said the admiral, testing his gouty foot with care, "I admire your friend's eye, but I don't like it."

Kathy laughed. It was a perfect laugh, free, light and easy.

"Candida? Doone's her first experience of the silent man—and she's rather breathless."

"He's silent enough," said the admiral, "but she's predatory as hell."

Kathy's breast rose and she half closed her eyes.

"I'm not afraid."

It was a whisper, and I heard it only because I was behind her.

They came back a little before luncheon—Blue Dandy in a lather, so we knew that Doone must have finished him hard; and John Callant shook his head and looked at me with a sourish eye, as much as to say, "If it was me brought in a horse that way, they'd string me to the handiest tree."

Doone laughed at him and looked at his watch.

"Fifteen minutes flat," he said.

"It was simply superb!" Candida cried. "I have never gone so fast in my life, and the way we came up the bank off the ice was like flying."

The front of Doone's coat was crusted with snow and bits of ice, and I glanced at her to see whether she had slipped under the robe the way I had the first time Doone had taken me out, but she was white as he. Even the two gold wings of her hair were dusted white and a sharp bit of ice had pricked her skin at the corner of her mouth. I saw Doone staring at the tiny dome of blood, and when she smiled stiffly at him, and the dome gave way and made a tiny trickle, he bent his head suddenly. But she turned her head to include us in her smile, and I saw that she did not need soft lights and a black dress to look beautiful. The wind seemed to have sloughed her of artifice. She stood there like a girl, with tiny laugh wrinkles just showing along the side of her nose; and she was excited, wonderfully excited, as though her blood were yet racing.

"Is there time for me to brush up, Kathy dear?"

"Plenty of time," said Kathy calmly, following her into the house.

Uncle Ledyard turned to Doone as we lingered on the porch.

"You brought in Blue Dandy pretty hot, don't you think?"

"It won't hurt him," Doone said. "John Callant needs something to do anyway."

His voice was thick, as though the taste of the wind was still in his throat, and his eyebrows twitched sardonically at the two old gentlemen.

"I imagine I'd better brush up too." He slapped his leg with his driving gloves as he stepped past us for the door.

The admiral's face was purple. He blew out his lips a couple of times at Doone's back, but as the door closed he found his voice and swore. Then, finding the door unresponsive, he turned back on Uncle Ledyard and me, still fiercely erupting, and for some reason it dawned on me that something had really disturbed him.

"What's the matter, sir?" I asked when he broke off to breathe. "What's wrong?"

"Matter!" he roared at me. "You're a damned filthy little beast! Go in and wash your face."

4

I did not think twice of the admiral's outburst at me—he had sworn at me often enough before for very good reasons, or for no reason at all; so I don't know what it was that started me worrying. I had not the remotest idea that anything was really going wrong; all I knew was that that day Kathy had lost her spirits. She did not act dejected in any way; but all at once she had become very reserved to all of us, almost wary. One always had a sense of her presence in the house, as though she were the heart of its living; but now with all of us in it, there were moments when it felt empty. I do not know how to explain it; but I felt it; and with a boy's instinct, I blamed Candida.

I couldn't think harshly of her, however. In the first place, she was a famous person, and in the second, she was beautiful enough so that even the horses followed her motions when Doone took her through the stable. And then, too, she seemed to have a genuine interest in horses, and that certainly wasn't anything bad. She delighted Uncle Ledyard at lunch with her account of the smithy; her nose wrinkled as she described the smell of burnt hoof, so that I seemed to smell it myself. She had sat on a box among the men, Doone said, and within five minutes she had all the loafers telling her how a horse ought to be shod, until old Darling shut them up and made her stand at his shoulder and see with her own eyes. Doone looked at her admiringly when he said that, and I saw Kathy watching them both. But it seemed all right to me.

It seemed all right that afternoon when she called to me from the stable door where Doone had taken her. Her color was bright in the cold wind, and she laughed over her shoulder at Doone's dark face.

"I'm just going to watch Adam milking," I called.

"May I come too?" Her voice was clear as ringing crystal. I blushed and nodded. And I felt very proud to see her running out after me.

It was fun showing her round the cow barn. She caught every smell. She spoke to Adam Fuess and reached over his shoulder and had him guide her hand as she tried to draw a little milk, so that the sweat came out on his neck with embarrassment. She stared at the big Guernsey bull through the bars, and then I showed her the new prize Guernsey cow Uncle Ledyard had bought that fall.

"Why is she all by herself?" Candida asked.

"She's going to have a calf," I said. "You can see that for yourself if you'll look."

"When?"

I turned to John Callant, who was coming along with half a

sack of oil meal. "When's she due?" I asked him in a professional voice.

"Her," said John, staring owlishly. "She's a chancy creature. The Lord Himself wouldn't know where she was at, at all, and myself would hesitate to say."

I disregarded his comment. "Doone," I said to Candida, "expects she'll come in next week."

She lost interest in the cow, so I took her to the two big farm teams and then up into the hayloft, and she jumped down from there after me with her skirts like parasols. I turned my back, though I had a great curiosity, remembering the admiral's words, and she laughed at me for being a gentleman, but her hand, when she put it in mine, was frank and friendly.

As we went out through the barn doors, she said, "I thought Doone was only interested in horses, Teddy."

"Oh, he runs the whole farm in winter," I said.

She was thoughtful, for no good reason that I could see, and we walked in silence towards the lights of the house. But suddenly she said, "It's rather a pity that Kathy wasn't a blonde."

"What do you mean?" I asked. And for the first time I felt angry towards her.

She laughed lightly.

"I was only thinking what a handsome contrast she and Doone would make then."

"They match well the way they are," I said. "They make a good pair."

"You're a horseman, too."

"We all are," I said importantly.

5

Whether she was tired, or whether the simple life at Boyd House had really had an effect on her, Candida was quiet that evening. She curled up in one corner of the red leather couch with her feet tucked up under her and her arms behind her head, and she hardly said a word while, from the rose room, Kathy played for us.

She played a strange mixture of things, at first bright glittery pieces, and then, with no warning, she sang a little song in French about a man remembering how it was when he was twenty, and I thought she was singing it for Doone, because almost on the closing note she broke into a wild storming piece of piano music that reminded me of the evening she had played, long before, when Doone was courting her, or she him, whichever way it was; and it made me think also of the way she had talked to me once in the rose room, about the Boyd women alone in the house, surrounded with care and at the same time emotionally neglected. It seemed a strange thing that with all the changes she had made in Boyd House, she should have left the rose room untouched; but she had, though whether as a reminder for herself, or for Doone, or because she felt that Uncle Ledyard would want it to stay as it was, I do not know.

When the piece she was playing had crashed to a stop, there was silence a moment in which the fire sounds came back to us from a distance and we heard the dogs sighing; and then she began to sing as she had that time before, the old-fashioned, romantic songs that Uncle Ledyard loved. But it seemed to me that this time instead of just singing for him, she was trying in some way to tell us a story, and I felt my heart aching.

I could not be sure if the others felt it. When I looked up, I found the admiral's eyes on me, but there was no recognition in them. Uncle Ledyard and Doone watched the fire, and anyone could see that Uncle Ledyard was wrapped in his memories. I think of them all only Candida listened with all her faculties; for from time to time she looked curiously over at Doone, and these times occurred, I noticed, according to Kathy's singing.

When Kathy came in at last, she said, as if she meant it, "Your singing's changed, Kathy. It's much, much better. Your voice is richer than it used to be."

Kathy smiled softly and sat down beside her. Her face was tender as she looked at Doone; and Doone smiled back, but it seemed to me that he included Candida in his smile. And for a while we all sat silently, letting the admiral doze and the warmth drug us.

Candida didn't talk about the simple life that evening, and she didn't speak about it next day. But as if she were adapting herself to a new part in a play, she followed the routine of Boyd House in all its details. She sat with Kathy in the nursery, when Fanny was having supper and discussed dolls' clothes with the little girl; and she went down cellar with Mrs. Callant to open preserves and left Mrs. Callant and Minna a-twitter with praise. She discussed the curing of hams with Benjamin Daniel and carried a sooty souvenir on her cheek out of the smoke house; and she had Doone take her down to the woodlot and rode back on the sleighs, standing up, like the men.

It was simple enough to entertain her. Whenever something different in the farm's routine occurred, Uncle Ledyard would ask her if she would like to see it, and as she always would, Doone was told off to show her. It came to be a natural thing, on hearing Doone's step on the porch, to listen to her quick, following footfall.

It was natural, that is, to all but the admiral.

We were sitting alone at tea, waiting for Uncle Ledyard and Doone to bring Candida in from a tour of the ice pond, and Kathy was behind the tray with her hands in her lap and her face turned from the fire.

The admiral got up as suddenly as his gout allowed him and planted himself on the hearth.

"For God's sake, Kathy! Why do you stand for it?"

"Stand for what, Jim?"

The admiral jibbered:

"Just stand. Look at you now. Holding your hands by the fire while she does her damndest to take Doone away."

Kathy sighed, turned her face slowly and examined the admiral.

"Jim," she said, "what on earth are you talking about?"

"You know well enough. What's more, it's been eating you for the past three days. Doone can't even see you any more. The poor sheep's eye is chock-full of Candida Brown." His voice soared unexpectedly: "What's more, he slights you. He's not uncivil. But I tell you I won't stand for it. Here you set him on his feet by marrying him——"

Kathy interrupted him quietly.

"Don't talk so loud, Jim. You know very well, Doone isn't that sort. Candida has to amuse herself, and it just happens that she came here when Doone had nothing to do with the horses. I was the first girl he ever looked at." She laughed a little. "So no wonder she fascinates him. She does everybody. Even me! Don't you see? —this is all new emotion to Candida. Fires, stoves, sleighs, cows, horses. But she can't see anything unless there is a man in it, and Doone's the eligible man, from her point of view."

The admiral cursed.

"Haven't you any pride in you, then—decent pride?" he demanded. "If you haven't, I have. I'll speak my mind to him!"

"Jim!" Her voice was like a whip, so sharp and hard that the admiral choked on his oath and pulled out his handkerchief. His eyes bulged like marbles over the top of it. Kathy lowered her voice again: "Jim, if you say as much as one word, I'll have nothing to do with you for the rest of your life. I have my pride," she said, "but I know there's nothing wrong with Doone—really wrong. It's horses and the Boyd inheritance. I knew my work was cut out for me when I married him. Do you think I'd have wanted him if I hadn't known that?" Her voice filled: "I want him a thousand times worse than Candida has wanted all her men put together. And I'm not going to let any vituperative, pompous old admiral put his foot in my affairs." Her smile took the edge from her words, her whole face softened, and then she laughed right out. "Jim, dear, do you know that when you swear you aren't a bit frightful? You're just pompous. Pompous Porter!"

The admiral started to curse her, caught himself, and stopped dead, looking very confused; and Kathy's laughter peeled out so freshly that Uncle Ledyard grinned at her as he came in through the door.

The admiral turned on him with relief.

"Where in God's name are those two?" he demanded. "We've been waiting tea."

"They wanted to come round by the footpath," said Uncle Ledyard. "There's no need of waiting."

"I'll go call them," I offered.

I went out on the side porch and looked into the twilight towards the line of woods on the far side of the meadow. There were flakes drifting from the gray sky, soft, large ones—a real snow beginning. It was cold but still. I stepped off the porch and started across the meadow towards the edge of the glen, where the foot path climbed up from the pond. A thin light that came from no discernible source edged the boles of the elm trees. But it did not make shadows. I wasn't looking for Doone and Candida. I wasn't even thinking of them, as I walked across the meadow with the sound of Kathy's laughter still in my ears. I was thinking of the admiral and why he was worried all the time; usually he didn't worry about other people. There was nothing the matter with Doone, I knew. There couldn't be anything really the matter between him and Kathy. I knew it. And then I heard Candida's clear, low voice.

I don't believe she said anything. She just made a sound; a soft, small sound, half out of breath, that clung to my ears. It made my heart pound to hear it, and I felt suddenly uncomfortable and queerly stuffed up. And then I saw Doone standing just in the break of the woods.

"Doone," I said, "we're all waiting for you."

He lifted his head and stepped back, and I saw that he had been standing in front of Candida. Her face was vague. I couldn't see it clear, except that her eyelids were heavy, and she smiled at me in a strange tentative way. I think I felt it rather than saw it. And Doone said suddenly, "Teddy's a good sort," and I blushed all over, for I was aware of his asking me under his hand, without even asking, not to talk. I felt weak and miserable as I followed them back toward the lighted windows.

When she stood before the fire, the snowflakes on Candida's coat turned to beads of water; and as Doone came in and Kathy looked at him and then at me, I felt that I must say something.

"It's snowing," I announced. "Is it going to snow hard, Doone?"

227

"Not hard enough to stop us from driving the south woods on Saturday, Teddy, if that's what you're worried about." He grinned at me, his eyes friendly, and I felt more miserable than ever. I saw what I hadn't noticed before—that he was carrying Kathy's .38 rifle, and now he gave it to me to take out to John to be cleaned.

"Dad and I had Candida shooting at a mark down at the ice pond," he said.

"They say I'm good enough to take a stand by myself!" Candida cried.

Uncle Ledyard nodded.

"She did very well," he said. "All she needs is practice."

Kathy said, "I didn't know you shot at all, dear." But she was looking at me as she said it and I felt myself flushing hotly. Kathy looked away then, as if she felt sorry for me.

Candida laughed.

"Oh, it really isn't so surprising, dear. We've taken it up in New York. It's quite the thing to end a party by going down to one of the galleries on east fourteenth street." Her foot tapped the hearth. "Of course it's not the same thing as shooting something alive. I don't know what I'll do when I see a deer running. But I must try. I must. If I did get one, I'd feel I really belonged in the country."

I went out with the gun to find John. He was coming into the kitchen with an armful of wood, which he dropped in the box by the stove.

"Can she shoot, really?" he asked, admiringly, taking the gun from my hands. "And her so delicate-looking!"

I thought that she wasn't a bit more delicate than Kathy; it was just her fair hair and dark eyes, and the way she used them that made people like John think so. But I kept my thoughts to myself.

They were arranging the hunt when I got back to the living room and discussing the best place for Candida.

"Let's put her just above the canal crossing," Doone was saying. "That way she'll have an open shot. Kathy can take the pond runway. I'll stand at the end of the woods beyond Candida, and

Dad will stay down at this end, a little above the canal bridge."

"That's four guns," Uncle Ledyard said. "All we need to take care of the line. But how about you, Jim?" He turned to the admiral. "Feel like coming out with us this time?"

"No thanks," the admiral said testily. "I'll eat venison, but I'm damned if I'll stand around in the cold for hours waiting for it to walk up to me."

Uncle Ledyard chuckled.

"Jim likes more excitement," he explained for Candida's benefit. "He wants to hear guns going off."

The talk shifted to earlier hunts, and then, naturally enough, to the big buck. There was always a big buck, but this one had been round the place longer than most—four or five years—and he had become almost a legend. A lot of men had hunted for him, but only one or two had succeeded in getting a shot at him, and then only a snap shot in the brush, so that as far as was known, he had never even been touched. But he was seen round the farm quite often in spring and summer, mostly in the early morning when the men were getting the cows. They said he had horns like a brush pile. They called him old Ephraim.

6

I hadn't expected to be given a stand, because there was only room for four guns on that drive; but as I listened to Uncle Ledyard's stories, I was seized by a wild idea of going after the buck by myself. I hadn't a rifle, except a small .22, but I did have two buckshot shells which John Callant had given me; and I thought they were all I should need, for if I did succeed in working up close to him, I'd be lucky to get in more than one shot with my old single-barrel. The fact that a good many men had had no luck hunting him meant nothing at all to me. I was deeply convinced of a providence that worked in favor of boys and beginners; and in my mind when I went to sleep that night, the big buck already lay as good as dead at my feet. My only concern was whether it would be safe for me to leave him unguarded in the woods while I returned to the farm for help in bringing him out.

I didn't get started next morning as early as I had planned. Kathy and Uncle Ledyard had things to do in Boonville and were taking the admiral with them; and it seemed to me politic to wait till they had gone before wheedling some sandwiches out of Mrs. Callant.

"What do you want to be eating for out in the cold like midwinter?" she asked me.

"I'm going hunting," I said.

"What for?" she wanted to know, and I told her, "Rabbits." And then in a slight access of truthfulness admitted that I might just possibly see a deer.

"Mister Boyd wouldn't like it," she said, shaking her head.

"Well, there's nothing for me to do here."

"You'd better ask Mister Doone," she said.

"He's gone off to look at some Guernseys above Talcotville," I told her. "Lord knows when he'll be back."

"What does Miss Brown say about it?" asked Mrs. Callant, but I saw she had already got out the bread and cold beef.

"She's gone out for a walk," I said. "But I don't have to do what she says."

"Well then, go along and stop bothering me," exclaimed Mrs. Callant, thrusting the package of sandwiches toward me. "And mind you don't go getting yourself in trouble!"

"How would I get into trouble?" I asked scornfully and walked out on her.

But when I had collected my gun and the two buckshot shells in the empty living room and had put on my jacket with the sandwiches in the back pocket of it and stood ready to leave, the idea of meeting the big deer by myself in the woods was suddenly too much for me, and I decided to take Leonidas. He cocked his head as if puzzled at being asked to go out with a shotgun, but he came along willingly; and five minutes later we were across the cow pasture and entering the edge of the woods.

I didn't know where to look for the buck nor had any idea of where he might have bedded, but I hoped to pick up his track near the pasture since he hung round there so much in summer. I found plenty of tracks right away, but none looked big enough to me, and as it had not snowed during the night, it was hard for me to decide which were fresh. So I kept straight on through the woods, with my eyes on the snow, while Leonidas skirted my route like a white ghost on pursuits of his own.

There wasn't a sign of the big buck anywhere, and I was bitter with disappointment and a sense of injustice when I saw the end of the woods ahead with the bare white of pastureland opening out. And then, as I came out of the trees, right in the open were the big prints, as John would have said, "As big as a cow," heading along the edge of the woods towards the canal and the river. The deer had been walking slowly; I was sure the tracks were fresh; and I turned to follow them with my heart pounding inside my ribs like a drum.

The wind was beginning to blow sharp from the north, but I hardly noticed it; and as the tracks soon led back into the woods, I should have been warm enough even without the racing in my blood. The deer had followed a gully down to the canal, moving through thick hemlock cover. Nothing had happened to disturb him when he crossed the open canal bed, and he had gone on up over the towpath and down the far side to the river. He had crossed there through the open rapids and I was forced to go up to the first stillwater where there was ice. But the tracks were waiting for me when I came down the other side and led me up a steep sand bluff to the back of our own land.

It would be pointless to describe all the country that deer track led me through. As far as I could see, the buck had just been walking. He had stopped now and then, but never for long, and I had no trouble sorting out his track and going on with it.

By one o'clock I was getting pretty leg-weary from plowing through the snow. I stopped in a sunny spot to eat two of Mrs. Callant's sandwiches, which made me feel better for a while; but by mid-afternoon I was played out. I knew I wasn't going to get even near that buck.

By then the track had circled the back of our place, so that I must have been a mile from the river and over two miles from Boyd House. The wind was biting colder, and I wanted to find a place I could rest in and keep warm for a while; and I suddenly thought of Maynard's sugar bush which was just off my route. It was in a curved gully that faced toward the river, with the maple trees growing along the slope of the ground and a little sugar shanty in the hollow below them. I thought I could go in there for a while and if there was any wood left in the shanty, I would light a fire.

But when I came over the top of the slope with Leonidas, I saw that someone else had had the same thought, for there was smoke threading up from the rusty stove pipe. I felt shy about going on down, but I was too cold to care much; and then Leonidas, who had plunged on ahead of me, began wagging his tail. I guessed it was someone he knew, and as I drew near, I saw where two people had walked into the shanty and out again.

They had not walked out right away, however. When I opened the door, the shanty was still warm inside, and I could tell from the pile of fresh ashes that the fire had burned for some time. Nor did I have to study the two sets of footprints, one long and one fine, to know who had made them. A small square of yellow silk that Candida sometimes wore round her throat for a scarf lay under the rough bench that faced the sugaring trough. She must have taken it off as the shanty warmed and forgotten it. It still smelled of her scent and I stood there holding onto it, with a harsh disillusionment growing in me.

I did not know what to do about it; I did not really know what I thought about it, except that it was no chance impulse that had brought them here. They had planned it to be by themselves; and except for my trailing the buck so far, no one would have known they had been here. And now that they had been together, I did not know where it left Doone in relation to Kathy.

One thing it had done: I had stopped feeling cold. The last thing I wanted was to stay in that place. I closed the door after me, dropping the wooden latch in place, and followed their footprints down to the river road.

They could not have been far ahead of me, or else they took it slowly, for as I walked up the lane toward Boyd House, I saw them ahead of me against the twilight sky. They parted there, Doone turning right toward the farm while Candida went on to the house; and I waited a while, so that they would not know I had come up the lane just behind them.

It was nearly dark when I reached the house finally, and I went in by the office to leave my gun. The lamps had not yet been lit, so the office was dark, and the living room beyond had only the light from the fire. As I moved to the door, I heard someone stir on the sofa, and Candida's voice said, "Doone," softly but with a quality of confident ownership that told me more than I wanted to know.

I walked in without a word and stood looking down on her.

"Oh, it's you, Teddy."

"Yes," I said.

She had looked away toward the fire, but after a moment she glanced up to find me still there.

"Do you want something?" she asked.

"I don't want anything," I said. "I brought this for you." And I held out the scarf. "You'd left it behind in the shanty."

She had started to reach for it but caught back her hand.

"It's not mine," she said sharply.

"Then I'll keep it," I told her. "I'll show it to Kathy and ask her if she lost it there."

"Go ahead," she said coolly, "if that's what you want to do."

But I knew, and I think she did too, that I wouldn't. I did not know whom I could talk to about it. It was not anything to be discussed with John Callant; I could not bear to hurt Uncle Ledyard or Kathy; and telling the admiral would only produce a volcanic explosion. I did nothing. But sitting that night after dinner and hearing them talk and discuss the hunt they would have the next day, made me feel as I did in a dream, when nothing was real except the sense of onrushing disaster.

7

We had breakfast early, but we were still at table when Morris and Pete Freelands came moseying up the road with their rifles under their arms.

"Come in!" Uncle Ledyard shouted at them. "Have a cup of coffee?"

They accepted the coffee but refused to sit down. Instead they stood side by side, handling their cups with great carefulness and looking at us from under their eyelids. They had been guides from way back, but now lived in Hawkinsville, taking a few parties into the woods every fall, and coming up once for old time's sake to drive deer for Uncle Ledyard.

"What's the weather look like, Morris?" he asked, cutting a kidney in two.

"It's quit snowing," Morris said. "It fell about three inches last night, between one and three-thirty, and the tracking had ought to be good."

"Think we'll see the old one?" asked Doone.

"Maybe you will," said Morris, stroking the coffee from his mustache. "I seen him this fall. He was fat as a hog. But he ought to be pretty brisk by now."

"Is he a big buck?" Candida asked, turning up her eyes at him. Morris made a slight gargling noise in his throat.

"Lady, if you see a big brown animal like a bull looking at you under a section of rail fence, you shoot. If you miss, maybe you'll see you've missed the old one. If you hit, maybe you'll find it's only Pete here. But if you see that rail fence, you shoot anyhow."

He studied her melting eyes somberly, then uneasily plucked the sleeve of Pete's brown mackinaw jacket.

"Me and Pete had better wait outside."

Uncle Ledyard grinned in his beard.

"We'll be right out."

We found them waiting for us on the back verandah, sitting out in the cold, smoking placidly. Pete looked at me.

"Teddy going to take a stand?" he asked.

"I'll stand with Kathy," I said. "May I, Kathy?"

"Of course you may, Teddy."

"I can carry the gun for her," I said, glancing at Candida, who had Kathy's own light .38. The old .44 was a heavy load.

"Thank you, Teddy. I wish you would."

"Then we'll start," said Uncle Ledyard.

"We'll set here till you get into the woods," said Morris. "Then we'll go down slow to the other end and see if we can shake anything loose."

The snow was feathery and came half way to our knees. There had been no wind, so every twig and broken fern carried its load of flakes. Our breaths made globular clouds that hung behind us like white balloons. Uncle Ledyard's face glistened red over his grizzled beard as we left him above the canal bridge, and we moved ahead into the white silence of the trees. Our feet plowed a winding furrow through which now and then the dead leaves turned up unexpectedly black and wet.

At the head of the pond, Kathy and I took our stand and I handed her the rifle. We stopped just under a hemlock that was bent down with snow, and against the white Kathy's hair looked black as a crow's wing. She took the rifle from me mechanically and moved a shell into the chamber. The breech closed with an oily, smooth click.

"Good luck," said Candida, her voice soft and clear, and she went away, a vivid figure in Doone's dark wake.

Kathy gazed after them for quite a while. There wasn't a sound in the woods. Not even a chickadee stirred so early. But as we stood there a golden haze from the increasing sun formed under the boughs.

I did not dare to speak. Kathy's face in profile was cold, like a cameo, with the warm coloring like paint beautifully brushed on. She breathed so lightly, so evenly, that the vapor from her nostrils was scarcely visible. But when she turned her eyes to me, they were not cold at all.

"Teddy," she said, "will you stay here for me?"

"Why?" I whispered.

I saw her face ashamed, suddenly, and yet as suddenly she put her shame aside. Her lips quivered.

"I can't bear it, Teddy. I've got to see for myself. Do you understand? I've got to know."

"What?" I started to say. But with her face so close, and her hand laid suddenly on my arm, I couldn't speak at all. I knew what she wanted. And my heart ached for her.

"Whatever I find, I don't want Doone ever to know I spied on him."

I nodded. And then I had a queer thought.

"Kathy," I said out loud, so that my voice shocked us both, "she doesn't know about the woods the way we do, even if she can shoot."

"I'll be very careful, Teddy," she said, squeezing my arm a little. "She won't see or hear me."

She started to move away.

"Kathy," I said again.

"What is it, Teddy?"

"May I have the rifle? Please?"

I can see her today, stopping, standing perfectly rigid, and then she faced me slowly. Her face was drained white. Her eyes seemed black in it, and they stared and stared at me. Suddenly she began to shiver.

"Kathy," I began, and I stuttered. "The big one, Kathy. He might come by here."

Her breast rebounded. The color waved up in her cheeks. And she laughed. She laughed very softly, but she kept on laughing, and I couldn't see anything funny at all.

"I can shoot all right," I said, "even if Doone won't let me take out that gun. I can shoot John's .45, Kathy. I did this fall at a woodchuck. John let me."

"Did you hit him, Teddy?" She had her hand at her throat, but she could not stop laughing.

I flushed.

"No, I didn't. But John said it was a shot any man might miss."

"Here," she said. "Here, Teddy. Take it. And if you see him, shoot. And I'll come right back."

I took the gun from her with hands that felt like puddings, and I tried to turn to watch the runway. But I could not take my eyes from her as she moved off. She went slowly, but just before she disappeared she said, "Thank you, Teddy."

And then, far off over the hill, I heard a murmur in the woods, and at the same instant a shadow passed through the trees, and, looking up, I saw a ruffled owl. A jay squalled. I heard Pete's voice baying deep down in his chest like a fearful and wonderful hound.

It was a marvelous noise, and he was very proud of it. It was known all over the county; and to me it was a perpetual wonder how a skinny man like Pete could bay so deep, all day, without getting hoarse. Once he told me that it was the tobacco he chewed. He said it acted like grease for an engine. I forgot all about Kathy. I listened and listened, but I could not tell at all which way Pete was moving.

His voice went on for a long time, and my eyes felt peeled, like onions, from staring into the still whiteness of the woods. The .44 became a leaden bar my hands could hardly hold off the ground. The world was a still, breathless space. The sky was like gold beyond the treetops, and it was still too.

Then, without any warning, away off to my left, an unbelievably shrill, fanatical yelping broke out, and I knew a deer had been started. He was running and Morris must have seen him, for I heard a heavy boom from his gun, and then the yelping broke out again like fifty beagles running straight at me.

My body stiffened. It seemed to swell inside my clothes. For a minute I was very hot, and then I was cold all over, and then suddenly I heard my heart beating. And just as I heard it, I heard also a stick crack smartly and I knew that the deer was coming my way. I tried to cock the rifle silently, but the click was like the crack of doom. But the deer didn't hear it. He was running hell-bent at me down the alley in the hemlocks. He would be at the bend of the glade in a minute. I lifted the rifle and aimed it just where I thought his breast would come. I knelt on one knee to do it and put my left elbow on the other knee, and I seemed to freeze there.

I could hear his feet now. And there he was. I never saw him clear. I pulled the trigger and the report was like dynamite, re-echoing from the snowy walls of the trees. The hemlock above me gave a whisper and all the snow it had slid onto my face. I opened my eyes and found that I was lying down in the snow with a sore shoulder. There was a mushroom of black powder smoke over me, with a strange hot smell in it. I had held the gun loose and it had keeled me over.

Then I heard someone coming, and in a moment Kathy was bending toward me.

"All right, Teddy?"

"Fine," I said. I felt very ashamed.

She picked up the gun and cleared the muzzle of snow. "Was it the big one?" She was standing over me now.

"I don't know, Kathy. I didn't see him clear. And I missed him."

A square grin trembled on her mouth. "Indeed you didn't, Teddy."

"I didn't?"

"No, there's a deer up at the bend."

I scrambled up and ran to her. There was a deer lying in the snow. I could hardly breathe as we walked up to it. I couldn't breathe at all as we looked down. It was the old big one, with his horns as Morris had said to Candida—like a section of rail fence. And he had a neat bullet hole right between his eyes.

For a long time I could only stare. Then I said, "Kathy!"

"Yes, Teddy."

"I shot him. I shot the old big one!"

She didn't answer.

But in a moment, as it seemed, the woods began to disgorge people. Morris was there, touching the big buck with a reverent toe. Pete came up and pulled the tobacco sock from his pocket and stuffed a chew into his mouth. Doone came with Candida and touched his horns, and Candida looked down in a troubled way, as if she wished that it were herself who had killed him. Last of all, Uncle Ledyard joined us. He was quite silent, and a little sad.

He finally spoke: "He was kind of an institution. But if he was going to be shot, I'm glad we'll have his horns in Boyd House."

I had hardly noticed them all; but when Uncle Ledyard said that I glanced up suddenly, and I was going to claim the deer. But my eyes fell on Kathy. She had moved off from us a little way; she was breathing fast. I could see that, though her back was turned to us. My voice shook so I could hardly manage it.

"You ought to have seen him," I said. "He was coming like blazes. And Kathy dropped him just as he hit the bend. He never moved."

Uncle Ledyard swung round.

"That was a fine shot, Kathy," he said.

"It was," said Doone.

"I wouldn't have minded making that shot myself," Morris said. Pete spat.

"Aren't you proud, Kathy?"

But Kathy didn't answer Candida. She turned slowly back to us all. And she looked at me, and her face was streaming with tears. Pete and Morris averted their eyes and set their rifles down and got to work bleeding the buck.

"I don't feel very proud," Kathy said in a queer voice. "And I do too," she went on, still looking at me. "Very proud."

Uncle Ledyard put his arm round her shoulders.

"I know just how you feel, Kathy."

"Do you, my dear? Thanks."

She managed to smile at him.

I didn't say a word, I couldn't have. I felt too sorry for myself. But at least I could watch Pete and Morris hog-dressing that buck. I did. And then Morris slung him on a pole and we carried him home.

Doone and Candida brought up the rear; and as we went I heard Candida speaking urgently to Doone. I did not catch her words, but I heard him laugh a little, and he said, "All right. In the office."

And she said, "We'll be by ourselves."

8

It had clouded over at noon, and now the wind was at the north and a driving snow had set in, tiny dry flakes that made against the windowpanes a sound like seeds. The long, sloped roof of Boyd House shuddered as it shouldered the wind off and a fine dust of ancientness was shaken from the walls. There was a slight smell of oats in the house, as if at one time one of the Boyds had used a room for a granary. The air became hazy with it; the candle lamps got themselves small dim halos after Mrs. Callant had lit the candles in them.

When I wandered into the living room the house seemed to be sleeping. The admiral was sleeping, there was never any mistake about that. And Kathy, I knew, would be in her room. Uncle Ledyard had driven Pete and Morris down to Hawkinsville, and he would be swapping yarns with them in the little house they lived in together.

There wasn't any sign of Candida; and though I thought that Doone was in the office, I didn't want to talk to him. Not just then, with the memory of Kathy's face as we looked at the old big one together. For the first time in my life I was angry with Doone. But I felt that if I were to say anything to him, or even to show how I felt, he would only laugh at me.

There wasn't anybody at all except Leonidas, and he was pretending to sleep, with his chin on his forepaws, at one side of the hearth. When I thumped him, he started and looked up at me as much as to say "Where on earth did you come from?" and I knew he had not much use for me just then. Perhaps he knew that I was upset; he had been avoiding the admiral. He didn't like worries in the family. But I thumped him again and said, "Well,

I guess maybe I'll just hang around here with you, old dog. Nobody can stop me hanging around where I want, can they?" He patted the floor very gently with his tail and dropped his chin back on his paws. And I sat down. I was spoiling for something to do.

And I kept my ears stretched for Candida in her room.

But the footfalls that finally broke the silence weren't her light-stepping ones. They were Adam's heavy treading, and with them came John Callant's, along the porch to the office door. The knock was full of foreboding.

"Mr. Boyd!" called Adam. And John said, "Say, Misther Ledyard!"

I had guessed right about Doone's presence in the study. I heard him swear softly and get up. The door opened and John and Adam entered. "What's the matter?" Doone asked.

"It's that Guernsey cow," said Adam. "She's begun calving and I don't like the look of things. I wanted to get you and Mr. Boyd over. To look at her."

His voice was stuffy with worry and apprehension.

"What's the matter?" Doone asked again.

"The calf's got its head turned back," said John Callant.

Doone swore.

"I'll be right over. Get me hot water out there."

"I've got it."

The door opened into the living room and Doone came in for his hat.

"Can I help any?" I asked.

"No," he said. He looked toward Candida's room.

"Sorry, Candida," he said.

She was standing behind me in her door, and I realized that she must have heard the whole business. She had put on a new dress—a clinging, soft, green thing, with lovely feminine frills round the flat yoke that was so low I stared at it, wondering how she ever kept it on her. In the candlelight she was amazingly soft and slim and full of grace. But her eyes were angry. And she gave me a glance that said plainly that she wished I would get out. But I wouldn't move. So she turned to Doone.

241

"Surely you don't have to go, Doone."

"It's a nuisance," he said. "But I have to."

"Why?"

"She's the best cow we have," Doone said. "And the calf represents a stud fee that would surprise you."

"Will it take long?"

"These things generally take quite a while."

He was getting his hat and pulling on his boots. Candida watched him. I thought that there was something like a panic working at her mouth.

"How long?" she asked.

"Two or three hours, if I have any luck."

She was very angry. She sucked her lower lip sharply against her teeth. And then she said, "Well, I'll come with you."

"Not on your life," said Doone.

"But I might be able to help."

"You?" he laughed. "Why, Candida, what on earth could you do?"

"I don't know," she said. "Whatever you say."

"Listen," he said. "You'd just distract me. This cow and her calf represent two thousand dollars to Dad and me. I don't want you on my mind too."

She put her hand on his arm.

"Doone."

The way she said his name made me think of her wordless voice in the twilight under the elms. But Doone shook her hand off.

"I've got to run," he said. "Sorry."

I could see that he wasn't even thinking about her.

"Teddy," he said, "run get my bag."

I ran, and as I went I heard Candida say, "Thank the Lord."

When I came back, I thought, "She's got something out of him." I thought he had kissed her again. For her color was up and she was saying, "Please let me come, Doone," as if she had hopes he would. But he said, "Sorry. Can't be done. You couldn't be any

242

use. Use," he laughed; "poor girl, Teddy would be better than you," and he turned and swung out.

Candida and I were alone in the room, except for Leonidas, and after he had stared at her for a minute, he got up quietly and slipped into the office.

She did not see him, she didn't seem to see me. She just stared at the empty space where Doone's back had last been, and she seemed strangely shaken. It was half fear I saw on her face and half a blazing passion. I think that he must have been the first man who had ever turned her down—and for a cow. I saw that she couldn't understand, and it made me glad. I forgot my worries and followed Leonidas into the office.

He was lying in front of the gun case, but I made him get up. I took out the old .44 and asked him to smell it, which he did. He wasn't much interested, but he was polite; and I worked the magazine for him and went down on one knee and shot the buck all over again. And then I looked over the barrel and saw Candida staring at me through the door. Her face was still angry, and I thought that it wasn't a bit like Kathy's rare blaze of wrath; it was a soft, smooth kind of anger, that picked petty quarrels.

"I thought I heard Doone telling you the other day not to take guns from the case."

But I was no longer troubled by anything Candida might do.

"I know it."

"Then why did you?"

I felt that I was vastly mature. "Candida," I said, "if you want Doone, you'll have to wait till he comes in from the barn."

She flushed and stamped her foot. "You're an impudent boy, aren't you?" Her foot made me think of a deer's; light, slim, and very, very vicious. "Put that gun back, or I shall tell Doone."

"Go ahead and tell him then."

"Put it back," she commanded.

"I won't."

"Why should he put it back?"

Kathy's cool voice sounded over Candida's shoulder. And when I saw her I sucked in my breath. She had put on an old dress, a simple red one she had worn the first time I had ever seen her at Boyd House, before she and Doone had married. I remembered Doone used to say it made her eyes look silver. And it still fitted her in a way that should have pleased her. Maybe it lent her something, for she seemed poised and calm.

"Kathy," I said, "I'll put the gun back, if you say."

Candida laughed. It was a brassy sort of laugh. But Kathy and I ignored her.

"Maybe you'd better, Teddy," Kathy said. I put it back. Then she turned to Candida and they stared at each other. Kathy's eyes were steady, but I could see what she could not—that Candida's feet were fidgeting. For I had sat down again with an instinct that warned me that they no longer knew I was there.

"Candida," Kathy said, "Teddy has a better right than anyone to handle that rifle. He shot that buck this morning. Do you understand?"

Candida paled in a queer way, the color leaving her cheeks, all but two small hectic spots.

"Then you were spying on us?"

"Spying?" said Kathy. "Why should I?"

"You know." And suddenly Candida smiled her loveliest and I hated her with my whole soul.

"Listen to me, Candida," Kathy said, but I saw her hands shake. "I left Teddy, and I went after you. I was ashamed to do it, but I am not ashamed to tell you that I didn't go the whole way. I never saw you, do you understand? I don't know what you and Doone did or said to each other. I don't want to know now. I don't really care. The Boyds have always picked up girls; you happen to be Doone's first—after me, I might say."

"We've done nothing," Candida said. Her hand went to her throat. "And if we had, you've had the best of him anyway."

Kathy fired up, but her voice held steady.

"I think I have," she said. "I'm going to keep it, Candida. You don't really know what you're talking about, because you're angry."

I looked up.

"She wanted Doone to stay with her," I said. "But that Guernsey's having trouble, Kathy. He had to go right out."

"I see," said Kathy, while Candida looked from one to the other of us. "You think he's turned you over for a cow. It doesn't matter. The important thing between you and me is Doone. Listen to me, Candida. Doone was like a man half dead, when I married him. I woke him up. And I had to use everything I had to do that, and I wasn't ashamed to, either. He thought and ate and breathed horse. I had to show him what a woman was." She laughed unexpectedly, and low and deep. "He still breathes horse in summer, all summer." She was looking at me and smiling. "Some summer mornings when I wake up I think I'm going to see a brass label at the head of my bed, with KATHY on it! Do you understand? It all seems quaint and different and exciting to you. It's gone to your head. You say its flavor is like caviar, but it isn't; it's good old corned beef and cabbage, or maybe Irish stew. And you haven't the stomach for it. Doone would make you sick. He needs handling. You wouldn't know how." She stopped a minute. I looked at Candida and I saw her eyes un-understanding. She was only thinking about Doone's going off. Leaving her for a cow. "If his eye veers," continued Kathy, "it's in his breeding. I accepted that when I married him. . . . Have you been inside the rose room, Candida? No, the men never sat there. But it would be an education, even to you. That's where the Boyd wives have spent their sorry hours. But I shan't spend my sorry hours there. I can hold Doone, and if he wants to wreck us both, I won't let him do it on a little thing like you."

The paleness still hung in Candida's face. Her eyes were black. "I don't know what you're talking about."

"Of course you don't," said Kathy. "I only realized it this morning. If you did know what I was talking about, I'd be scared out of my wits. Now, I'd like you not to be hurt too badly. That's all. You see, Candida, he's made you drunk. Like a little girl at her first real grown-up party. Even though you think he's just a kind of superior rustic. But he's an awful lot more. And if you found out you'd be ashamed of yourself. And that wouldn't suit you at all."

Candida drew a long breath.

"This seems pretty trivial, this talk. And a little sordid."

"I suppose you're right," said Kathy. "Don't you see, though, mad as you are? He hasn't thrown you over for a cow, really. He's just busy. It wouldn't make any difference if she was old Gretel, and Lord knows what that cow's breeding is. He'd have to go just the same."

"Why doesn't he get a vet?"

"Vets are hard to come by in a hurry in this country. And Doone can do anything a vet could, anyway. It saves him money."

Candida stared at her hard.

"I don't see," she said. "I don't see what you're talking about."

"You don't even see why I should choose to live here, do you?" Kathy's voice was gay. "But I do choose. I don't know why myself, but I do. That's all that matters to me."

She turned out through the living room. Candida stared after her until she had disappeared through the parlor door. All at once, I felt sorry for Candida.

She made a quick snatch of her lower lip. Then she went to her own room. When she came out she was dressed for the snow.

"Where are you going?" I asked.

She looked at me disdainfully.

"If you're going after Doone," I said, "I shouldn't if I were you."

But she opened the door and stepped into the cold. I saw the wind pick at her pale hair, and then the flakes and darkness hid her.

I waited a moment more with a strange feeling of trouble for her, and then, in the rose room, I heard the piano start under Kathy's hands and she played a rousing march. A gust of it swept past me as I opened the door, but she did not stop playing. She looked over her bare shoulder at me like a girl, and her lips said, "Shut it, Teddy," silently. And she had a grin for me.

Then, as the march hushed for a moment, she laughed.

"It's Candida's funeral," she said, and the tune became solemn.

And then all of a sudden her hands dropped and the tears stood in her eyes, and she said, "Just think of the blasted fool I've been, Teddy, to trouble myself at all. What does it matter, if Doone isn't in love with her? He has to amuse himself, I suppose. You're a dear boy, Teddy. What shall I play for you?"

"Anything," I said. "Anything at all, Kathy."

I sat down on a chair away from her and watched, while she played anything at all—I don't know what—and I thought that she was happier than she had been in a long time. She played for me until we heard Candida's slippers running through the living room and her door slam. Kathy's face was tender.

"Poor child, Boyd House is no place for her."

She dropped her hands from the keyboard and rose, and came over to me and kissed the top of my head lightly. Then she went out, and I heard her tap on Candida's door and open it, and I was left alone in the rose room, looking at the print of Sacred and Profane Love.

When I went into the living room, I could hear Candida crying. I stood there listening and wondering what to do, until Leonidas pressed nervously up against me. And then Doone came in. His hands were red from cold after washing and he looked worried.

"Is she all right?" I asked.

"She's fine. A dandy heifer calf," he said. Then he heard Candida.

"What's the matter with her?"

"I don't know," I said. "She ran in like that."

"Maybe I was a bit rough with her. She came into the barn and asked for me, and I couldn't move. So she had to talk to me over the pen rail, and I couldn't be bothered. I got rid of her."

He grinned with a queer boyish embarrassment. Then he sobered quickly as Kathy came out of Candida's room. She closed the door stealthily, and she looked very girlish in her old red dress.

She looked at Doone with her level gray glance.

"Candida's upset," she said, "and she thinks she'd better go home tomorrow."

"Oh, Lord!" said Doone, and his sheepish grin returned. "That's too bad. Can't I do anything?"

"No," said Kathy, "nothing."

Doone looked at her for a long minute.

"Kathy," he said, "why did you get that dress out?"

Kathy's color rose slowly.

"A whim, maybe. I didn't think you'd remember it."

247

Doone smiled. And the admiral opened his door.

"Do you realize we can have venison for Thanksgiving dinner?" said the admiral. "With the Romanee Conti? Is Fanny too young for it, Kathy?"

"The meat or the wine, Jim?" she asked with a smile.

9

So we did on the last day of November. There were just the six of us, once more, round the table, with Uncle Ledyard carving the saddle and the admiral toasting him, and all the rest of us for that matter, in the Burgundy. Doone sat across from me, responding a little bit absently; but I knew that his mind and heart were back on the place, the horses, and home. And Kathy knew it too. There was strength and contentment in her face as she watched him; this was the home of her making, and she had it safe again.

Then her eyes turned to mine with a radiant understanding that she never showed me afterwards. At the moment I only smiled, a little uncomfortably; and as soon as dinner was over I went out to the back pantry, where John Callant was cleaning and polishing the big buck's horns. He needed a rag for the oil, so I gave him the yellow silk piece from my pocket.

"You wouldn't want me to be using this," he said.

"Yes I would," I said.

"Well," he allowed, "it's a great deer, to be sure;" and he dipped it into his saucer of oil.

It was long ago; and it seems unreal in this world of today. But I remember the way she looked. For we all were in love, whatever our age.